THE BLAKE LE(

A FRACTURE IN TIME
by
I.C. Camilleri

First Edition

Kindle Edition
ASIN:

Cover designed by Tracey Sammut.

Dedicated

To Brian
To Luke and Sarah
To Mum and Dad.
I will always love you.

TABLE OF CONTENTS

THE BLAKE LEGACY

Prologue

She looked down across the collapsing stairway. The burning inferno raged below; red, relentless and hostile. She clutched her soft brown teddy bear close to her chest and squeezed her eyes shut. That welcoming darkness engulfed her, but she could still feel them consuming, she could still hear them advancing, she could still smell their acrid destruction...those marching amber flames. She could hear her mother's cries too...and the man's.

"Take my hand. Come on. Reach out. You can do it. I can haul you up."

The resounding *NO* was followed closely by the distinctive rasping sound of creeping death. "...too late for me...I'll slow you down. Save her...my daughter."

"Take my fucking hand." His hissed command snaked high above the crackle and the crunch. "I can get you *both* out of here, I promise. Trust me for fuck's sake."

Take his effing hand, Mummy, the girl wanted to scream out. She wanted to offer her tiny hand too, but the tall man had told her to move back to her room and stay put. There was that authoritative ring in his deep voice. He was someone used to giving orders and having them instantly obeyed. She wouldn't dare cross him. In some strange way his intense coal-black eyes made her feel secure...but they deeply scared her too. She felt the gush of warm urine going down the insides of her thighs. She cracked her left eye open, peeping tentatively down at the spreading puddle around her feet. What was she doing? She was a big girl now, just had her fifth birthday the week before, big girls never wet themselves. *When this is over, Mummy is going to be so mad*, she thought.

A second blast rocked her off her feet, smashing her skull against the doorframe of her bedroom before knocking her to the ground. The first blast had fractured her perfect tiny world apart, rapidly consuming the entire ground floor, tearing her mother's left limb apart. She dreaded to think what the second blast had done. She squinted through the billowing grey swirls of smoke, concentrating hard on the very spot on the landing where the man had stood a few seconds earlier. He had been trying to reach out across the gap in the stairway to the other side where her mother had collapsed. But he was there no more, his reassuring dark presence now replaced by the dancing red flames rapidly advancing along the first floor. She was truly alone, lying there, immobile but still gasping in that choking world of grey, her soft brown teddy her only companion in her final ordeal. Should she be crying? Should she be praying? Should she be running, or at least crawling? She didn't know. She was too numb to move. Closing her eyes and slipping into oblivion was all she could do to escape that piece of hell.

The touch of a sticky hand broke through that slipping state of bewildering numbness. The man...he had survived the second blast. He'll get them out of there. He had promised. She believed in him. He could be trusted...but was she dreaming?

"Becca, honey, please open your eyes. Oh, please dear God, let her be alive. Becca, honey, please, look at me."

She forced her eyelids apart and she stared deep into his coal-black eyes, just inches above her, the dancing grey smoke giving them that ethereal feel.

"Thank you, God," he gasped in relief. "Thank you, God." She felt his sticky hand grab a fistful of her red pyjamas and drag her along as he crawled beneath the doorway of her bedroom. She could hear his laboured breath and smell the stench of his burnt flesh. He was in pain but he kept on crawling, finally kicking the door shut behind him. Her solid bedroom door should deter the dreaded flames and offer temporary asylum. *Hey, no*, that wasn't right; her mother was still out there.

"Mummy, Mummy," she started to scream.

He swooped down on her, roughly shaking her out of her sudden hysteria, restraining her flailing arms. "Becca, listen to me, Becca. Your mother wanted you to survive this. You are going to honour her life and do exactly what I tell you to do. Understood?"

She could not fully comprehend what he was trying to tell her but the crucial message in the tone of his imposing deep voice was unmistakeable. She couldn't ignore it. She quickly nodded, her eyes wide with dread and fear, resigned to the fact that the flames had probably taken her mother away to some place far far away, a place this man didn't ever want her to visit.

"That's a good girl," he sighed in relief, registering her nod of acceptance. And he loosened his tight grip on her arms. "Becca, honey, if we work together we will survive this..." He stopped as he coughed and wheezed his way through an intractable bout. With every jerk of his head, ash flowed down from his straight black hair, peppering her face. "Right," he finally choked out, "Let's try to get out of here. You are to stay close to me at all times. Understood?" He dragged himself up on his feet and, treading through the gathering smoke, he staggered towards the window. He peered out into the moonlit back yard outside and he nodded. "Yes, we can do this, we can definitely do this," she heard him murmur to himself.

She stood on her tiptoes, trying to see what he was seeing. The entire first floor was a converted attic whose windows opened out onto a sloping roof, making the final drop down to the ground a mere storey high. The man was right; they could definitely do this especially if they were lucky enough to hit the lone laurel shrub to the left.

He pushed her behind him and started smashing the glass down with a chair. The much needed fresh night air came hissing in, reviving them, giving them purpose. But then, the wooden floor groaned and listed to the right. With that final burst of energy, he demolished the rest of the spiking shards, making way for their grand exit.

"Take my hand, Becca, quick." He held out his left hand and she let out a little scream of horror. The pale moonlight was highlighting the raw gaping tendons peering beneath the charred skin. No wonder it had felt so sticky; it was oozing gallons of yellow stuff. In fact his entire left arm looked chillingly morbid. She couldn't possibly touch it...too ghoulish. She was about to step away in fear when, wincing in pain, he stooped down and scooped her up on his good arm, leaving his wounded arm free to manoeuvre them both out of the window...and all that just as the floor started to collapse beneath their feet.

"Help me out, Becca," he gasped, "...can't hold you too well. It's up to you to keep holding on." And that was what she did; she clung on to his neck collar for dear life as he slithered down the sloping roof. Down and down they went, his movements precise and self-assured, just as if he had mentally practiced that exact escape route a thousand times before. His angle of direction was shrewdly calculated too so that as soon as his foot hit the gutter he swung down and there was the lone laurel shrub miraculously breaking their fall.

He lay still for a second or two, his back on the grassy lawn, grinding his teeth in agony, clutching the little girl close to his chest. She was looking down into his coal-black eyes and she saw them widen in fear of the spectacle unfolding before him. She followed his line of vision and, craning her neck, she saw the red flames lapping around the very window they had just escaped from. The what-could-have-been was indeed too scary to contemplate. What a very lucky break! A third blast shook the ground and the roof caved in, the very roof they had slithered down a few seconds earlier. A shard of glass hit her forehead but the man was quick to react, instinctively rolling to the side, pushing her fragile body together with her teddy beneath him, shielding them both from the raining debris.

A deafening silence ensued but slowly and surely the worldly noises started puncturing her dark bubble again; the roar of the flames, the soft patter of falling glass and lastly the man's rapid shallow breaths. The girl poked him in his chest. He did not move. It was her turn to pray. *Please dear God, don't let him die*, she whispered. She started to squirm and push on his dead weight. He was slow to react but her presence must have kept him from falling over the edge of his oblivion. He groaned and shifted his weight around, debris clinking down from his back.

A distant wail of a siren was added to the cacophony of noise. It grew louder and louder, eventually dominating the night. Some vigilant passer-by in that deserted piece of land must have called for help. What were the chances of him passing by in the dead of the night? Just another lucky break; but whatever it was, help was good. Her heart soared. The firemen...yes, they would be able to help. She had met a fireman once, during a school trip to the local fire station. He was so good and kind, letting them play on his fire engine as he explained the dangers of a house fire. Yes, firemen were good people. They would be able to help her and this man...and perhaps her mother too. But the sound of approaching help struck a wrong chord in the wounded man above her. She heard him swear softly beneath his breath as he staggered up to his feet. This time he offered her his uninjured right hand.

"Come, Becca, quick," he panted in pain, "It's time for us to leave."

He was swaying unsteadily before her, so close to collapse. She didn't want him to collapse, not after everything he had done for her. They didn't have to move from that spot. The firemen will find them and help him before he collapses. Perhaps he wasn't thinking straight because he was so badly injured. She felt that it was her duty to explain things. "It's OK," she said, trying to sound much older than a five-year-old. "You can sit down again. The firemen will find us and help us."

"Please Becca, we have to leave before they see us."

"Why? Firemen...the police...they are good people. Our teacher said so."

"They usually are...but not today, I'm afraid. These were far too quick to react. Please Becca, I'm asking you to trust me."

Yes, she could do that. She could trust him. Her mother had always told her that the eyes were the true reflection of the soul, and this man's eyes were good and kind, though somewhat too stern. But yes, definitely kind. Clutching her teddy close to her chest, she took his offered hand and followed him out of the yard and into the ghostly lane at the back of the house. His movements were painful and laborious but carefully calculated, keeping to the shadows, skirting away from prying eyes...not that there were any because there were hardly more than a couple of seemingly barred-up houses dotting that vast British farmland.

"I'm sorry, I can't carry you. I'm not strong enough right now," he wheezed after ten long minutes of laboured walk. They had been trudging the edge of a ploughed field, exposed on the left but shielded on the right by a wall of tall evergreen trees. "We're soon there, though. My friend is waiting for us in a car just across this field. He's a good guy. He's a doctor. He'll be able to fix us up. Are you hurt? Are you OK with walking?"

She shrugged. "I'm OK," she said. She kept looking back over her shoulder, spying the column of angry grey smoke swirling up towards the night sky, trying to decide whether distancing herself from it had been a wise choice. She looked up at him and met his eyes.

He sensed her discomfort. "So, what's the name of your teddy?" he asked, trying desperately to win her trust and put her at ease.

"Just Teddy. He was my birthday present. I had a birthday last week. I am five now." She stifled a sob; her birthday party had reminded her of her mother. She so wanted her to be there. She so wanted to curl up on her lap and cry. She looked back over her shoulder again and she secretly wiped her eyes with her teddy, hoping that the man had not seen her tears.

"Hey, it's OK to miss your mummy," he said in a soothing voice, suddenly deciding to tackle the problem head-on and discuss things like adults. "But please try to remember that she would want you to be safe and happy, and moving away from that burning house is the hardest but the safest thing to do right now. You are being so strong and brave, she would be so proud of you. And besides, wherever you go she'll always be there in your heart, looking after you, as I will too. You don't need to worry about anything; I'll find a nice family for you...a mummy, a daddy and a pet or two. Do you like dogs?"

"I don't know. I've never had one." She paused to think for a while, trying to picture the secure portrait he was trying to paint before her eyes. "I've never had a daddy either, but that doesn't mean that I don't want one....mmmm...a daddy and a dog...can you really?"

"Sure, I can do that. You wait and see. Your mother was right, you're a good kid, Becca, and very clever too. She was always talking about you and how well you were doing at school. She was really proud of you, you know." He smiled down at her, a nice wide and genuine smile that touched his stern eyes. She liked him when he smiled. She screwed up her eyes in concentration, trying to remember if she had seen him before that night, but she had no recollection of ever having met him before. However, he seemed to know her mother well, enough for her to brag about her clever daughter. And she was indeed doing very well at school, proving the fact that he wasn't bluffing about knowing her mother either. He had even known that her name was Becca; she didn't recall introducing herself to him.

"How did you know my mummy? I've never seen you before, and I've met all of my mummy's friends."

"Ah, not all, you hadn't met me. Your mother and I, we were good friends, we worked together."

"Mummy never went to work," she quickly interjected, knowing that her mother was always at home, looking after her, unlike her friend's mother who had this all important *work* to do and was always away, leaving her child with a nanny.

The corner of his mouth curled up in a smile. Dodging this child's questions was proving to be much harder than he anticipated. "She worked with me a long time ago, way before you were born," he finally explained in an offhand way.

"But she used to talk to you about me, so you must have seen her after I was born," she insisted.

"You're a sharp one, Becca," he laughed out loud, amused by her quick and inquisitive mind. "You'll definitely do very well for yourself. You mark my words." He was saved from offering any further clever comebacks by the presence of a tall hedge at the end of the field. He shuffled his way around and went through a narrow gap, pulling her hand along. They emerged out onto a long and narrow country lane palely lit by nothing but the silvery moon. The man hobbled out to the middle of the lane and, using his uninjured arm, he started to wave wildly at a car parked some distance away.

"Come on, Jake, wake up, do your bit," he wheezed into the night. The excruciating pain had finally caught up on him and he wanted to be spared from the insurmountable ordeal of the last few metres. The car's headlights eventually lit up, dazzling the night, and slowly they started crawling their way towards them. The man's legs gave way just as the car halted to a stop.

The car door opened and slammed shut. The elongated shadow of a tall and well-built man loomed over them. He was shaking his head in disbelief as he pulled on the lapels of his elegant dark blue suit. "Bloody hell, what did you do to yourself? When will you ever stop playing god?"

"I'm sorry, I just had to intervene this time round. Look at her, how could I not?" the wounded man gasped as he nodded towards the little girl in her red pyjamas. She was clutching her teddy, her beautiful big brown eyes wild with fear, her dishevelled dark brown hair cascading down her shoulders and her fine features darkened with raw grief and soot.

The sight of her touched a tender spot in his heart and the blue-suited man immediately sank on one knee before her and held out his enormous hand, "Hello little girl. I'm Jake. What's your name?"

"I'm Becca. Are you a good man too?" she asked as she shook his outstretched hand.

"Yes, I would like to think that I am," he smiled.

She looked at him bathed in the headlights of his car, trying to weigh up the validity of his claim. His dark blonde hair was wild and tousled, his features strong and rugged, but it was his eyes that grabbed her entire attention. They were so vividly blue and bright, so open and honest, so hypnotizing, washing her with that inexplicable sense of gentle tranquillity.

He shifted those entrancing eyes away from her and started assessing the wounded man lying on the ground. "Fine, you're forgiven for summoning me to this ungodly place," Jake smiled at his friend. "But next time, try to be more punctual. You said that you would be back in fifteen minutes max. And here I am more than half an hour later." He sighed and shook his head in mock annoyance. "Right, I suppose that you're expecting me to do the impossible and put your mangled self back together...yet again."

"You're the doctor, your turn to play god." Flashing lights sped past the main road at the far end of the long and lonely lane. Reinforcements were being called in to tame the fire. "Come on, Jake, let's get out of here fast." He nodded towards the billowing column of smoke a fair distance away. "*They* are probably thinking that both the mother and the child perished in the fire. I want them to continue thinking that way until I sort the girl out. And no one will think about knocking on my door either because as far as they are concerned I'm still in Paris enjoying a relaxing family holiday with my wife and kids. I'm doing all this for Luca's sake...trust me...just don't ask why."

"You know me. When do I ever question your infallible logic? Come, I'll help you up."

The girl watched the doctor half lift his friend up and drag him towards the waiting car. The dark-haired injured man winced in pain as his battered back touched the back seat, but he swallowed hard and stoically shouldered his agony just as he had been doing ever since that fire broke out. The girl looked deep into his intense coal-black eyes; she wanted to thank him for saving her life, but his eyelids drooped down and he immediately slipped into that bottomless dreamless sleep. As she sat down beside him, she realised that she didn't even know his name...

1. Peer Pressure and Intimidation

Alina flicked back her long and shiny dark brown hair as she swayed to the loud music, her hands in the air, her legs apart, her hips gyrating their erotic moves, just as her best friend Lizzy had patiently taught her the week before. She had taught her the meaning of style too, telling her what to wear on a fun night out; a tight black dress that barely fell three inches below her backside, revealing her slender legs in all their glory, and at a little under six feet tall Alina had a lot of leg to show off. The demure blue dress her mother had bought her especially for the occasion was quickly booted out by the skimpy black dress. No competition there; this dress would be smooth and slick, convenient for what she hoped would be a momentous evening for her. Lizzy had kindly offered to do her makeup too, dark red gloss for her full and sensual lips, black luscious mascara for her dark brown eyes and the perfect tone of blusher to highlight her exotic sun-kissed complexion. She looked and felt like a million dollars. And all that artwork had to be done in the sanctuary of her friend's apartment an hour or two before she met her date, Steve. Her cosy bedroom in her parents' house wouldn't do; her mother would never have allowed such a blatant carnal display of her only treasured daughter.

Raised in a catholic and highly sheltered environment in a small rural village in the heart of the Mediterranean island of Malta, Alina Spiteri had virtue and love deeply ingrained in her doctrine. Her parents had always shared this selfless and exclusive love for each other despite living in a modern world full of carnal temptations. As a result of that mutual fidelity she had experienced nothing but security and happiness in their little tight-knit family of three, or four if one counted Alaska, her dog. She had hoped that she would one day find that type of pure love, a love untainted by monetary gain or sexual intentions, a love for the sake of love itself, but, at twenty-one years of age she had finally admitted to herself that it was too elusive to find. She was being coerced by the world around her to move with the times.

She had always been highly observant of her parents' wishes, never causing more than a tiny ripple of disagreement at home. She was what any mother and father would proudly call a perfect child; alluringly beautiful yet humble and considerate, dutiful, clever and diligent, acing her GCSEs and A levels and going on to study maths and computer science at the university on the island, freshly graduating with a first-class honours degree. Her tutors fully recognised her high IQ and her exceptional aptitude for numbers, and they encouraged her to open her horizons and further her studies abroad. But the concept of leaving the security of that tranquil Mediterranean island was too daunting for her.

Also daunting for her was the prospect of forming new friendships. Even though she had, what Lizzy would say, the smoking body of a model and the exquisite face to die for, Alina was a shy and self-conscious individual, coming across as somewhat aloof. Hardly anyone dared approach her and she had very few close friends, well two to be exact; her cousin Max and his former girlfriend Lizzy, whose breakup a few months back had been traumatic and bitter to say the least. Nonetheless, the *wounded* Lizzy harboured no ill feelings towards her ex's cousin and in fact their friendship had only strengthened as she made it her personal mission to coach the shy girl out of her protective shell. After weeks of learning and adapting, Alina had a breakthrough, her first ever date. The campus heartthrob, Steve, had bravely approached her and asked her to accompany him to their overhyped graduation party. She wasn't particularly interested in him, having seen him for three years sampling every other girl he could get his hands on, but she was curious to know what it felt like to go on a date with the handsome boy everyone craved, and to be kissed by him.

"Alina dear, boys want to do much more than just kissing, and that feeling should be shared by any *normal* girl. You really need to loosen up," Lizzy had told her the other day. And so began that last week of arduous training where Alina transformed herself from a demure and innocent young lady into a sensual and accommodating girl Steve was expecting her to be. Her graduation party was meant to be a milestone in her life, the day she would lose her inhibitions and virginity, not for love as she had once hoped but for the sake of doing what everyone else was doing.

She felt Steve's hands slide around her backside and pull her towards him. Lizzy had been right, that erotic wriggling of her bottom would drive boys mad and apparently Steve was no exception; she could definitely read through his mood as he kept grinding himself against the flimsy material of her short black dress, shamelessly oblivious to the crowd around them. It wasn't long before he sought her blood-red lips, his tongue brutally forcing them apart, invading her space. She wondered if he could taste the strong shot of alcohol Lizzy had made her down before meeting him. She had said that it would help calm her down, but it did more than that, it had started to make her feel reckless. One shot was all it took, having never before drunk alcohol in her life, in any shape or size, for no reason other than she absolutely hated the potent stinging taste. But, that day, she felt obliged to ignore her fastidious taste buds, just to get through the evening. She couldn't help wondering why the whole thing felt like an unpleasant chore that just had to be done, not at all what she had dreamed her first sexual experience would be like.

She forced her wandering mind back to what Steve was doing to her. The slimy feel of his darting tongue in her mouth had not made her heart race, and neither did it knock her off her feet with ecstasy, contrary to what Lizzy had guaranteed. What was wrong with her? She should be enjoying this; every other girl craved Steve, so why didn't she do too? And it was not as if she was in love with anyone else. She panicked. She had to act fast before this handsome demon devouring her mouth realised that she was as frigid as ice. She closed her eyes and let out a soft moan, pretending that she was in her seventh heaven.

Her moan excited him even more and he squeezed her bottom hard with both hands, hurting her. Apparently she was expected to like that because he broke his dirty kiss and looked back at her, giving her one of his confident seductive winks.

"Hey, do you want to go somewhere more private?" he whispered in her ear.

Her big brown eyes widened in fear. She had not expected the invitation to come so soon, a mere fifteen minutes into the party. Her hands started to shake as she flicked her hair back. "Now?" she croaked out.

"No point in postponing. Come on, there's nothing to be afraid of. Lizzy did tell me that you've never done it before and that you're bound to be a bit anxious. But don't you worry; I will be very gentle with you. You couldn't have picked a better pro for your first."

She gasped, feeling betrayed. "Really? Did Lizzy really discuss such intimate things with you?"

"Chill, it's not as if it's the best guarded secret in the world. Don't you know what everyone else calls you? *The Virgin Beauty.* Very apt, don't you think?" He let out a malicious laugh. "It's high time you got your pretty head out of those maths books and shed that terrible title, grow up and live the wild life while you can still call yourself a student. Remember that in a month or so we will all be busy working our arses off in a boring adult life with no time to party. So tell me, do you want to do it or not?"

What she really wanted to do was to slap his face and call him a jerk, but she did nothing of that sort. Instead she looked deep into his cold grey eyes, trying to, at the very least, *like* what every other girl *loved* and *adored*. She had always held the belief that the eyes were the true reflection of the soul, and Steve's eyes were just that, cold, empty, soulless. She could never like them, no matter how hard she tried. In the end she just shrugged her shoulders in defeat.

He took that as a sign of weakening resolve and he continued to apply pressure in that condescending tone of his. "Alina dear, you are a very beautiful girl, easily one of the hottest I've ever dated. And I'm not just saying this to flatter you or to get into your pants. Believe me, I could easily find another girl to shag this evening if you want to walk away, so either way I'm sorted. But I would really like to help you release that wild devil inside you. I'm doing this for you." He let out a small sigh of exasperation. “Listen, do you want to try having a drink first, just to get you in the mood?”

She let him take her hand and lead her to the crowded bar. As was typical of him, he arrogantly jumped the queue and ordered shot after shot for her. He just stood back, one elbow resting on the bar, drumming his fingers in impatience as he waited for her to down them all, one after the other. She was grimacing her way through her third or fourth, she just couldn’t remember, when she glimpsed her cousin Max a few paces away, snaking through the dancing crowd, his tall broad frame head and shoulders above the rest. He looked livid as he craned his neck here and there, desperately looking for someone. She ducked out of sight before he could spot her. Thankfully he didn’t; instead he spotted Lizzy dancing with a couple of other girls, and after exchanging what looked like a few foul words with her, he roughly grabbed her elbow and propelled her away from the dance floor. Alina sighed sadly, those two were always arguing so bitterly and she just wished that they could be able to talk through their differences. But now, as far as she was concerned, she had better make a fast exit. She didn’t want Max to see her dressed like a whore and report everything to her parents. It would break their heart with disappointment.

“OK, Steve, I’m ready,” she giggled, feeling strangely elated by the cocktail of spirits churning within her. “Where is this private spot you’re taking me?”

He beamed at her and started to walk away. She quickly followed, wanting to keep up with him, but her ridiculously high heels were impeding her already undignified chase. She was aware of fellow graduates gawping at her as she elbowed her way through the crowd, obviously envious of her; she was Steve’s chosen one for the night, an unlikely coupling given their different *cool* status, but it was still happening just the same. Two minutes into the chase, she managed to grab hold of his hand and lock her fingers firmly around his, trying to infuse some tender sentiment into the intimate experience they were about to share together.

He eventually stopped by the men's room, and once inside, he headed straight for a locked cubicle. After a few seconds of fiddling around with the lock, he reversed its occupied position and opened the door. He put his hand on her waist and ushered her in, firmly relocking the door behind them.

She stood still, in that narrow claustrophobic box with barely any space to stand, her left leg brushing against the toilet seat smelling of strong bleach. Was this where she would lose her virginity? Really? "Here?" she finally gulped out.

"For a maths genius you can be pretty dumb sometimes. Seriously, what did you expect? A king sized bed with velvet red cushions filled with soft down feathers? Zip it girl, you're killing my mood. I would have given up on you a long time ago hadn't you been so hot."

She saw him smirk with satisfaction. He knew that his cruel words had the exact intended effect on her; to intimidate her, to humiliate her, to make her feel grateful that he had even considered her for such an honour. Something at the back of her mind told her that he should be the one feeling that humiliation, but at that moment in time it was she who was fiercely blushing with disgrace. Her big brown eyes welled up with tears and she mouthed her humble *OK.* Happy with her willing consent, he hooked his index finger around the hem of her tight black dress and jerked it up to her waist. She shrunk back against the wall, conscious of the fact that she had no underwear on, just as Lizzy had strongly advised. *One less thing to worry about*, she had emphatically told her. And she had been right; Steve seemed to like it that way too. He gave her a curt nod of approval and he pulled down his trousers, expecting her to gape in wonder.

She didn't; she looked away and started fidgeting with her hands, not knowing what to do with them. She was suddenly aware of a faint humming noise as the awkward silence stretched on, but his loud grunt of disapproval shattered the string of logical thoughts that were struggling to add up in her mathematical mind. She looked into his cold grey eyes, silently asking him to show her what he wanted her to do. He huffed in annoyance and he lifted her left leg up, placing her stiletto heel on the toilet seat.

Then he took both of her fragile wrists in his strong hand and pinned them high above her head as he moved closer, preparing himself for the onslaught. Her heart broke into a million pieces; he wasn't even going to try to woo her or kiss her. It all felt so impersonal and cold. She hated it. But this was something that she absolutely had to live through, for her own sake, just to feel *normal*. She squeezed her eyes shut, her lower lip trembling, bracing herself for a vicious and painful experience; she expected nothing less from a guy like Steve.

But things never progressed; his brutal intentions were interrupted by the ferocious slamming of the door to the men's room, followed closely by three powerful kicks which smashed down the flimsy cubicle lock in mere seconds. She was stunned. It was all happening so astronomically fast; Max's livid face, she pulling her dress down in embarrassment, him grabbing her arm and jerking her out of the cubicle and throwing her against a urinal, Max reaching inside the cubicle again, smashing glass, Steve's charge and bellow, Max's strong fist locking hard on Steve's nose, blood dripping out onto the sterile white tiles, and finally Max's strong grip roughly dragging her out of the men's room amid the stares of fellow graduates...

2. Luca Snell

Luca swiftly locked the door and stood still, hardly breathing, trying to blend within the dark shadows of the tiny windowless room, fervently wishing that he could make himself invisible. A drop of sweat broke through a pore in his forehead and started its slow sliding way down his cheek. He cursed his impulsive nature. His gamble was about to backfire. It would cost him his cover and in so doing kill the beating heart of this operation. The lives of so many depended on its precise and tediously slow execution, and it seemed as though his impatience had just wrecked it to pieces. He listened closely, and he heard the throaty cough again, this time much louder. Where the hell was his wingman? Bloody Tom. He should have received his distress signal by now and called in the diversion.

A few metres away, heavy footfalls echoed across the bare hallway and up the groaning stairs. Luca fixed his vividly blue eyes on the shaft of light seeping in through the base of the locked door. All too soon that ray blinked as the heavy boots walked past. He almost whooped with joy, but his jubilation was short-lived; the heavy boots had decided to retrace their steps and halt to a stop, partially blocking out the shaft of light. *Shit. Shit. Shit.*

He transferred his watchful eyes onto the door handle. In the next second or so it would start to rattle. How long would it take for Dr Throaty Cough to realise that the door wasn't just jammed but locked...from the inside? Five, six seconds, perhaps fifteen, he reckoned, and another fifteen to break down the flimsy lock and confront whoever had locked it. With nowhere to hide and no weapon to defend himself, Luca's chances were slim. If he were lucky enough he would be granted a swift execution in that very room. Was this where he was going to die? Was this how he was going to die, wearing a tattered black hoodie and looking and smelling like a tramp? He had never seen this coming, but again, he had meddled with destiny so many times that he could hardly blame the stars for wanting to strike him down...for good this time.

His heart started to beat faster and faster and the burst of adrenaline surging through his veins made him think of *the girl.* He had never met her in the flesh but he had so often seen her image invading his conscious and subconscious dreams. Apparently the stars had predestined that their lives would be closely intertwined. He had obviously changed that now, just as he had changed every other thing in his life. He wondered what she would be doing at the time of his demise. Would she subconsciously feel his loss? It seemed fitting that he should see her for one last time and he closed his eyes and reached out for a hasty glimpse into her own dimension in the existing present...

...Her tall and graceful form was gliding towards the calling sea, her short tight black dress riding high with every spellbinding movement of her perfectly shaped legs. She had that peaceful look on her face as she relished the simplicity of the heavenly fingers embracing her senses; the fine golden sand crunching beneath her bare feet, the fresh salty smell, the hushed sound of the waves, and last but not least the divine picture painted before her with the stars and the moon shimmering on the glassed surface of the water. She stopped by the edge of the sea and closed her beautiful brown eyes, leaning her head back and letting the delicate breeze play with her flowing dark brown hair.

A stray tear escaped the confines of the brave face she was trying to maintain.

"Don't cry, Becca, don't cry for me," he whispered, and he tried to wipe that tear but he was nothing but a shadow of a ghost in her dimension...

The door handle rattled. He opened his eyes and started to count...one second, two seconds, three seconds...the reflexive act of locking the door had merely bought him precious seconds. He prepared himself to lunge forward and attack with his bare hands. He had every intention to go down fighting hard…But the impatient ring of the front doorbell shrilled through the darkness, and again, and again, and again, short sharp bursts that couldn't be ignored. The rattling of the handle stopped and the shaft of light beneath the door reappeared in all its welcoming brightness.

"About fucking time," he mouthed to the shadows of the darkened room. Tom had to leave him hanging on till the last freaking second. As it happened the locking of the door had not only bought him seconds, it had in fact bought him back his life. He had chosen wisely.

He waited patiently for the jingle of the keys and the opening creak of the front door which would be closely followed by the introductory statement, then the polite denial, then the assertive insistence, and it would ping-pong like that for a couple of serves. Ah, there came the introductory statement... "*Pizza delivery, Sir.*" That was his cue to act fast. He was kindly given only two to three minutes of grace because the game could hardly be expected to last any longer than that. He had unlocked the door and sneaked down the stairs by the time the polite denial came... "*I'm afraid you've got a wrong address. I haven't ordered anything.*"

The doctor's back was a mere three metres away from him and he could see him fingering the gun in his back jeans pocket, the gun he would have used on him had he found him locked in that room, the gun he would not hesitate to use on the pizza delivery boy should he find him suspicious. Silence was of the essence; only it separated life from death. Luca shrunk back against the shadows and soundlessly entered the darkened kitchen, the pale light of the moon beckoning him forward towards the window he had used to access the house some fifteen minutes earlier. He never heard the next serve, the assertive insistence; within the next second or so he had nimbly slid out of what could so easily have been his personal torture chamber.

He headed straight for the flimsy wooden fence and, with all the agility of the athletic twenty-two-year-old that he was, he jumped into the neighbour's back yard. He stood there for a minute or two, grinning and recuperating, breathing in the heavy London night air. Despite the odds he had lived to see another day.

The stars had so far always smiled upon young Luca Snell. He was born in comfort, wealth and love. He was the sixth and last child of Jake and Emma Snell. His father had the cumbersome title of the eleventh Earl of Yorkley, but he was also an experienced and bright cardiac surgeon working in a prestigious hospital in Cambridge with a string of research papers and innovative life-saving procedures to his name. His mother was a retired Oscar-winning Hollywood actress who dedicated her life to her husband and children, lavishing them with love and support. From his father he inherited his shrewd and creative inner energy as well as his vividly blue eyes, his most arresting physical feature. Everything else he inherited from his mother's side of the family, the Blake gene pool. Like his uncle, Ben Blake, and his grandfather, Josh Blake, he was endowed with a tall and slim-built frame, jet-black straight hair, finely chiselled aristocratic features and an infallible photographic memory. Unfortunately the *Blake Curse* gene was also thrown in the mix. By some chance weird wiring of their brain cells, the three men were often plagued by premonitions in the form of short sharp images. The two older Blakes treated this ability with respect and tried to refrain from playing god and meddling with the natural course of events, too fearful of upsetting the balance and unleashing a catastrophe. The younger Luca, however, rebelled against it, making it his personal mission to destabilize the entire universe.

The short sharp images he had always had of himself were of him living the life of a successful lawyer working in a magic circle law firm in London, but also happily sharing a family life with *the girl* and the two children they had together. But he could never accept the unpalatable fact that his life had to conform to some predestined plan. He set out to disrupt everything he saw and the first thing he attacked was his choice of career. His photographic memory would have guaranteed a secure place in one of the most competitive law schools in the UK had he actually sat his GCSEs and A levels. He didn't; he went on a holiday and was partying hard on some Greek island at the time when he was supposed to be sitting at a bench pouring everything he knew on a piece of paper. And after that he took that approach to everything else in life. If his compass pointed north he would turn and go south, doing the exact opposite of what was expected of him.

His mother started to despair; Luca was by then aimlessly going round in circles, squandering his incredible talents and bright mind, kicking opportunities aside time and time again just to prove a point to no one other than himself and his grossly immature teenage brain. She turned to her brother, Ben, for help. Having the same abilities himself, he was in the best position to understand what the rebellious youth was going through, and he immediately took him under his wing, offering him a lifeline in the form of a job that would help him channel his inner energy. Ben was the chief agent in charge of an elite and highly secretive branch of British Intelligence dealing with security matters of state and answerable only to the Prime Minister. Luca had no official certificates to his name but he possessed an abundance of potential, and the most his uncle could formally offer him was a menial office position within the agency which was based in a secret location in the back streets of London. Luca had never seen images of himself within that role and he immediately accepted it, knowing that the stars hadn't planned that one for him. It had been his choice and his alone.

And so, at nineteen years of age, he packed his bags and kissed his mother goodbye, leaving his family mansion in Cambridge and moving into a luxury one bedroomed apartment in London owned by his father. He immediately fell deeply in love with the vibrant city, with its sounds and its smells and its divine fast-paced beauty. He instantly knew why his original predestined working life would have been based in the capital. It would always have been his first choice of lifestyle. The high-speed city life ran in his veins. Ironically he had gone round in a full circle and ended up at the same point, with London as his home base. But he chose to shrug off that minor detail, knowing that he was not some stiff-collared lawyer in a magic law firm, but a humble agent doing his small bit to protect the city in the country that he loved.

And he took to his new calling in life like a fish to water. He was a fast thinker, bright, fearless, hard-working, rapidly assimilating a string of ideas and offering plausible strategies and solutions. He was a risk-taker but he always seemed to land on his feet and win big whichever height he chose to jump from; true traits of the lawyer he should have become, but traits which were just as vital in the intelligence role he had chosen. His uncle (the Chief of British Intelligence) as well as the Prime Minister, Larry Wills, recognised his true potential and they started to rely heavily on his opinions and recommendations. Luca quickly rose through the ranks and, while still in his first year of service, he was handpicked to actively participate in the monthly highly covert intelligence meetings. It was after one such trip to the ministerial offices that he happened to bump into Jessica, Larry Wills' only daughter.

Besotted by the mesmerizing effect of his deep blue eyes and charming smile, she could not stop herself from wanting him, just as she wanted everything else she fancied. She was never one to mince her words and she asked him, in a very suggestive tone of voice, to accompany her on a *crazy fun night out*. That was nothing unusual; he was more than used to hearing that same invitation from the tons of girls who took him home after a wild night of clubbing. However, he always firmly kissed them goodbye after he had shared their bed, sprinting out of their door and out of their life for good, never really liking anyone enough to stay the morning. He didn't particularly like Jessica either, recognising her as the rich spoilt brat who was always in the news for the wrong reasons; drinking and driving, smoking pot, indecent exposure, you name it and she did it. But her wild spirit intrigued him, her rebellious nature matching his own, and, more importantly, she was part of this new future he was weaving for himself, knowing full well that he would never have met her had he still been on his original intended path. For that reason alone he accepted her proposal and the *fun night out* turned out to be much more stimulating than he had anticipated it to be. Both were not keen on exclusive relationships and they settled in the habit of phoning each other for a random crazy night together here and there whenever there happened to be a mutual free spot in their diary.

Larry Wills was not happy with that arrangement. He desperately needed his daughter to tone down her wild ways which were beginning to seriously hurt his political career. She needed someone mild and sweet to neutralize her unruly taste and keep her in line, and that someone was not Luca. He pointed out again and again the obvious fact that the two were not good for each other; they were both too wild and fiery. After all, opposite poles were meant to attract and like poles repel. But both were hard-headed, never taking kindly to doing what they were told, and the concerned father had to resort to underhand tactics to break the two apart. And that was the main reason why Luca was offered his first undercover assignment out in the field. His talents were best suited for office intelligence and strategic planning, but, being young and enthusiastic, he longed to be out there in the thick of the action, thinking on his feet, adrenaline pumping in his veins. Larry knew this and he opened up an opportunity for him on the proviso that he had to completely let go of his previous identity and take on a brand new one where he was expected to infiltrate the dangerous territory of drugs, firearms and their potential links with terrorist activities.

Luca seized the opportunity with both hands. Without a second thought, he gave up his erratic affair with Jessica, knowing full well that she would never mean more to him than a very amusing way to spend the night, and he was sure that she shared that same opinion of him too. After one last fling with her, he told her that he had decided to move abroad. She was under the impression that he was some sort of diplomat working with her father and she never probed any further than that. She accepted his decision and kissed him goodbye, wishing him luck.

The following morning, Luca firmly closed the door to his father's luxury apartment and to his old way of life, and he went down the one way road leading deep into the underground chambers of British Intelligence. With much enthusiasm, he embarked on an arduous and compressed training programme whereby he gradually transformed himself from Luca Snell, a stylishly dressed, upper class and well articulated posh aristocrat, into David Black, a despicable lowlife criminal. His appearance was the first to change; that was the easiest. His stylishly cut hair was left to grow unchecked and so was his jet-black beard. He refused the permanent tattoos offered but accepted a henna of a vicious snake creeping up his neck. He thought that it looked rather intimidating. The only snag was that he had to refresh it every so often but he would rather live with that than having something permanently done. His new accent and mannerisms took a little longer to grasp, but he must have inherited his mother's acting talents because he was in top form to be released out on the streets of London within just four months into his intense training. Not even his mother would have recognised him then.

To complete his ensemble he needed a trusted wingman whose job was to discreetly follow him around and adapt to the needs of whatever difficult situation he landed himself in. Luca wanted to choose his own wingman and he asked for the reliable and thoughtful Tom who had shared an office with him in his early days within the agency before he had started to rise through the ranks. In fact, Tom was the first person he had befriended after his move to London. He was a quiet and reserved individual, a sharp contrast to the boisterous and full-of-life Luca, but both boys hit it off immediately, their different characteristics complementing each other. They often went clubbing together, with Tom relying heavily on Luca's outrageous confidence with girls to help him with those painful first introductions. Over time their friendship matured, forged on mutual trust and goodwill, the very ingredients needed for a successful relationship between a good wingman and his leader.

After that important addition to his operation, Luca was set loose. He rented a squalid studio flat and immediately started blending in. He was a fast learner and he quickly infiltrated the underworld. His incredibly deep insight together with an astounding gift of the gab (another trait for the brilliant lawyer he should have become) made him a true natural. People were easily convinced by what he said and all unwittingly gave him full access to their private lives and thoughts. Like the winner he had always been, he seemed unstoppable, thwarting plots faster than they were hatched up without ever implicating himself in the process. He started with petty drug dealers and moved on to smuggling of firearms and dangerous weapons and he eventually unearthed their deep-seated link with terrorist activity. And all that in a year, and he was still going very strong.

Luca could not stop himself from grinning smugly into the night as he made his way out of the back yard. He had won yet another battle, another step towards conquering the big war. He crossed the road and headed straight for the homeless man huddled beneath a filthy duvet at the far corner of the littered street. He slipped in beside him, taking refuge beneath the warm cover smelling of stale sweat.

"Bloody hell. That was close. I nearly died in there. What took you so long?"

"Fuck you, Luca, what did you expect? You impulsively marched in there, giving me less than fifteen minutes to rouse the backup team. You should know the rules by now. Plan first and act later. Besides, you shouldn't be the one doing the breaking and entering. Your job is to pass on the address and let the pros do the rest. You could so easily have blown your cover."

"But I didn't. Chill out, Tom. I just needed to feel that adrenaline pumping in my veins."

"Freaking hell, you are a loose cannon. Your impulsive decisions are beginning to piss people off, especially the Chief, your very own uncle. And I can tell you that he is usually one cool dude, not so easily pissed off, so well done to you for achieving that. He is giving you your final warning and then you're out. He also told me to tell you that some of your methods are bordering on the unethical, so you had better tone it down."

"Really?"

"Really."

"What did I do?"

"Jeez man, the list is endless but I'll start with the most recent offence; sleeping with the doctor's wife," Tom bickered as he nodded towards the quarry who was by then firmly closing the door on the tenacious pizza delivery boy.

"I never forced her and she was a very willing participant. What part of that is unethical? And besides, that doctor has forsaken his Hippocratic oath, planning to end life rather than preserve it. He is a bloody terrorist," he finished with a hiss.

"But his wife isn't. She shouldn't be used like a commodity. If this ever gets out, the media will have a field day."

"I needed to get her on my side because her hubby does not trust me with all his plans," he protested strongly. "Here, pass these on to my uncle...that little ungrateful prick...and tell him that I called him that." Luca dumped some gadgets onto his wingman's lap. "There is enough evidence in there that the doctor has recruited outside help; an orderly and two nurses. The orderly inherited this dump of a house from his late mother and they've been using it as their quiet plotting space. The hospital is their target. They are building something in a small windowless room at the back of the house on the upper floor, which I've bugged so that my prick of an uncle can keep his eye on its construction. I think that it is still in its early days, so we have time on our hands and perhaps, in the meantime, I can uncover who is behind his radicalization. Someone bigger than him is definitely pulling all the strings. Am I making sense, or not?"

"Sure, Luca, you always make sense. Your intentions are always impeccable and you do deliver every single time, I know that, everybody knows that. But the Chief still wanted me to pass on his final warning." He let out a loud sigh of accumulated fatigue. "I'm sorry, Luca, I didn't mean to snap. Are we good?"

Luca looked at him, understanding his frustration. Being a wingman was not an easy task; he had no life of his own, being always at the beck and call of his leader, constantly changing and adapting his appearance, being a homeless guy one minute and a well dressed customer drinking coffee in a cafe the next. He slept only when the leader slept and he ate only when the leader ate. He had to coordinate backup teams and act as that vital messenger between the two sides, staying perpetually alert, his one aim being to preserve the life and false identity of his leader. Luca gave him a friendly nudge with his elbow. “Sure, Tom, we’re good. Bloody hell, we’ve been doing this shit for over a year now. We need a break.”

“Yeah, sure do. I desperately need a shag too.”

Luca gave him a look of utter surprise. “Hey, I’m not such a slave driver. I do try to stay at home peacefully doing nothing on a Friday and Saturday night, and I do that for you. It’s your free time. Haven’t you been going out? After all, a wingman has his advantages; he isn’t shackled down to any identity, like I am.”

“Yeah, I know. I do go clubbing but it’s not the same without you.”

“Are you still shy with the ladies?”

“Yeah, I guess so.”

Luca thought for a moment or two before offering him a big mischievous grin. “You and I, my friend, we’ve been working too hard. We need a break. We deserve a break. Give me your phone, quick.” And he nicked Tom’s phone out of his breast pocket and, after putting it on speaker phone, he punched in a number he had so often used the year before.

“Hello,” came a sweet voice on the other end of the line.

“Hi Jessica, it’s me, Luca, Luca Snell. Remember me?”

“Sure...Luca...Luca sexy blue eyes, how could I ever forget you? How are you? How’s life?”

“Great,” he answered curtly, wanting to get to the point and avoid the niceties. “I’m in London for the night. Are you free?”

“Ermm, no. But I’ll clear my diary for you. Do you want to call at my place in an hour or so?”

“I was rather hoping that your father will never get to know about this. I would rather meet at my place, just a quiet night in, nothing too crazy. I’ll get some takeaway and booze, and we can watch stuff and do stuff.”

“OK. That sounds interesting.”

“And Jess, do you remember Tom, my friend? He’ll be there too. Can you bring a friend? Perhaps Mel? He likes Mel.”

“OK, will do. See you in an hour.”

“Make it two. I still need to sort some things out.”

"Sure, see you soon." And the line went dead.

Tom frowned. "Oh man, that's a bad idea. You should never make contact with anyone from your previous life. Not even your parents. They can't ever see you in your new skin. Man, they'll have your balls for this. And with Larry Wills' daughter too! Here in London! Oh, man, that's suicide."

"Chill. No one will ever get to know. Jessica Wills is our safest bet, safer than a hooker. She doesn't ever ask anything and she won't ever say anything. But she'll do everything. Believe me when I say *everything*. I really need to sleep with someone for the pure sake of sleeping with someone rather than for the sake of extracting information from their unsuspecting little brain. Believe me, I'm doing this for both of us, for our sanity, we both need it. Go on, Tom, crack on, deposit the stuff on my uncle's lap; he'll be very happy with it. You and I are heroes today and he won't think of checking on us and he'll just dismiss you with a smile. I guarantee that. Then all you have to do is run home and have a bath and change those smelly clothes, pick up some takeaway and lots of booze for the girls, Jess likes it that way, and meet me at my old place in two hours. Don't be late."

And he flicked the hood of his tattered hoodie over his shoulder length jet-black hair and walked briskly down the road, looking forward to his first holiday break in more than a year. The intelligence agency owed him that much.

3. The Truth about Alina Spiteri

"Let me go," Alina screamed at her cousin. But her shrill cry was diluted by the loud booming music reverberating back from the walls enclosing them. Max tightened his grip on her fragile wrist and continued to mercilessly drag her out across the dance floor, never pausing, never stopping, forcing her to run just to match his quick long strides. The crowd quickly spread out, making way for his charged exit, too frightened by the angry fumes bellowing out of his nostrils to intervene. Not that she expected anyone to step forward and help her; Max's sheer athletic bulk was just too daunting for anyone to challenge. She stumbled and twisted her ankle, and again, and again. She hadn't yet fully grasped how to walk in high heels, let alone run. She quickly kicked off her brand new black stilettos, leaving them lying in her wake, and she scuttled barefoot out of the venue and into the warm Mediterranean night air.

Max continued to storm down the lonely road, pulling her along, creating space between themselves and the prying eyes peering out of the front door. When he reckoned that they were a safe distance away, he stopped and roughly slammed her back against a rubble wall, knocking her breath out. Ever since she could remember, Max had always been there by her side, viciously protecting her from physical as well as emotional harm, his fiery Mediterranean temper quickly flaring up against anyone who dared taunt her. Their mothers being sisters, they enjoyed that unbreakable family bond that was typical of that small island of Malta, and this was more than strengthened by the fact that both had no other siblings or cousins. Knowing how protective he was of her, she had expected an angry tantrum from him that evening, but not to that extent. She had never before seen him so furiously out of control. The sheer wrath in his chocolate brown eyes was beginning to seriously scare her. She looked away and rubbed on the fresh bruises around her wrist.

"What the hell were you thinking?" he boomed in her face, using his full staggering height to tower above her.

"That's none of your business," she dared scream back. "And you're not one to preach either. Lizzy told me about everything that you two got up to in the past and from what I heard you are not an innocent virgin."

"That's peer pressure for you. But I thought that you were much bigger than the rest of us."

"Well, I'm not. Please stop butting into my life. We are not kids anymore and I no longer need your constant protection. I am old enough to make my own choices, be they good or bad."

"Fair enough. But I'm sorry, I just couldn't let you make that choice with that jerk. Why Steve? Are you in love with him?"

"Of course not," she answered with disdain.

"I thought so. How far did you two go? Did he hurt you?"

She was about to tell him, yet again, to mind his own business, but she hated confrontation. "No," she said meekly as she nervously played with her fingernails. "He hurt my pride and dignity but nothing physically."

He let out an audible sigh of relief; the two lovers had been so closely intertwined together that he had not been sure at what stage he had intervened. But the fact that they hadn't yet engaged was, at least, one positive aspect of the whole horrific nightmare. And on another positive note, she was not in love with Steve, and that should make the brutal betrayal he was about to reveal a bit easier to stomach. He moved away from her, raking his fingers through his thick brown wavy hair, deliberating how best he could break the rest of the news without shattering her already fragile self-esteem. But, however painful it would be, he just had to tell her the whole story because she was the only one who had the brains to potentially erase what had been done.

He took in a deep breath, "Alina, honey," he said in a surprisingly soft voice, "That whole thing was a cruel set-up, a malicious hoax performed by Lizzy who wanted to hurt me by hurting you; her cruel revenge for daring to break up with her."

"Sort your own life, Max, before trying to sort mine out. Stop blaming Lizzy for everything that happens. She was only trying to help me."

"Bloody hell," he swore. "You choose to believe in her, but not in me. Fine, let me show you her true colours." He took out his phone, his thumbs flitting across the screen as they accessed a website on the internet. Without another word, he slammed the phone in her hand.

The Virgin Beauty and The Generous Stud...place your bet now, read the title of the webpage. She scrolled down, quickly absorbing the sheer number of bets that had predicted that *The Virgin Beauty* would lose her preciously guarded virginity to *The Generous Stud* in less than an hour into the party. The memory of the soft humming sound she had heard in the cubicle surfaced on top of her ravaged emotions. Her heart started to hammer inside her chest as she scrolled further down, fearing the inevitable. She eventually encountered the footage of her experience in that box up to the point where Max had grabbed the recording device and smashed it beneath his foot. To her utter dismay, she was caught on film in all her explicit glory, Steve having wittingly positioned her exactly where he wanted her to be. Had the whole thing been allowed to run to completion it would have made a pretty erotic piece of work, leaving nothing to the imagination. Nonetheless, despite being cut short, the footage seemed to be an instant hit, already having thousands of paid downloads by those who wanted to add the piece to their private collection. The number of such downloads was increasing by the second, and the price of each purchase wasn't cheap either.

She gave him back his phone, completely lost for words, too traumatized to cry. Turning away from him in embarrassment, she started to stagger along, leaning heavily against the rubble wall. After a couple of paces she fell to her knees and she retched and retched, emptying the entire contents of her stomach onto the narrow grass verge, the alcoholic shots and all. She needed that, as much as she needed her cousin's sympathetic arms around her shoulders. She felt strangely stronger for that, and the anticipation of sweet vengeance started to take centre stage on her mind. She staggered back up on her feet, feeling reborn. After hitting rock bottom there was only one way to go...and that was up.

"So Steve wanted to make a quick buck," she hissed.

"And so did Lizzy. But it was revenge, rather than cash, that drove her."

"You're the lawyer; tell me, can we prosecute?"

"I don't think we can. When I questioned her, under duress I might add, she did vaguely admit to knowing about the presence of a recording device in that particular cubicle which transmitted live footage to that porn betting site. However, it's her word against mine. Why would anyone believe me? After all, everybody knows that we are always at each other's throats and that we would trip each other up if we possibly could. They would just think that I'm trying to frame her...just as you thought before I showed you that clip." Now that his blinding anger had subsided, the young lawyer inside him had started to think rationally. He had graduated the year before but he had enough knowledge of the ins and outs of the legal system to know that his claim wouldn't stand in a court of law. He shrugged sadly, "That's Lizzy, quite untouchable as far as this is concerned."

"And Steve?"

"Steve could easily claim that he, like you, had been duped into the whole thing, having no knowledge of the presence of that recording device. In that case, he did nothing illegal in the eyes of the law because you gave your full consent to have sexual intercourse in that cubicle. It definitely wasn't rape. And I'm positive that both Steve and Lizzy were not stupid enough to allow the recording device to be traced back to them. In fact Lizzy has already hinted that they commissioned some professional thugs to set the place up."

"What about the porn betting site?"

"Yes, that site, another blind alley, I'm afraid. It is foreign registered, very elusive to pin down as all illegal sites are. Apparently it is the playground of the very rich from all over the world. The clients are loaded enough to pay good money to see explicit and uncut filth on their laptop, especially a beautiful young girl going through her first experience. The fact that you were unsuspecting and scared would give an enticing slant to the piece, making it raw and natural as opposed to the acted out versions generally available on the net, certainly worth that extra dollar. And from what I saw, you were not the first to be duped into their scheme. They have been doing this for quite some time now, keeping their clientele of millionaires very satisfied."

Max paused as he evaluated the logical string of thoughts that were forming in his mind. "My guess is that Steve, with his affluent background and having used the site before, knew what sells most. After the unexpected demise of his father's wealthy empire last month, he decided to make a hefty sum of his own by performing in his own *movie* and selling its rights to that site. I'm pretty sure that he was clever enough to cover his tracks during any transactions that might have occurred; after all, he's a freshly graduated lawyer, certainly well trained in the cunning department. All he needed was a beautiful innocent virgin and you happened to fit the bill, but you were far from being accommodating. At that point he must have recruited Lizzy's help to quickly convince you as well as groom you for your first sexual experience. She seized the idea. I think that she would have liked this to go public, for maximum humiliation, but she must have been sworn to secrecy due to the obvious legal implications. However, just the knowledge that she had corrupted you in such a vile way was enough revenge for her. It is probable that you were never meant to get to know about the existence of that footage; I mean, what are the chances of you coming across a well protected illegal porn betting site based on the other side of the world and whose wealthy clientele can only access the site via their yearly membership subscription, which, I might add, is by invitation only and costs the earth, much more than you and I could ever earn in a year."

"But you just accessed it now," she accused as suspicion started to edge its way in. "Hey, how did you get to know about all this?"

"All thanks to a drunken brawl and a good Samaritan in the unlikely form of Mark Deliri." He saw her eyes widen in surprise. He nodded, "Yes, that Mark, Steve's best crony, son of the island's richest billionaire, and an active member of the select Campus Populars, as they like to call themselves. Apparently, he has always harboured this great crush on you...or love as he called it...but he found you to be too unapproachable. Even so, an association with a middle-class campus bookworm, no matter how beautiful she might be, would go all against the Populars' ethos; you know how they are, all coming from highly affluent families, all marrying into money, class and power, all doing what they bloody like thanks to that privileged status. So he kept his feelings tightly bottled up and did what he was expected to do…get himself engaged to a politician's daughter, you know, that arrogant Sophia."

"And the rumour is that she is heavily pregnant and they are getting married next week before she pops."

"Indeed...typical of all Populars; trapped in a loveless marriage, all for the sake of power." Max shrugged his shoulders, unable to fathom the way the mind of the rich and powerful worked. "But I feel sorry for Mark; there is a decent side to him too, decent enough to do the right thing when it mattered most. Apparently, yesterday while the two boys were stinking drunk, prowling that porn site, Steve let slip his intentions. Mark was furious that he had even dared ask you out, let alone plan to seduce you in such a crude way, and a terrible brawl broke out which spiralled out onto other grievances between them. The night ended with Steve being kicked out of Mark's villa but both were too intoxicated to remember anything and they met the next morning as if nothing had ever happened between them. It was only after Mark accessed the site again this evening and saw the webpage accepting bets that he vaguely remembered what had occurred. He liked you enough to betray his best friend, and he immediately called me, asking me to be discreet about his snitching. At first I wasn't too worried about it, brushing him aside, thinking that a graduation party wasn't really your scene, but he insisted and he gave me his membership password to access the site. After seeing the title, *The Virgin Beauty*, I panicked. I'm sorry, it's what everybody calls you and I knew that, but by then I had given up on breaking every nose who said it. Anyway, I called you on your phone, trying to warn you, but Aunty Lillian answered, saying that you had forgotten it on the kitchen table yet again, and she immediately confirmed that you had indeed gone to the graduation party with Lizzy. And here we are now...." he finished with a sigh.

She gasped in horror, "Does Mum know?"

"No, of course not. She doesn't know a thing, and she will never get to know either. And that is one valid reason why we shouldn't go down the public legal route, apart from the obvious fact that we will probably achieve nothing if we do. But we could still have our vengeance...just hear me out. I have destroyed the hard copy in that recording device in the cubicle but I could do nothing about the stuff that has already been transmitted live. But *you* can."

He smiled at her and grasped both of her arms in encouragement, trying to make her glimpse that tiny flicker of light in the darkest cave. "Go on, Alina," he urged, "Pay them back for what they did to you. You're the maths nerd and computer geek. Use your talents. You can do it. Infiltrate the site and wipe it out. Wreak complete havoc and destroy Steve in the process. Here, use this," and he put his hand in his pocket and conjured up a mobile phone. "Steve's phone. It was lying on the floor of the cubicle, probably having slipped out of his pocket when he pulled his pants down. I nicked it on an impulse and he was too stunned with the intrusion to notice. I'm pretty sure that he has used his phone to access the porn site at some point or other. All you have to do is flick through his history and breach his defences, accessing the site via his membership account. And then you can play revenge to your heart's content. True, we can use Mark's account to infiltrate the site, but that might implicate him, and that's not right."

"I wouldn't even think of doing that, I don't want to hurt Mark, not after his generous gesture." She stopped to think for a moment or two, evaluating the plausibility of Max's proposal. Then she threw back her head and laughed out into the starry night, suddenly feeling elated. "You're a genius, Max. Whatever will I do without you? If we can't use the legal door, then we will have to use the back door. Justice will still be served."

She eagerly grabbed Steve's phone and, hooking her long flowing hair behind her ears, she set to work, her thumbs flitting across the small screen, performing her magic. She could do anything she wanted with the simple device in her hand. Her exceptional skills with numbers made her see things that others easily missed. She was one of the fastest computer hackers in the world, breaking security defences within minutes. She had often experimented on a wide range of different sites, cracking open files; from local bank accounts to the island's protected government dossiers, from hospital notes to a random individual's innocent love-declaring emails...anything she could get her hands on...just to see how far and how fast she could go. Max was the only one who knew about her little illegal secret. He had so often watched her, dumbfounded, as her fingers clicked away on her keyboard. But she had never meddled with anything within the contents of the files she opened, always retreating quietly without disrupting a single digit. Her strict catholic upbringing forbade her to use her extraordinary talents for any malicious intent.

Her thumbs momentarily stopped their dance. She looked at the screen; she had already accessed the porn site using Steve's freshly cracked account. Her conscience nagged. Were her actions malicious? If so, she could choose to retreat now and try to go down the legal route, however difficult it would be, but at least her conscience would still remain intact. Her eyes darted across the faces of the unsuspecting girls on the site. Quite a few were barely adults, their cruel exploitation definitely bordering on the illegal. She ground her teeth in anger. She owed it to them to do something. It wasn't her who was malicious; this site was and so were the wealthy clients who derived pleasure from the humiliation of others.

With fresh determination, she resumed her magic, conjuring up a technologically lethal virus within Steve's account. It quickly permeated through the whole site, irreversibly corrupting it as well as the thousands who happened to be connected to it at that moment in time, whether they were downloading or just ogling at the erotic images on the screen. And she went further than that, flagging those *oglers* she encountered and tagging them onto a police watchdog site, exposing their filthy habits for the world to see. She smiled...that should cause quite an uproar; she just hoped that Mark hadn't been using the site at the time because he would certainly have been caught in her net.

Fifteen minutes spilled on to half an hour and on to even more minutes. "Hey, aren't you done yet?" Max asked, a hint of apprehension in his voice. He had been staring over her shoulder, witnessing the bloody battle which had only one victor, Alina, but the whole thing seemed to be going too far now. "I think that we had better stop. We don't want to make them too mad."

"I'm almost done. I just found the route through which all the clients' transactions are being channelled. They seem to end up in an iron-clad Swiss account. But it's nothing that I can't handle." Within the next fifteen minutes all that wealth had been distilled onto a children's charity. She giggled into the night, satisfied with her achievements. She had used her talents to steal from the rich and give to the poor. Did that make her a criminal? Probably not; Robin Hood was a hero, and so was she. She gave Steve's phone back to Max who immediately wiped out all fingerprints. He then headed for the car park and started to weave his way through the cars, looking for Steve's open-top flashy convertible. It should be easy enough to slip the phone inside. Trust Max to think of all the legal loopholes. She turned her back on the imposing venue the students had chosen for their graduation party, and she strolled down the road, barefoot, towards the sandy beach gracing that silent Mediterranean evening.

She took in a deep breath as she glided further towards the calling sea, relishing the simplicity of the heavenly fingers embracing her senses; the fine golden sand crunching beneath her bare feet, the fresh salty smell, the hushed sound of the waves, and last but not least the divine picture painted before her with the stars and the moon shimmering on the glassed surface of the water. Golden Bay, that idyllic beach on the north side of the island, a piece of heaven; she had always liked it there, it never failed to take her back to her happy carefree childhood summer days where she and Max would storm the beach and ride the waves. She stopped by the edge of the water and closed her eyes, leaning her head back and letting the delicate breeze play with her flowing dark brown hair. She wanted to stay like that forever, frozen in time...

She was dimly aware of Max's approaching presence somewhere behind her and she quickly wiped a stray tear that had escaped the confines of the brave face she was trying to maintain.

"Hey, are you OK?" he asked in a hushed voice as he put his hands on her shoulders and slowly turned her round to face him.

"Why, oh why did I ever let myself get involved with those loathsome Campus Populars? I've always hated them and everything else they stood for, all muscle and no brain and definitely no soul. I'm so stupid." She needed a comforting human hug and she put her arms around his waist and rested her head against his chest, listening to the calming beat of his thumping heart. He held her close, one hand on the small of her back and the other playing with her dancing hair in the breeze. She felt his heart rate rise a notch as he bent down and buried his face against her neck, his warm lips brushing against her delicate skin...Something did not quite feel right. This was way beyond the boundaries of an innocent and good-will friendship that she knew they shared. She started to push on his chest but he held her in a tight grip.

"Let me go," she hissed.

"Alina, honey," he said in a hoarse voice laden with the emotion of the insane moment that had just passed between them. "At least hear me out. I *think* that I'm falling in love with you...I *think*...but Lizzy seemed to think that I am too and she hated you for it. She was so damn jealous of you and she was always begging me to sever all ties with you. But I could never do that. I care too much about you. And that was the reason why I chose to leave her."

"You're confusing care with love. You can't be in love with me; you're my cousin, for Christ's sake."

"I am not your cousin."

"You're crazy. Lizzy was right, you are sick in the head. Now, take your hands off me."

He lifted his hands up in the air and moved away from her. "You are NOT my cousin, and I am NOT sick," he said, using a deep forceful tone of voice. "We are NOT related by blood, and what I just did was a normal reaction that any man would have for a beautiful and intelligent woman wearing that kind of dress. I am NOT sick," he repeated again for emphasis. "I've been begging Aunty Lillian to tell you the truth...but she won't. She is always putting it off, saying that you had exams and then it was this and that and the other. But if she won't tell you, then I will...Alina, honey, I'm sorry...you were adopted."

"Nonsense."

"I still remember the first time Aunty Lillian got you home. You were this scared five-year-old, clutching a brown teddy, saying nothing, doing nothing for weeks on end."

She closed her eyes and tried to remember back in time, looking for a string of truth in that absurd claim. She shook her head. She knew of no other life apart from the happy and secure one she shared with her parents. "Why are you lying to me? How come you remember and I don't?"

"I am three years older than you. I was eight at the time and I guess that three years can make a lot of difference to childhood memories. Besides, I think that you wanted to forget that part of your life. I once heard Aunty Lillian say that your real parents went through a very traumatic death and that was why you refused to speak for weeks and weeks. Eventually the child psychiatrist you were seeing broke through your wall. Little by little you opened the door to your heart and started to let people in. Your parents were the first to be invited in. Then your father bought Brandy, your first dog, and that made a big difference. Then you and I became the best of friends, quite inseparable. But you never trusted anyone else, no other child, no other adult, no other friend. And, to this very day, you're still doing the same thing. Alina, honey, you have no other friends at Uni. Lizzy had to force her way into your life when she and I were engaged and you only let her in because you thought that it might please me. It did at the time. But then we broke up and she started to claw in on that budding friendship and poison your mind. I tried to warn you about her but you wouldn't listen."

She turned on her heel and started to march away. He was right on just one thing; she struggled with friendships, she knew that, and she even went as far as calling herself frigid when Steve had kissed her earlier that evening. She had never before felt inclined to fall in love and she had somehow always considered herself as emotionally stunted, thinking that that was something which came hand in hand with her extraordinary mathematical talents. But it had nothing to do with being adopted. That was a lie, a cruel lie. She was bright and sharp and she should have remembered another life had it really existed.

"Alina, I'm not lying. You are just refusing to remember. Please Alina...the nightmares...do you remember the nightmares? Aunty Lillian said that you're still having them from time to time."

She stopped in midstride. Ever since she could remember she had been plagued by a sharp nightmare. It was always the same; a man's coal-black eyes hovering above her, the dancing grey smoke between their faces giving those eyes that ethereal feel. She would wake up screaming and screaming until her mother took her in her arms and rocked her back to sleep. And at twenty-one years of age she still needed her mother's comforting hug to help her out of her hysterics. But as time went by the frequency (though not the intensity) of the nightmares got less and less and she hardly bothered reflecting on them anymore.

She turned round to face Max, tears streaming down her face. "I see a man with these intense coal-black eyes. Is he my real father?"

"I don't know. Aunty Lillian doesn't speak of your past, not to me, not to anyone else."

She wiped her tears with her hands. "I'm tired; please can you take me home now?"

He hesitated for a while, wanting her to delve deeper inside the subject and talk about it, scream about it, cry about it, vent her emotions. Bottling them up like she wanted to do was not a healthy option. He felt guilty for throwing her in at the deep end without having some kind of professional emotional support at hand. He had been selfish to do so, driven only by the self-centred desire to prove a point, that the romantic moment he had experienced was not sick. "Alina," he began, "I'm sorry for telling you. Can you forgive me?"

"Don't worry about it. I'm fine. Subconsciously I have always known the truth. You telling me won't make a difference to anything in my life. Mum and Dad have always given me security and love and they will always be my parents as far as I am concerned. But now, I just want to go home. Please can we go?" She held out her hand and he took it, and they both started to tread through the golden sand.

They reached the edge of the beach where it touched the roadside. Alina looked back over her shoulder at the silent idyllic stretch of heaven. The ghosts of the past were still there, building sandcastles, playing tag, riding the waves of that glorious Mediterranean blue sea. She had shared many happy summers there with Max. She looked at their hands casually locked together. They had so often walked that way. Her feelings for him ran very deep and she loved him like a brother, but nothing else.

"I'm sorry, Max," she whispered. "I don't think that I can ever see you as anything but a loving cousin."

"That's OK. We don't have to talk about it now...or ever."

"But I want to talk about it now. You're not in love with me; you just think that you are. You care for me just as much as I care for you. But it's not love. I recognise love when I see it. You were deeply in love with Lizzy once, it showed in your eyes, I saw that, everybody saw that. But her malicious jealousy smothered that love and she planted that seed of doubt in your mind, brainwashing you into believing that you love me. And I know that I'm right on this one. Sometime down the line I'm positive that you will fall in love again with someone who is worthy of your heart much more than Lizzy ever was."

"Yes, all right, if you say so." He gave her an uncomfortable smile and, shaking the sand off his shoes, he led her to his waiting car at the end of the road.

4. The Priceless Lure of the Unknown

Luca opened the door to his former apartment. Everything inside was sparkling clean and in order thanks to the professional cleaning crew his mother had commissioned on a monthly basis. After more than a year away it still felt strongly like home and it was good to be back. He absolutely loved the place with its prime location overlooking the fantastic views of the river Thames with Big Ben and Westminster against its backdrop. A place like that would cost millions for its view alone, but his father could certainly afford to have it and keep it. It was a small place, just one bedroom, but more than enough for Luca and the bachelor life he relished. He took in a deep breath, feasting his eyes on the expensive and luxurious furnishings, a hallmark of his sophisticated and stylishly obsessed mother. It was a far cry from the squalid and damp studio flat his new identity had been forced to live in that past year. At that moment in time he was struggling to comprehend why he had chosen to live undercover when he could so easily afford to live in sheer luxury thanks to his overwhelming family fortunes.

But the reason behind that logic was simple enough. He hated his orderly predestined life and, because he had seen it all beforehand, it lacked that element of surprise and adventure. He needed that burst of adrenaline, he was addicted to it, and he was determined to do everything in his power to infuse that priceless lure of the unknown into his life. So far he had succeeded in doing that with his choice of career, and the next thing he needed to tackle was his choice of life partner, *the girl.*

Her image had invaded his conscious and subconscious dreams so many times that he felt that he already knew her inside out; there was just nothing new left to discover. And from what he had seen he could not understand why or how he could ever fall so deeply in love with her, so deeply so as to ask her to marry him. He was certainly not the marrying type, so why choose her of all people? True, she was very pleasing to the eye, but so were a whole bunch of other girls he knew, and some were far better looking than her, and certainly more accommodating and adventurous. So, again, why her?

He had always seen her living this quiet and simple life somewhere in the Mediterranean...at least he thought that it was the Mediterranean; the backdrop of the images he had seen looked that way. He reckoned somewhere in Italy or Spain or Greece, somewhere near the sea, somewhere sunny, somewhere deeply catholic because she sure did pray a lot. And she looked Mediterranean too, with her brown eyes and hair and an exotic sun-kissed complexion...though she spoke English, good and well articulated English with a hint of an accent, hard and elongated, not quite guttural but putting a lot of emphasis on all consonants, an accent he had never heard before, an accent not quite Italian or Spanish nor Greek, but a very pleasant accent nonetheless. But that was the only anomaly. Otherwise she was definitely Mediterranean.

She seemed to have two favourite spots close to her heart, the local cathedral and the sea. He had lost count of the number of times he had seen her kneeling down at a gilded altar as she shot prayers up to the sky. And she seemed to have an equal deep fascination for the crystal clear deep blue sea which she would religiously visit and worship, night or day, winter and summer, whatever the weather. Whenever he consciously dipped into her world, he always saw her alone and it seemed as though she never bothered to socialize with anyone. Her life seemed otherwise dull and colourless. If she was not praying or lusting for the horizon, he would invariably find her with her head stuck in a book, usually boring maths books with a lot of numbers, equations and theories. She also liked spending time alone on her computer. That was all she seemed to do...certainly not his choice of lifestyle. He worshipped noise and crowds and parties with their fast heart-pumping thrill rides. So, again, why her?

Her choice of attire wasn't quite him either. He liked his women well perfumed, well dressed, revealing but subtle, enticing and sophisticated. He had always seen her wearing tight jeans and a loose sweater or shirt or T-shirt, whatever the climate at the time permitted. Flat shoes were her constant companions and she never wore any jewellery. And neither did she wear any makeup. She enjoyed being as plain as Mother Nature intended her to be.

But she had looked different when he had invaded her world earlier that night at the time when he thought that he was about to die. The backdrop was the all-too-familiar seashore setting, but, for the first time ever, he had seen her wearing a dress, a nice short sexy dress revealing a pair of splendid legs, and she wore loads of makeup too. Perhaps she was hoping to get lucky that night, perhaps a good tumble on the beautiful sandy beach he had seen. He grinned to himself as he slumped down on his comfortable sofa and closed his eyes, curious to know who was igniting her fire that night. He cleared his throat and concentrated hard, reaching out into her dimension, invading her private space...

...She was still wearing that short black dress, but she was curled up on a bed, fast asleep, clutching a soft brown teddy bear close to her chest...

Seriously? Really? This girl still slept with her teddy bear! Freaking hell. But he had rather liked the way the short black dress had partially ridden high up her hips, revealing the naked rounded curve of her backside. She was either wearing nothing beneath that dress or else she was wearing thongs the size of nothing. He couldn't really tell from the way she was all curled up. It was certainly a refreshing change from her usual frumpy night-time T shirt and shorts. He felt *obliged* to go back there to have a better look and perhaps wait for her to move about in her sleep. He cleared his throat again and closed his eyes...

She had moved. She was by then lying flat on her back, her long brown hair splashed all over her face and pillow, her brown teddy bear loosely held by her right hand. But her evident distress grabbed his entire attention and he neither wished nor could do what he had come back in there for. It did not feel right. Her breaths were coming in short sharp bursts, her strangled moans only partially escaping the confines of her constricted throat. She was obviously reliving a nightmare. His eyes caught sight of the blue bruises on her fragile left wrist lying on the pillow beside her face. He shifted his gaze and he quickly registered the black smudges of makeup beneath her eyes. She had definitely cried herself to sleep. Her big evening had not gone quite as she had planned. Someone had hurt her. A great sadness descended upon him, crushing him down. He felt her pain. It hurt him, it hurt him so badly. He bent down and tried to kiss her lips.

"Becca, baby, please wake up. He won't hurt you again. I promise. As long as I live no one will ever hurt you again."

Her voice finally broke through the restraining chains of her nightmare and she started to scream and scream and scream, her whole body trembling with fear, writhing in pain, rocking the bed, her eyes open wide with terror as they stared vacantly up at the darkened ceiling. He could do nothing to calm her down because she could never see him or hear him or feel him in her own dimension. He just stood there, hopelessly trying to hold her, enduring her screams for help which were wrenching his heart out of its ribcage.

The door behind him burst open and a petite woman in her late forties passed through his shadow, wrapping her arms around the writhing mess on the bed.

"Alina, honey, it's OK, it's only a dream. Wake up, honey," she said.

The girl blinked, once, twice, and a thread of life started to diffuse through that vacant look. Slowly, her big brown eyes started welling up with tears. "I was so scared, Mum. That day I was so scared," she sobbed. "But he was there and he saved my life...I didn't want him to die...I know everything, Mum...Max told me...he told me the truth...Why didn't you ever tell me?"

Luca turned his back on the scene. There was nothing else he could do. The mother will sort the daughter out. And he retreated back to his own world...

He was clutching his chest in agony, his heart beating dangerously fast, his own body contorted as he shared the girl's pain. He was scared, very scared. What had just happened to him? He had never experienced anything like that before. In the past whenever he had consciously dipped into her world, it had always been calm and serene, quite unremarkable, just ordinary everyday emotionless settings. Similarly, whenever he had been subconsciously taken to some place into that future they would share together, it had always been equally as calm and serene. This was the first time he had experienced any negative emotions and it seemed as though his feeling were closely connected to hers. He didn't understand it. He was not in love with the girl; he refused to be in love with someone he had never talked to or even seen in the flesh. He hated his grotesque ability with a deep passion. His uncle had so often tried to discuss it openly with him, similar to having that uncomfortable sex talk with his father, both using the rationale that an open discussion would lead to better trust if and when problems arise. He did have that sex talk with his father, he had no choice, but he categorically refused to have the premonition talk with his uncle. Discussing it could only make it feel more real and all he wanted was to brush it under the carpet and ignore it. His uncle respected his decision and backed off but not before strictly warning him against disrupting the natural course of events.

Luca knew that his uncle would always be happy to discuss things at any time of day or night, and he could well try to contact him that evening. A part of him wanted to. But he couldn't, not that day anyway, he had to avoid his uncle at all costs because of the planned illicit rendezvous with Jessica.

He closed his eyes and leaned his head against the sofa, trying to calm that wild beat of his heart. Something was nagging at his logic. Ah, yes, the mother had called the girl Alina. He knew her as Becca, he had always called her Becca, she had told him that her name was Becca in one of his dreams which depicted the day they were originally destined to meet in the flesh. In that dream he should have been a big shot lawyer and she a lost tourist in an elite area in London. But he had obviously meddled with that dream by changing his career path, and it was highly unlikely that it would ever come to pass in its original raw form. He recalled it in all its finest details...

...He was walking home from work, taking the familiar route from the law firm to the multimillion pound house he himself owned deep in the heart of Mayfair. He liked it there, living shoulder to shoulder with the elite of society. His big shot job allowed him to live that lifestyle without having to rely on any financial help from his wealthy father. That day, the crowds around him were fairly thick but he still managed to spot her as she stepped out of a top-end toy shop in the iconic Burlington Arcade. Her simple low-cost attire rather jarred with the affluence of the toy shop she had just exited. She stopped in the middle of the busy pavement, people jostling her about. But she didn't seem to care. She wore a dejected expression on her face, just as though she had just reached her checkmate, trapped with no place to go.

"Do you need any help? Are you lost?" he felt obliged to ask.

She looked deep into his vividly blue eyes and she must have liked what she had seen because she cast aside her introvert tendencies and, instead of lowering her head down and scuttling shyly away, she held her head high and decided to talk to him. "Yes, I suppose I am lost."

"I can help you there. Tell me, where do you want to go?"

"I'm not literally lost. I know where I am...physically," she said with that unique accent of hers. "I'm just lost, mentally, if you know what I mean. I came to London looking for answers but everything here is so vast and huge, it's like looking for a needle in a haystack. And this is just the tip of the iceberg. How on earth am I going to comb through the streets of the rest of Britain if I can't even tackle London? Perhaps I should go back home...but I really can't do that either because that would be suicide. They are bound to hunt me down and corner me, exploiting my skills. And here I am now at this single point in time, I can't move forward and I can't go back. So, yes, does that answer your question? I am lost...lost in that sense," she finished

with a big smile on her face. She had never before exchanged such a philosophical and ambiguous string of sentences with a stranger she had just met on the street. But it sure felt good to unload her worries onto his sympathetic ear.

He threw back his head and laughed heartily. "OK, you lost me at your very first sentence. Shall we start a little bit slower? I'm Luca Snell. What's your name?"

"Ermm....Becca...I think."

"You think? Do you have other names?"

"I might. But the unique privilege of calling me Becca goes to you. This might be the beginning of something new, so why not start afresh...new life, new beginning, new name."

Was she flirting with him? He thought so. "Wow, I'm honoured," he teased, playing along. "And why, may I ask, am I the privileged one?"

"I like your eyes. They are so captivating, sharply reminding me of the deep blue sea back home where I come from. They are actually making me feel quite homesick."

He rolled his eyes up to the sky. There came the usual response. All the ladies liked his sexy come-to-bed eyes. He started to mentally count in his head, wondering how long it would take for her to pop the same old question and ask him out. But he could never have anticipated her next response.

"You see, the eyes are the first thing I look at when I meet someone. I have this ingrained belief that they are the true reflection of the soul. Perhaps it was something my biological mother taught me. I don't know. I can't seem to remember. But in any case, I think that your eyes are open and honest, luring me into revealing things I shouldn't be telling a stranger. But what the hell, I've reached my rock bottom, yet again, and I don't think that I can go any lower than this. This must be the end of the road for me. I might as well go home and wait for those hounds to hunt me down." She sighed sadly. "Well, I had better get going. It was really nice of you to listen to me. Good bye Luca Snell. Wish me luck. I'm going home." She turned on her heel and started to walk away from him.

It took him a full minute to recover, and after that he snapped into action and weaved through the crowd, desperately searching for the unique shine of her straight brown hair. He managed to grab hold of her hand and jerk her round to face him.

"Hey, hey, stop. I'm curious, who is hunting you down?"

"Some seriously big names with seriously big money."

"Why?"

"Because I hacked their account and fiddled with their well of gold, siphoning it all onto some charity for a great cause."

He laughed, "You're kidding me, right?"

She looked him straight in the eye. "Do I look like I'm kidding? They tried to mess with the law, and with me and a whole bunch of other naive girls, and I just had to pay them back. Ironically, they liked what I did so much that they are all hunting me down, trying to coerce me into using my skills for illegal purposes."

"Why are you telling me all this?"

"I don't know. I feel like the condemned man with a noose around his neck; his desperation would make him start to talk to anyone who cares to listen." She paused. "Damn, I feel like such a loser. Listen, Luca Snell, you look like the type of guy who has reached the top of his mountain of success. I don't want to drag you down with me. Forget what I just told you and let go of my hand so that we can both go our separate ways."

He was Luca, and Luca never took kindly to doing what he was told. He squeezed her hand tight and offered her one of his big charming smiles. "I live just round the corner from here. Do you want to discuss this further over coffee?"

"No."

"Come on, Becca," he said, stressing out her name and letting the cheeky twinkle in his eye do all the convincing. "Come home with me. You know you want to. What happened to your 'new life, new beginning, new name'? You like me; you were flirting with me back then, weren't you?"

"Yes, I suppose I was. But that was the condemned man talking again. Had you met me in normal circumstances you

would immediately know that I am very shy and awkward with people. No, I'm even more than that; I'm actually frigid, emotionally stunted. You wouldn't want me in your fancy home...or bed, if that's what you're thinking. I'll let you in on a little secret...I am twenty-one years of age and I've never had sex. Hell, I haven't even had a decent kiss...well only Steve and Mark, and in my book their attempts were far from decent. I really hated the slimy feel of their tongue in my mouth, yuk...and they were supposed to be the most popular guys on campus, irresistible heartthrobs, but they did nothing for me...zero, nada, zilch...and that's exactly how frigid I am."

Ah, a naive frigid virgin. The vast majority would find that repugnant. He, on the other hand, found it challenging. He gave her an impish grin. "I can see why you've never got laid. Are you always this honest on your first date?"

"I don't know. I don't usually date, and I don't think that this weird conversation between us could ever be defined as a date."

"Freaking hell, you talk too much." He tightened his grip on her hand, not wanting her to walk out on him. He was about to take a gamble; he could either get slapped in the face or get laid by this intriguing virgin. He calmly put his leather briefcase down on the ground and slid that free hand through her silken brown hair, jerking her head towards him. He went straight for his instant kill, gently stroking his lips against hers, his tongue slowly teasing its way in, performing its tender erotic play. Once again, she was that condemned man on the scaffold, awaiting execution, with nothing to lose, forsaking all inhibitions, and she returned his sensual kiss as if all her life depended on it. The minutes ticked by, pedestrians streaming past them, some staring, some frowning, some aroused by the naked passion.

He eventually had to pull back because she herself had no intention of ever doing so. He grinned as his finger stroked the deep scarlet flush on her face. "You are definitely not frigid, my dear. Mark and Steve were probably just two dweebs who couldn't even kiss. Am I right in thinking that I just knocked your socks off?"

She looked down, suddenly overwhelmed by an emotion that was virtually alien to her. "Yes, you did," she mumbled. "Phew, that was out of this world. It looks as though you've got tons of experience in the kissing department."

"Yes, I have...but I can honestly tell you that that was the best I've ever had in all my years." He could see that she had started to fidget now that her inhibitions were slowly returning. It was time to start his reassuring speech and take her home...to his bed. He was Luca, and Luca always managed to sweet talk people into doing whatever he wanted them to do, his infamous gift of the gab. "But enough of this sex-talk. Believe me, I wasn't taking advantage of your vulnerable state; I just wanted to prove the point that the word frigid doesn't exist. Everything hinges on meeting the right guy. Now, Becca dear, what I really want to do is to take you home and sort out your other department, this hacking problem that you have. Try me out, and who knows, I might actually be able to help you."

"I very much doubt that." She sighed. "Oh well, OK, lead the way. I am a dead man walking anyway, so I might as well take my chances with you."

He smiled inwardly. That was a relatively easy task to do, needing only a dirty kiss and a few short sweet sentences. He picked up his leather briefcase and led her into his home and into his life and eventually into his heart...

And that was the way the stars had originally destined their chance meeting, in a busy street in London on some random evening. But all that became nothing but a whisper of a fractured dream the day he turned his back on law school. No law school meant no big shot law job, no Mayfair house and no walking back home at that random spot in time. It was virtually impossible to reproduce or pinpoint the exact year, month, date, hour, minute or split second of that single chance meeting. Not that Luca ever wanted to. Yes, that first meeting would have been energetic and flavoured and he could see why he would have been drawn in by her unique enigmatic appeal, but that day she would have acted out of character due to desperation. It was her real self that had him cringing and the more he saw of her in her actual everyday life, the more he doubted the good judgement of what was written in the skies.

But it seemed as though destiny was too tenacious. Even though he had thwarted that first meeting, Luca knew that his future was still closely linked with hers because he still had images of their life together: their wedding, the birth of the children they would share together, and several other family images. Destiny was determined that they should still fall in love and it had somehow found another way for the two to meet. The fact that he had gone round in a full circle and ended up living in London should make that feasible. And perhaps deep down inside him he already loved her. The image of her screaming in pain and fear during her nightmare had ripped his heart to pieces. The fact that he had reacted that way scared him, really scared him because he coveted the lure of the unknown too much to ever blindly accept with whom he should fall in love. He wanted to make his own choices and preserve that element of surprise, that surge of adrenaline, something he would never get with this girl, Becca.

With that in mind, he stood up tall and walked purposely towards the bathroom. He had less than an hour to prepare for Jessica's arrival. He looked at himself in the mirror. The elitist Jessica was in for a shock. He had ceased to look like the suave and sophisticated Luca. The shoulder length jet-black hair, dark shaggy beard and creeping snake up his neck made him look even more ferocious than the drug lords and terrorists he was hunting down. All he could do was try to clean up. He quickly groomed his beard into a stylish stubble; that was a risk worth taking because it would soon regrow to its unmanageable state in the next couple of days. He could do nothing about his hair but tie it up in a neat ponytail. He discarded his tattered black hoodie and took a quick shower.

He was walking towards his bedroom with a towel around his waist (intending to choose one of his expensively labelled suits to compensate for the rest of his appearance) when the doorbell rang. He looked through the eyehole. It was Jessica. She was early. Damn.

He opened the door for her, grinning widely. "Hello Jess. It's still me, Luca. Don't worry, most of it is reversible."

"Bloody hell, why would you do that to yourself?" She flicked back her long blonde hair and haughtily sailed inside, scrutinizing his new look.

"Just don't ask," he said as he closed the door and turned round to face her. He hardened his chest muscles, trying to divert her attention away from his snaked neck and onto his well maintained torso and ripped abdominals. That strategy worked well on the sex-obsessed Jessica, just as he knew it would. She moved closer and shamelessly unwound the towel from around his waist and let it fall to the ground.

"Let us see if you're really Luca," she teased as she calmly stood back and devoured his nudity with her beautiful and cat-like green eyes. She finally gave her nod of approval. "Yes, OK, it's all been confirmed, you are definitely the same old Luca."

A strange thought flashed through his mind. Had Becca been in Jessica's position, she would probably have chosen to look deep into his eyes to confirm his true identity in a stranger's face. He remembered what she would have told him on that original predestined first encounter...*The eyes are the true reflection of the soul.* He couldn't help feeling soulless and shallow at what he was about to do. Where these actually pangs of remorse? Why now after all those years of voracious sexual experiences? Why had the image of her crying in her sleep affected him so badly so as to make him feel guilty? For goodness' sake, he hadn't even met the girl and therefore he was not cheating on her, and more importantly, he was NOT in love with her.

He had to break free from destiny's chains. He had to make his own choices in life. And he chose adventure and the lure of the unknown.

He dragged his thoughts back to Jessica standing in front of him, and he mentally forced himself to offer her a wide suggestive smile to hide this newfound discomfort with his stark nudity. “You’re early,” he said.

“Yes, I know. I was hoping for an appetizer before Mel and Tom arrive. Are you up for it?”

“Sure.” And he wrapped his hands around her slim waistline and dragged her close to him...

5. Hunted

Alina looked at the watch on Max's wrist as he parked his car outside her house. It was still half past ten, way too early. Her mother was not expecting her back until the early hours of the morning, more than convinced that she would be having so great a time at the graduation party that the hours would just sail by. She had been so wrong.

"Hey, do you want me to come in with you?" Max asked. "You don't have to go through this alone. Knowing how cagey Aunty Lillian can be about the...the...the adoption, it would probably need both of us working together to persuade her to dish out all the fine details."

"No, I'm not going to discuss that tonight. I still need to mull over it. Thank you, Max, you can go back home. I'll be fine, and if I'm not I'll call you, I promise."

Alina gave him a quick friendly peck on the cheek and slid out of the car. She looked down at her attire and scowled. Pulling down the hem of her stretchy dress would be futile; it would only ride back higher with every pace she took. She thought of the demure blue dress her mother had bought her especially for the occasion. Coming from a working class family, Alina knew that her parents had saved very hard for that dress. But she had still chosen to heartlessly dump it for one of Lizzy's sexier outfits, with the original intention of going back to her friend's house at the end of the party and changing clothes again before returning home. She shrugged sadly. Her parents would be so disappointed in her to see her all dolled up in her slutty costume. At least her father was working the late night shift at the local hospital and she would be spared the embarrassment, and if she were lucky enough her mother would be in her usual position on the sofa in the lounge, fast asleep in front of the running television programme.

She sent up a little prayer to the sky before inserting her house key in the lock and opening the door. The jovial sound of the TV permeated out of the lounge, and so did her mother's loud snores. She sighed in relief. She had been spared. She silently closed the door shut and was about to run up the stairs to the sanctuary of her bedroom, when Alaska, her puppy Labrador padded out of the lounge and started to circle her ankles, yapping happily.

"Shush," she whispered as her bare feet skipped the frisky dog and tiptoed up the first few steps. But it was too late. The commotion had disturbed her mother.

"Alina, is that you?" came a sleepy voice from the lounge.

"Yes, it's me, Mum. Sorry for waking you up. Go back to sleep." She continued to skip up the stairs, out of sight.

"No, that's fine, I wanted to wait up for you but, you know me, I just dozed off, like I always do. Come back here and give me the details. How was the party? Did you meet anyone interesting?"

"I'm tired, Mum, I'll tell you all about it tomorrow," she shouted down the stairs.

"Ermm...OK, dear. Have a good night." Her mother was not convinced but she had decided to give her that space.

Alina opened the door to her room and slid inside. It had been a close call. She stood still, her back against the door, and she couldn't help but feel uncomfortable. Dishonesty was never her thing. She had to go back down and face the music. Her parents deserved that much. With tears in her eyes, she opened the door and padded down the stairs again.

"I'm sorry, Mum," she sobbed as she entered the lounge and patted down her short black dress. "I borrowed this from Lizzy."

"Oh, honey, that's OK, I should have let you choose the dress, but you were never interested in shopping and I had to go and buy it myself. My tastes are not so modern, I'm afraid. You're right, looking back, the blue dress was a tad old fashioned."

"No, Mum, no, it wasn't. It was beautiful and modest. It's just that ...the other girls all wear these short..." She shrugged, "I was only trying to fit in."

"That's OK honey. I can understand that. I was young once too and I know that trying to fit in can be quite overwhelming. Come, come and sit with me, let's talk." And she patted the sofa next to her. She had registered her daughter's bruised left wrist and blackened bare feet, the latter the obvious result of running around barefoot in the streets. The mother jumped to her own conclusions. "Alina, honey," she began, her heart thumping wildly, dreading hearing about that apparent abuse, but at the same time wanting to approach it calmly and sensitively. "You shouldn't have to change yourself to fit in anyone's circle. If the boy doesn't accept you the way you are, then he is not worth knowing. Let him love you for what's inside you, not for the way you look or dress. Remember that looks fade away with time, and when that's gone, it's your soul that will remain, and it's your soul that he should be in love with." She softly touched the bruised wrist. "Did a boy hurt you, Alina? You can tell me."

"He was going to, but Max saved the day and broke his nose. He won't be asking me out again, for sure." She gave her a weak smile. "Don't worry, nothing happened in the end. Actually, it was Max who bruised my wrist, but he did it with good intentions. He was so angry with me that he dragged me out of the place...it was so embarrassing...everyone was staring at me and laughing. All that shame for nothing. And it's not as if I enjoyed the evening. I hated every second of it. I never liked Steve, my date, but he is so popular with all the girls and I wanted...well you know. Mum...is there something wrong with me? I've never been in love and it feels as if there's this emotional void somewhere inside me. Perhaps something bruised my soul when I was little..." She left it hanging in the air, hoping that her mother would seize the opportunity and have the courage to approach the sensitive issue of adoption. She didn't. She just took her in her arms and hugged her close to her chest as she embarked on her usual sermon about pure love. Alina had heard it so many times that she could have recited it off by heart.

"No, honey, there is nothing wrong with you. You just haven't met your other half yet, and when you do eventually meet you'll know it in your heart. You'll feel that click. I know what I'm talking about because I have felt that same click with your father. He means the world to me and I'll die for him. It is love for the sake of love itself, and for no other reason, not for wealth or sex or beauty. One day you'll feel that love too. Just don't do what so many others do and settle for anything less than that. Those relationships never last."

"Thank you, Mum," she said, deeply disappointed that her mother hadn't taken the hint. Perhaps Max had been right, she did need him there. She herself was not assertive enough to broach the sensitive issue. Her shoulders sagged. "I'm dead tired and I think I'll just go to bed and sleep the horrendous night away. Goodnight, Mum." She kissed her on her cheek and quickly flitted up the stairs to her bedroom.

Her eyes roamed the familiar space and her gaze fell on her soft brown teddy bear occupying its usual prime spot on her bed. She had had many toys over the years and all had been given away to charity, but she could never bear to be parted from her brown teddy. What sentiments did she harbour for it in her subconscious mind? She must have some sort of memory hidden somewhere deep inside her head. She thought hard, really hard as she rubbed her cheek against the soft brown fur. That simple act evoked a single previously suppressed childhood memory...

"So, what's the name of your teddy?" the man asked as he held the girl's tiny hand and continued to drag his laden feet around the perimeter of a ploughed field.

"Just Teddy. He was my birthday present. I had a birthday last week. I am five now." The girl stifled a sob and looked back over her shoulder, spying the column of angry grey smoke swirling up towards the night sky, and she secretly wiped her eyes on the soft brown fur of her teddy...

It was the same man again; the man in the nightmares she had been having ever since she could remember. Was he her father? If so, he must have died shortly after their escape from the fire, otherwise she wouldn't have been given up for adoption. After all, he had been in pain, in great pain in her memory, so his demise would seem reasonable. She tried to piece together an unbroken image of him in her mind. He was tall; well, in that memory she had been a five-year-old girl and every man would be bound to seem tall from her diminutive vantage point, so that was not a reliable attribute to build the picture. He had dark hair and dark eyes. But that was all she remembered. He was otherwise featureless in that childhood memory because the fine details must have been lost with the passage of time.

She turned the teddy round and round in her hand. It had been a birthday present, a fifth birthday present. But gifted by whom? Obviously, not by the man. By her mother perhaps? She looked at the label on its side....Harveils...she had never heard of such a company. She booted up her laptop and she gasped in surprise. Harveils was an elite toy store deep in the heart of Mayfair, an affluent part of London. She had never been outside her Mediterranean island of Malta, certainly never to the UK, her parents never having enough spare cash for holidays, but she knew of Mayfair, who wouldn't, it was the most expensive site to buy on her old Monopoly game. She went on the Harveils' website. It was immediately evident that it only catered for the very rich and famous. The prices were ridiculously high, totally laughable. A teddy similar to hers cost over a thousand pounds. Gosh, what was it made of, spun gold? Even that would not justify the price. No one in their right mind would ever spend so much on a child's toy...unless they had millions stashed away and, in that case, a thousand pounds would be their equivalent of five pounds.

"Who am I?" she murmured. She didn't want to think of herself as a rich privileged kid. She was proud of being Alina Spiteri, a humble child raised on good principles by working-class loving parents. They had always encouraged her to applaud hard work and respect the value of money. She didn't like the way her investigation was heading. It somehow scared her. She clutched her teddy close to her chest and slumped down on the bed, consciously draining all disturbing thoughts out of her head. She yawned and curled up on her side. The fatigue of the eventful evening was finally catching up on her. She was just too tired to change into her nightclothes. She yawned again and closed her eyes, slipping into that welcoming world of dreams...

*

...The touch of a sticky hand broke through that slipping state of bewildering numbness. The man...he had survived the second blast. He'll get them out of there. He had promised. She believed in him. He could be trusted...but was she dreaming?

"Becca, honey, please open your eyes. Oh, please dear God, let her be alive," the man prayed. "Becca, honey, please, look at me."

She forced her eyelids apart and she stared deep into his coal-black eyes, just inches above her, the dancing grey smoke giving them that ethereal feel.

"Thank you, God," he gasped in relief. "Thank you, God." She felt his sticky hand grab a fistful of her red pyjamas and drag her along as he painfully crawled beneath the doorway of her bedroom...

Her voice finally broke through the restraining chains of her nightmare and she started to scream and scream and scream, her whole body trembling with fear, writhing in pain, rocking the bed, her eyes open wide with terror as they stared vacantly up at the darkened ceiling.

The door of her room burst open and her mother wrapped her arms around her. "Alina, honey, it's OK, it's only a dream. Wake up, honey."

Alina blinked, once, twice, and a thread of life started to diffuse through that vacant look. Slowly, her big brown eyes started welling up with tears. "I was so scared, Mum. That day I was so scared," she sobbed. "But he was there and he saved my life...I didn't want him to die...I know everything, Mum...Max told me...he told me the truth...Why didn't you ever tell me?"

"Oh, Alina, honey, please forgive me. I wasn't being deceitful. It was fear that held me back, fear for your well-being. You had such a rough time adjusting after the accident and I didn't ever want to take you back there. And I also had my own selfish reasons too; I was scared that once you knew the truth you might want to leave. I'm so sorry, honey. I may not be your biological mother but I love you more than life itself, and I hope that you will remember that love and keep it in your heart wherever you may decide to go. Forgive me, Alina."

"Mum, there is nothing to forgive. I couldn't have asked for better parents and you don't need to worry about losing me. I'm going nowhere. My place is here, with you and Dad. But I'm just curious to know who I really am."

"I understand, honey. I'll tell you everything I know. Wait here, I'll get all the documents." And she left the room and came back holding a black box file. She sat down on the bed and started rummaging through the papers within the file. "Your real name is Alina Bruni..."

"Alina? Are you sure?" she blurted out. She was positive that the man in her nightmare had called her Becca.

"Yes, dear. Your father and I thought it best that you retained your Christian name. We just gave you our surname when we signed the adoption papers and from then on you were registered in the name of Alina Spiteri. Here, this is your original birth certificate...from the Italian registry."

Alina looked at the piece of paper in her hand. She was born in Pisa, Italy, twenty-one years ago. She was the first and only daughter of Gina and Luigi Bruni. She frowned and slowly let the paper slip out of her hand. This did not feel right. She was positive that she didn't have Italian origins and the biggest clue supporting her conviction was the language itself. The vast majority of Maltese were multilingual, speaking the local Maltese language but also having both English and Italian as their strong second language. Out of the three, English was her strongest language, her first language of choice, preferring it when communicating with her parents, and she spoke it with the accent typical of her Mediterranean island. She understood Maltese and Italian and she spoke them too if need be, but she was nowhere near as fluent in them as she was in English. At school she was naturally gifted in maths and sciences but her language skills were ordinary and she had really struggled hard to get that A star in Italian. Had she really been Italian, she would have found the language easy to master having spoken it for the first five years of her life. She dragged her mind back to what her mother was saying.

"...you were on a sailing boat with your parents off the coast of Italy, when you ran into trouble. Your father radioed for help but it was too late. They eventually found the wreckage at the bottom of the sea some two days later. Inside they found the corpse of your mother and...bits of your father. The lower half of his body was missing, probably shark attacks. They never found your body and they initially assumed that you were dead. Some three months later a fisherman came forward, saying that he had found you floating on a piece of wood and rescued you. You had trouble remembering things and that was the reason why it took him so long to identify who you really were."

Alina shook her head. "Mum, I dream of a fire...not water. It was fire that killed my parents. I'm positive about that." She flicked the birth certificate aside. "This is not me; I know it in my heart. Mum, tell me, who brought me here?"

"A man brought you here to our house and personally handed you over to us with all the documents. He said that the family lawyer had handpicked us from the long list of potential parents. Luckily, just the month before, we had registered with an adoption agency. We were told that it would take months and sometimes years to get a child, and we were rather thrilled to be given the opportunity to become parents so soon."

"Can you tell me anything about the man who brought me here?"

"He was a tall man, fair hair, blue eyes, very courteous, very friendly."

"Was he Italian?"

Her mother hesitated for a second or two before answering truthfully but against her better judgement. "No. He had a very posh British accent."

"British? Mum, what language did I speak when I first came here? I don't think that it was Italian. I have always struggled with that language."

"You didn't speak much for weeks and even months...but the few words you said here and there were in English."

"In what accent? Was it English with an Italian accent?"

"Ermm..." The mother's discomfort was mounting up to a dangerously high level. She kept rubbing her chin again and again. "No, it was a British accent. But you lost that over time, adapting it to the way we speak English here in Malta."

"Didn't you find that British accent odd? I was meant to be Italian. Both my parents were Italian."

"Yes, it was odd. But, Alina, honey, please understand that it wasn't our place to probe and ask...we were *told* not to probe and ask...discreetly *warned, cautioned*, even *threatened*...and we had to oblige because we wanted you so badly. We had been trying to conceive for years but it was one disappointment after another. We desperately wanted a child to love. Adoption was our only chance. As you know, we are not wealthy and all we could offer the child was a humble loving home. We would have been way down the list of eligible parents. So when you came along, we grabbed the opportunity, blindly accepting the terms, and we tried to raise you in the best way we could, infinitely grateful to whoever had chosen us as parents."

"My real name is not Alina Bruni. She probably died in that sea tragedy. Months later someone stole her identity and gave it to me. Why? Mum, I think that my real name is Becca and I think that I'm British."

"But, on the other hand, you don't look British. You don't have the right colouring. You skin tone is definitely Mediterranean. And that was why we finally *accepted* the story we had been told."

Alina clasped her head in both hands, deep frustration getting the better of her. "I dream of a man with dark hair and eyes. I think that he was my father. We both escaped a house fire but my mother probably died there. The man was badly injured and I think that he succumbed shortly afterwards." She glanced up at her mother who was looking more and more uncomfortable with each passing second. "What, Mum? Please don't hide anything from me."

"Some three or four months after you came here, a man, a British man with dark hair and eyes, knocked on our door. His left arm was heavily bandaged. He introduced himself as the lawyer representing the late Gina and Luigi Bruni, and in fact it was he who had handpicked us from the adoption agency. He apologised for being unable to accompany you here at the time, saying that he had been involved in an accident, hence his arm. He asked how you were getting along. I told him the truth; that you were still struggling despite us doing our very best. The next day he turned up on our doorstep with Brandy, your first dog. He thought that it would help you recover quicker and he suggested that we should tell you that the dog was something we had bought for you. It somehow worked, and you started to flourish after that."

A sharp flashback shone through the dark mists of her memories. "*...I'll find a nice family for you...a mummy, a daddy and a pet or two. Do you like dogs?*" the man had asked her. Her heart leapt with joy; he had survived his injuries and he had kept his promises, all of them, dog and all. "Do you think that he is my biological father?"

"Mmmm, I don't think that he is. He had his wife and three children with him in his car. They came to Malta for a family holiday and I invited them all in. His wife was so charming and friendly and his children were so well behaved. He had two boys and a girl, all a good ten years older than yourself. Had you been his child, a secret love child at that, he wouldn't have brought his wife along."

"Perhaps they weren't his real wife and kids. He just wanted to create that illusion to..."

"They were his children. His eldest son, a young man, sixteen or seventeen perhaps, was his spitting image. He was not lying about them."

"Ah, OK," she said as disappointment washed all over her. She had rather liked entertaining the thought that he was her father. "How come I didn't get to meet him and his family?"

"On both occasions you were having your sessions with the child psychiatrist at the time he called. Perhaps he had timed it, I don't know. Perhaps he didn't want to reopen your old wounds. But the main reason behind his visit was to give me these." She started to rummage through the papers in her box file and she held out two official documents, bank documents.

Alina gasped. There were two nameless bank accounts; Swiss bank accounts, highly secure and secretive, a haven for dodgy money, as she knew only too well. Each had over two million pounds deposited in them. "What are these?" she croaked.

"Apparently your parents were wealthy. The man, their lawyer, wanted us to have half their wealth, two million, to help with your upbringing, and other two million were for you when you reached the age of eighteen."

"Mum, both accounts are still intact after all these years, if anything the amount has increased with added-on interest. Why didn't you ever use them? You and Dad were always struggling with your finances. It would have helped you a lot."

Her mother shrugged, giving her an uncomfortable look.

"Ah, I understand," Alina murmured. "Deep down, you knew that the story he had spun had a lot of gaping holes. But you wanted the child so badly that you never challenged anything, in fear of having her taken away from you and given to another couple. So you welcomed the child into your home but not the money which could well be dirty money."

"Alina, I'm sorry. We couldn't use that money. We were scared to. Instead, we tried to raise you with what little we had. And I would like to think that you grew up stronger for that."

"Yes, I did. You made the right choice, Mum." She paused to think for a while. "I'm curious, did he ever give you his name?"

"Plain David Smith, one of the commonest names in the UK, so common that it must have been made up. You needn't bother looking him up. It's not his real name. I knew that, and he knew that I knew, but we both left it hanging in midair. But having said that, despite his deception, he looked like a genuine man and I'm sure that he did what he did because he had your best interests at heart. I mean, he was honest enough to give us the money, he didn't have to do that, he could have kept it himself and no one would be any wiser. And buying Brandy for you was a nice thoughtful gesture, showing that he cared about you. Alina, honey, I don't think I was ever meant to tell you the whole truth. We were cautioned and now I'm cautioning you. You may not like what you uncover if you delve too deep. Please, can you try to let this go? Can you do that for me?"

But her answer was drowned by the desperate ring of the front doorbell. "Alina, Aunty Lillian, open the door." Max's frantic voice carried through the open window of that warm summer. What was he doing out there in the early hours of the morning? It had to be something big. Alina ran down the stairs, two at a time, a heavy feeling in the pit of her stomach. She opened the door and Max staggered in, white as a sheet, breathing heavily, sobbing like a child.

"Lizzy is dead, stabbed, half an hour ago, they found her body just outside the venue. Steve is in a coma, in intensive care unit, they beat the shit out of him because they initially thought that he was behind the hacking..." He stopped to catch his breath. "But he must have talked before going down, naming you, the obvious computer geek. Soon they will be after your arse like crazy."

"Who?"

"The Mafia, a Sicilian Mafia family, the people behind the site you messed with last night. What you did was beyond anything they could ever do. They crave such talent within their circle. They will eventually hunt you down and corner you and they will beat the shit out of you too unless you work with them, hacking sites and doing their filthy work. Mark Deliri called me ten minutes ago, warning me."

"How does Mark know all this?"

"What do you think? His father is the wealthiest businessman on the island. How do you think he got so rich? He is part of some brotherhood here which has links with that Sicilian family. Mark wants you to go into hiding. He knows them well. They will intimidate you really badly and even target your family if you don't do what they ask. But if they can't find you, they can't threaten you. You have to leave the island for your parents' sake. Malta is too small; you can't hide from them here. But Mark has offered to help smuggle us out in his yacht tonight."

"We can't possibly trust Mark; we have to report this to the police."

"The brotherhood...they infiltrate everywhere...the police, the government, the very law itself. We can't escape them. We have to trust Mark and do what he tells us to do. He has already saved your arse once and he is going to do that again. He will be sailing off in the next fifteen minutes or so, and you had better get dressed and pack a small rucksack. I'll give you a couple of minutes to get ready. Quick, go, and in the meantime I'll explain things to your mother."

Alina bounded up the stairs, past her bewildered mother, feeling as though her inner self had just been wrenched out of her. Her soul was somewhere out there, broken and crushed, while her body went through all the mundane rational moves of putting on a pair of jeans, T-shirt and a black hooded jumper, as well as stuffing extra clothes and a small laptop into a rucksack. She was about to exit the room when she retraced her steps and, on an impulse, she stuffed the brown teddy in her bag too. She felt her mother's presence behind her.

"Alina, honey, take these with you. You'll need them," her mother said as she pushed some documents in her bag, amongst them the Swiss account statements and their associated access codes, never-used-before debit cards and all their works.

"Mum, I can't."

"It's OK, honey. That man would want you to use them in times of need. It's a sin not to. These will help you survive out there. I have nothing else to give you."

She wrapped her arms around her mother, her heart breaking into a million pieces. "You've already given me everything in life. Your love was enough and I'll always carry that around with me. I'm so sorry, Mum. I'm so sorry. I've let you down. But when all this settles I'll come back to you and Dad. I promise. I love you, Mum. Tell Dad that I love him too."

She didn't ever want to let her go, but Max gently pulled her away and, taking her hand, he firmly marched her out of the house.

She heard the front door close shut behind her, a closed chapter of her life, a chapter she didn't ever want to leave behind. But leave she had to do, for the sake of the mother and father who had wrapped her in so much love for all those years.

6. Love for the Sake of Love Itself

...Luca played with his glass of wine as he half listened to the rough boyish banter circulating amongst his two brothers and a group of close friends. In normal circumstances he would have been the alpha male of that jovial and witty repartee, but not that day, that special day, his wedding day. He had thoughts only for his new wife and that single exquisite moment when she had slipped the plain wedding band on his finger. He was not an emotional person by nature, far from it, but her vows had really touched the very depths of his soul, and the more he thought of them the more his heart glowed with peace and bliss.

He stroked the golden ring on his finger. The concept of settling down had seemed so daunting before he had met her. She had certainly taken his life by storm, radically changing his beliefs, his feelings, his reckless habits, everything he had previously regarded as gospel truth. And he was comfortable in his new self, loving the way he had changed, loving the way he loved her. He wanted nothing else but to share every single day of his life with her and he had proposed within less than a year of meeting her. He was lucky in that she shared his strong feelings and she had said yes without ever mulling over it.

He looked over his shoulder, craning his neck, trying to catch a glimpse of her amongst the guests. She should be with the girls, his three sisters and his over-bubbly mother who was probably proudly showing off her new daughter-in-law to all. Luca smiled. If he knew his new bride well enough, she would almost certainly be tagging along, trying to look confident, trying to look interested, but failing miserably on both attempts. She had cringed at the idea of having a wedding reception but she didn't want to disappoint his mother who was rather keen on celebrating every occasion big time, so she had reluctantly agreed.

Ah, there she was; he had finally spotted the brilliant white of her wedding gown glowing against the shades of colour. She had her back to him and he let his eyes devour the way the fine lacy material kissed all the contours of her divinely-shaped backside. All too soon she clasped her hands behind her back, obliterating the main focus of his scrutiny. Her fingers started the all-too-familiar nervous play as she twirled them round each other, her discomfort with social crowds manifesting through her not-so-subtle signs. She was always so awkward around people. But he loved that side of her too. He loved everything about her, all of her tiny imperfections...and perfections of which she had quite a few.

She seemed to sense his eye on her and she slowly turned her graceful neck and met the full blaze of his stare. Her face lit up in a radiant smile, the smile she reserved only for him. "I LOVE YOU," she mouthed across the crowded space. That was his Becca; losing all vestiges of inhibition whenever she was embraced within his bubble.

Guided only by the beat of his heart, his legs started their hypnotic walk towards her, but his brother's hand on his shoulder held him back.

"And to think that Mum had almost given up on you ever being tamed," he teased in his ear, having just witnessed the tender exchange between the newlyweds. "Look who's feeling the sting of that whip, now! Ttisshhhh."

Luca threw back his head and laughed. He had so often thrown that same lashing sound of a whip at his older brother, mocking his blind devotion towards his wife. "What can I say...I like being whipped by her." He shoved his wineglass in his brother's hand and, fixing his eyes on the radiance of her smile, he made his way towards her. He took her hand and pulled her away from the chattering crowd where her silent contribution would definitely not be missed.

"Hey, Mrs Snell," he said as he wrapped his hands around her waist. "You look so beautiful tonight; I just can't take my eyes off you."

"I don't want you to. I like it when you look at me that way."

"What way?"

"That way...your lustful stare. It makes me feel so..." and she leaned against him and whispered in his ear, "...wet and horny."

He cupped her face and his thumbs stroked the pink flush on her cheeks. He loved the way she always blushed so heavily whenever she talked dirty. "I'm at your service, madam. Shall we ditch our own party?"

"We can't. They are expecting us to cut the cake or whatever in an hour or so."

"When do I ever do what I'm expected to do? Come on; let's check out the wedding suite in this grand hotel that my mother so kindly booked for us for the night. I'll try to make it worth your while, I promise."

"OK, I'm convinced, let's ditch this circus. It's high time I do something that I really want to do on my wedding day. And, Luca darling, I will be the one making it worth your while." She gave him a sweet innocent smile and took his hand as she started to weave through the guests, she leading, he following, his presence giving her that assertive burst she would otherwise never have possessed. He smiled to himself. He liked following her. He, a dominant leader by nature, had surprised himself again and again at how often he enjoyed taking the back seat when he was around her.

The wedding suite at last! Overcome by impatience, he pressed her hard against the closed door, kissing her wildly, his hands roaming for the fastest way to relieve her of her very tight wedding dress without resorting to tearing it to pieces. She had inflamed his thoughts and his overwhelming hunger had to be satiated.

"Hey, not so fast, Mr Snell. This is our first legal...ermm..." She stopped as she searched for an appropriate word in her head.

"Shag," he offered with a teasing smile, knowing how much she struggled with propriety. "But why use the word legal, are you seriously suggesting that all the others were unlawful?"

"Yes, they were...unlawful and very sinful, yet divine. Right, as I was saying this is our first legal...sexual encounter,

and I want it to last forever." She slipped out of his arms and turned her back on him, swaying slowly across the room, her hips dancing their tantalizing rhythm, teasing him. "No, no, don't move. I want you to just look at me for now," she rebuked when she heard his first few steps forward. "Go on Luca, give me that infamous stare."

He moved back and leaned against the door, loosening his cravat. He could do this. He could rein in his lust long enough to do what she asked of him. There he was again, taking his place in the back seat, like he always did whenever they started to play together. She had her moods; sensual and romantic one day, and wild and dirty the next. He always obliged, knowing full well that they would always take each other to different heights of ecstasy every single time.

She turned round to face him and smoothly slid open the hidden zip down the side of her chest. Ah, that was the way he was meant to relieve her of her dress. How was he, the poor frantic groom, meant to know of its concealed existence? With all the patience he never knew he possessed, he watched the gown slowly slip to the ground and his eyes feasted on her brilliantly white lacy lingerie highlighting all her beautiful curves. He swallowed hard.

"Do you like it?" she asked. She was blushing heavily as her fingers lightly traced her laced bosom. "Your mother gave it to me at the bridal shower she hosted. She thought that you might like it."

He rolled his eyes up to the ceiling and put his hands together, sending a thought across the space, "Thank you, Mum," he said with a lopsided grin on his face that he knew his new wife loved so much. He started to walk slowly towards her. This time she didn't stop him, instead she blatantly basked under the naked lust in his vividly blue eyes, never flinching from her erotic pose, her shy reservation withering away into the stillness of that room. He stopped in front of her.

"Can I stop with the looking and start with the touching now," he asked in a mock timid voice.

"Can't you do them both?"

"I can try." He placed his hands on her waist and slid them slowly down her backside, and down her thighs, and up again, seeking refuge beneath her lacy thongs. He heard her sharp intake of breath as she closed her eyes and leaned her head back, thinking of nothing but his wandering hands skilfully playing their intimate erogenous dance.

"How does that feel, Mrs Snell? Do you like the touching too?" he teased.

Her body started to spasm and shake. She clawed at his satin cummerbund around his waist, her hands trembling in her sudden newfound haste. She had apparently abandoned all her previous intentions of a leisurely encounter. "Take me, Luca, take me now," she gasped.

He had been very patient and it was time for him to reap his rewards...but something far more important than his sexual gratification was taking centre stage in his mind. He had to tell her before he went any further. "Honey, I love you. I love you so much. And I don't just love you for the sex and the fun. I love what's inside you too. During your vows you mentioned something about a love, a unique type of love that lasts forever, a love for the sake of love itself. I liked that. It touched my soul. It made me feel all warm inside. I hope that you know that that is the kind of love I have for you too, despite my wild demeanour and sexual overdrive."

She circled her arms around his neck. "I know, Luca. I wouldn't have settled for anything less than that. But I can't take credit for the words in that vow, they were my mother's. She was always speaking of this raw kind of love. Deep down I have always mocked it, thinking that it couldn't ever exist, but then it found me the day I met you. Bless you, Mum, you were right all along," she sent out across the miles.

He kissed the lines of pain on her forehead that always crept in whenever she thought of her parents. "You miss your mother, don't you?"

"I wanted her to be here. She would have loved the wedding, and so would my father...but, I know, we can't ever meet in public, not just yet, I have to stick to this new identity. It's the

price I have to pay for one really stupid mistake I did a year ago."

"I am infinitely grateful to that one single mistake. We wouldn't have met otherwise. If you were given a choice, would you go back in time and undo what you did?" He could not help that sharp bolt of anxiety that spread through his whole existence. Would she want to undo meeting him?

The gripping fear must have shown in his eyes because she leaned forward and gave him a sweet reassuring kiss. "Don't worry; I wouldn't undo anything that would jeopardize our chance meeting."

He let out an audible sigh of relief. "Thank you, Becca, that means the world to me, and I will do everything in my power to fill this void in your heart. Would you like me to arrange another undercover meeting with your parents next week, before we come back from our honeymoon? You can show them your ring and a couple of wedding photos. They will like that. How does that sound?"

"I'm OK, Luca, really. I know that the meticulous planning takes a lot of your time and energy. We just met them two weeks ago. That was enough."

"Hey, no problem. Intelligence and strategic planning is what I do for a living, it is what I'm good at. I'll quickly think of something that will be safe for both you and your parents. No problem at all. You should know by now that I'll do anything to make you happy, my darling." He pulled her close to him. "I love you, Becca, I'll always love you." And he kissed her, a heartwarming tender kiss...

Luca opened his eyes. The cosmic space around him was whirling round and round and all he could hear was the deafening thumping beat of his heart...boom, boom, boom...Where was he? Where was he? Panic gripped his insides and twisted hard. Where was he? His disorientation was making him feel sick. He closed his eyes, and he reached out and grabbed hold of a worldly tangible noise, the humble faint coo of a pigeon that seemed to be a million miles away. He held on to it until it gradually got closer, and closer, and closer, finally dimming the aberrant thumping noise of his beating heart.

He slowly opened his eyes again, fixing his gaze on the breaking dawn seeping through the open window, and he silently thanked the pigeon out there whose call had brought him back to sanity. His eyes started to roam in their sockets, scrutinizing the rest of the familiar place. He was lying on his left side, on his bed in his bedroom in his luxury apartment in London. He could feel Jessica's naked body pressed hard against his back.

OK. OK. He had got his bearings back. The night before he had overindulged in alcohol...and sex, and this was the morning after, his hangover. Heavily intoxicated, he had simply gone to bed and dreamt the vivid dream that he had so often dreamt before, a dream that took him to some place in his future, a dream that jarred heavily with his feelings of that present day. He felt completely dissociated from that Luca in that dream. He was everything that he himself was not. That Luca was in a monogamous relationship, he had deep feelings for a girl, and even more than that he was in love, he was altruistic, caring about her feelings more than his own, and he actually had a soul. He still enjoyed sex but had preferred a long winded declaration of an alien kind of love, a love for the sake of love itself, rather than getting on with his sexual gratification, the latter being something the present day self-centred Luca worshipped above everything else. It was hard to believe that any girl could change him so much.

The bed creaked as Jessica shifted around somewhere behind him. He could tell from the rhythm of her breaths that she was awake, and it seemed as though she was waiting for him to completely surface from his sleep and turn around and face her. But he did not; he kept his back turned to her, hoping that she would take the hint and leave quietly, like she had so often done in the past. The minutes ticked by, no one wanting to be the first to make a move. It was a battle of wills. Eventually, Jessica lost, but she had no intention of leaving early that day. He felt her hand slide over his ripped abdominals and down towards his groin. Quick as a flash, he grabbed her hand and rudely flicked it aside.

He was not in the mood for an early morning fling, not after *that* dream. He gingerly lifted his head from his pillow and sat up, swinging his legs down the side of the bed, his toes digging deep into the plush red carpet of his room. He sat still for a moment or two, his head down, trying to overcome the lightheaded feeling of his hangover before walking away.

"You talk in your sleep, did you know that?" Jessica asked. "You call her name and you tell her that you love her, that you'll always love her. Who is Becca?"

That's a good question, he thought. *Who is Becca?* He tried to piece together the fragments of information he had gathered from his wide range of dreams. Becca was a timid, introverted, self-conscious girl who would one day make a single mistake in the form of something illegal in her own country. What had she said in his other dream? Ah yes...she would hack a computer or something, drawing the attention of some criminals to her unique computer skills. As a result she would flee her country and she would end up in London, where she would meet him at her personal lowest point, the point when the noose around her neck tightened to a critical level. He would take her home with him for no reason other than to bed a naive virgin, something he had never done before, but instead, for some bizarre reason, he would fall deeply in love with her. He would make it his mission to protect her and he would apparently give her a new identity to help her escape whoever was hunting her down. And he would go even further than that, using his intelligence skills to organise undercover meetings with her parents, just to make her happy. Eventually, he would propose, get married, have two children with her and live happily ever after. The end.

Did he really want that life for himself? He shrugged. That morning a big part of him seemed to want it. Perhaps, for just this once, he could try to let things take their natural course. He would allow that chance meeting to take place and see where it would lead.

He felt Jessica's finger trace a delicate line down his spine. "Poor, Luca," she mocked. "He is in love."

"I'm not," he said with fervour, more to convince himself than Jessica.

"Prove it, come back to bed with me."

"I would love to but I'm running late. I really have to go." He stood up and started looking around for his boxers. Ah yes, he didn't have any. The four of them had decided on a naked all-night party until, totally washed out, he and Jessica had stumbled to his bedroom and Tom and Mel had taken the sofa bed out in the lounge. He walked over to his chest of drawers and selected a clean pair of boxers, putting them on, immediately feeling better now that his decency was restored.

"I've missed you, Luca. I would really love to take this thing between us up to the next level."

He slowly turned round to face her. Her naked body was sprawled across his bed, her pose suggestive and inviting. But instead of enticing him, as it would have in normal circumstances, it somehow repelled him. Perhaps, he was finally growing out of his rather prolonged wild *teenage* phase which had continued to run well into his early twenties. "I'm sorry, Jess," he said firmly. "I can't do the next level. And more importantly I don't want to. I haven't changed, Jess. I'm still only interested in good sex with no strings attached. I only called you last night because I thought that you still shared those same interests. I wouldn't have called otherwise."

She laughed, a loud sarcastic laugh. "I'm not interested in anything serious either. By the next level I meant getting together once a week rather than once a year. The sex last night was out of this world. So, shall we meet again same time, same place, same play next week?"

"I don't know. I'll call you."

"Fine by me, but just for you to know, Mel won't be seeing Tom again unless we are there too. And Tom, your best mate, seemed rather keen on Mel...so..." and she left it hanging in the air.

"Are you threatening me?"

"No, of course not. Last night I had a pretty rough time convincing Mel to come along and she only did so because I reassured her that we'll be there too. Don't get me wrong, she likes Tom, he's a decent looking guy, tall, dark, handsome and rugged, all his boxes are ticked. Hell, I like his good looks too, but after a few drinks he is rather aggressive in bed, bordering on the sadistic. Apparently he knocked her about pretty badly the last time they met alone at his place, a little over a year ago."

"Bullshit," he said. "Tom is too shy with the ladies to even ask them out. If you ask me, Mel begged to be manhandled. Didn't you see her last night; she was the wildest one of the lot. Listen Jess, I really have to go. Thank you for last night. It was nice seeing you again. I'll call you." And he nimbly slid out of the bedroom, not wanting to squabble with her, especially knowing that his entire career rested on her kind discretion. A word about their illicit rendezvous to her father and he would be deeply fried.

He averted his eyes away from the sleeping naked bodies on the sofa bed in the lounge and he made his way to the bathroom, reluctantly retrieving his tattered black hoodie and jeans. The novelty of undercover work and its associated adrenaline surge was wearing off. For the second time that morning he felt that he was once again maturing out of that wild reckless phase that had gripped his life for so long. As he looked at himself in the mirror, he made two important decisions. One; his affair with Jessica was strictly over. Two; he was done with undercover work out in the field. He would tie up the last few loose ends, namely the terrorist doctor and the identity of his puppet master, and then he would retreat to office intelligence and go back to living the life of the suave Luca Snell.

With that in mind, he strode out to the lounge and headed straight for the sofa bed. "Hey, buddy," he said as he gently rocked Tom's shoulder and waited for him to crack his eyes open. "I'm leaving. Can you lock up the place and see the girls home when they eventually return to planet earth?" He smiled and nodded towards the stoned-out Mel. That smile froze on his face as his eyes lingered on the girl's breasts. They were horribly bruised and bleeding with three or four very nasty looking bite marks. Jessica had been telling the truth.

"Oh man," Tom groaned as he followed his friend's line of vision. "I just got carried away...what with all the booze and...oh man, I hadn't had sex in over a year. What do you expect? And it's not as if she complained about it at the time, if anything she wanted it rough."

She didn't complain at the time because she was probably too stoned out to do so, Luca wanted to say. But instead, he shrugged. Mel probably deserved what she got. She was a vicious tigress and he knew that. She had incited him pretty badly last night when they had swapped partners for a while. He still had her deep scratch marks down the side of his back.

He heard the door of his bedroom creak open. He looked up. Jessica came gliding over towards them, wearing nothing but her astronomically high heels as she calmly smoked away some pot. She smiled at him and lifted her left eyebrow up, giving him that I-told-you-so look. He ignored it and, after pulling the sheet up to cover Mel's mistreated breasts, he turned to go.

"Good morning, Tom," he heard Jess say. "I'm so horny and high, but Luca here won't oblige. Are you man enough to take me on this morning."

Luca threw back his head and let out a loud booming laugh. Was she trying to make him feel jealous? If so, she had failed miserably. He didn't have a shred of jealousy anywhere inside him. "Sure, Tom, go ahead, take her on. I expect to see you around midday, so that should give you hours of fun and play." He impishly slapped Jessica's bottom and headed for the front door. By the time he closed it behind him the high-on-pot Jessica was already happily riding the lucky Tom while the stoned-out Mel slept peacefully beside them. He snorted in disgust. The hypocrisy. Why complain about Tom's manhandling when the first thing she did that morning was to incite him. Both girls deserved to have their breasts bruised hard by Tom.

And as far as he was concerned, he strongly felt that that chapter of his life was finally over; he *wanted* it to be over. That morning felt like his rebirth. He didn't know what had changed him overnight. Perhaps it was the dream and *her* wedding vows...but on the other hand he had had that same dream for months and months and it had never moved him as much as it had moved him that day. Why? Perhaps that chance encounter was imminent. To hell with the lure of the unknown; he now wanted that chance encounter. He was ready for it. He was ready to give it a go. He was ready to see whether this girl could really change him so much so as to make him love her for the sake of love itself...

7. The Binding Promise of the Ring

"Alina, please. Every extra second you stay out here might be your last. Let's get on that fucking yacht and sail away before dawn breaks."

"Your swearing won't intimidate me, Max. I'm sorry but I'm not dragging you into this. It's my problem and mine alone. I'm the only one they are after and I'm the only one who needs to hide. I'll die if I have to but I will not board that boat if you come too."

"Hey, will you two shut the fuck up," Mark shouted above the running purr of the engine. The two cousins had been arguing on the wooden pontoon for the better part of five minutes. He just had to intervene because apparently no one had fully grasped the gravity of the situation. "Just in case you haven't noticed, my neck is on the line too if someone sees you here. We have to leave NOW."

"Max, listen to me," she hissed. "I'll be on the run for God knows how long. You have a life here; you've got a good job in the career you love. I can't take that away from you. Please, Max, stay here and have a good life, find that girl who deserves your love and settle down. Besides, I need you to stay here and look after Mum and Dad. Will you do that for me, please?"

He could see that it was futile arguing with her. He had to let her go, otherwise she was prepared to stay there and face the death of a martyr if need be, and death would certainly catch up on her one day because just as the vengeful Mafia had murdered Lizzy they would have no qualms murdering her too if she wouldn't cooperate. He finally nodded, "Go on then, take care, Alina."

She stood on her tiptoes and kissed him on his cheek. "I'll keep in touch. I'll find a way to contact you without them knowing. I promise. I'll hack your email account if I have to," she said with a weak smile on her face. She gave him a friendly punch on his chest and turned her back on him, walking the plank towards Mark Deliri, the affluent and daunting Mark Deliri, with his open white shirt billowing in that light breeze of that warm summer early morning.

He took her hand and helped her down onto his luxury yacht. "Go down below deck. Quick. I have to stay up here with the captain for now, but I'll join you as soon as we leave port."

With a final yearning glance at the starry Mediterranean sky, she swiftly went down the polished stairs. A spacious lounge welcomed her below deck and the sheer splendour around her made her gasp in awe. She couldn't help but feel out of place there especially wearing her old trainers, worn-out jeans and hooded zipped jumper. Why on earth was Mark even bothering to help her? She obviously didn't belong to his world. She felt too drab to even sit on his couch and she stayed standing up, clutching the shoulder strap of her rucksack, feeling inadequate and awkward. This was going to be a very painful journey; she had no words to converse amicably with anyone, let alone the confident and wealthy Mark. She wondered how long the journey would last and she fervently hoped that he would stay up on deck for the whole duration.

But she was not so lucky. Barely five minutes had passed when she saw his costly boat shoes approach the top stair, and with despair she saw the rest of him slowly descend before her; his white knee-length shorts followed closely by his open white cotton shirt which contrasted heavily with the brown tanned colour of his chest. Finally, her eyes encountered his wide confident smile in a deeply tanned sun-kissed face. His appearance had always reminded her of some Greek mythology god with his pumped-up chest and dark gelled hair, heavy eyebrows and dark eyes. She had known him ever since she was nine or ten, having gone to the same co-ed private school, the very best on the island. Her parents had saved very hard, even selling family gold heirlooms, to give her that good but expensive education, while his parents had simply sent him there because their status required them to. In all those years she couldn't remember ever exchanging a single word with him; she had found him daunting then as much as she did at that moment in time.

"Alina Spiteri," he said with a big smile on his face. "I never thought that I'll ever see the day when I would entertain you on my boat. Please, make yourself at home." And he slipped the rucksack off her shoulder and flicked the hood of her jumper off her head, the hood she had purposefully worn to mask her appearance on the way to the marina.

She looked down at her worn-out trainers, finding his closeness uncomfortable as was the overpowering smell of his costly body spray. "Thank you, Mark," she mumbled. "I really appreciate what you're risking for me."

"My pleasure. Come, let's get out of the way. I think that we had better stay in one of the bedrooms, safer there, just in case they decide to check the number of passengers." He took her hand and led her into one of the three spacious bedrooms, firmly locking the door behind them. As her eyes fell on the luxurious king-sized bed before her, she wondered if Mark expected her to pay her fare with sex. There had to be something in it for him. He didn't seem like the type of guy who did anything for free and out of the goodness of his heart. Her suspicions were immediately confirmed when he turned on her and slid open the zip of her jumper, purposefully grazing his knuckles across her breasts in the process.

"It's too warm for your jumper in here," he said as he slipped it off her shoulders and let it fall to the ground.

Say something, say something, say anything just to postpone that inevitable start, her mind screamed inside her head. "Ermmm....Ermmm...wwwhere are we heading, Mmmark?" she finally stammered out.

"I've asked the captain to head for Marzamemi, a small fishing village on the south side of Sicily. It's pretty quiet there, easy to smuggle you on shore. From there you can go anywhere you want; the whole of mainland Europe is at your disposal. If you play your cards well they will never find you."

"How long is the boat trip?"

"It should take four or five hours, perhaps three if the captain is fast enough. So, we have plenty of time to get to know each other and make up for the lack of words between us over all these years."

His hands were caressing the curve of her hips now, playing around the hem of her T-shirt. Her mouth felt dry with fear. "Wwwill they check passports?"

"Not if we're lucky. Malta is part of the Schengen Area and we don't need passports to cross borders. So you'll be OK. Sometimes they do spot-checks on random boats here and there, but everyone knows me well in these waters. I do this trip at least once a week, and they know that I always have an illicit cargo in the form of a girl or two in my bedroom. Italian patrols are heavily bribed to turn a blind eye on my yacht. Besides, I'm good business; I always take the girls out for a lavish meal in Sicily and always return home, taking the cargo back with me, within that same day. I'm just a harmless playboy in their eyes. If they see you with me, they will think that you're just another girl I'm entertaining."

Her T-shirt had joined her jumper on the floor and so did her plain black brassiere. She was not assertive enough to stop him. She looked down in fear and despair, and her eye fell on his golden engagement ring on his left ring finger. "Bbbut aren't you getting mmmarried next week?"

"So?"

"Does ssshe know that you entertain girls on your boat?"

"Oh, yes she knows. Sophia definitely knows. She has her own hobbies too. I don't stop her and she doesn't stop me. Hell, I don't even know if that baby she's carrying is mine. It probably is, but I can't be sure unless I run a paternity test." His shoulders sagged, and for the first time in his life, he let his guard down, allowing the deep unrest to seep out of the solid mask of confidence he had built around his wide assertive smile. He turned away from her and walked towards the bed, lying flat on his back, his eyes staring vacantly out at the ceiling. Money had certainly not bought him any happiness.

His pain was tangible and Alina felt sorry for him. Mark was a decent guy deep down inside his heart, otherwise he wouldn't have bothered helping her twice in less than twenty-four hours. She picked up her T-shirt and slipped it over her head before walking towards the bed and lying down beside him. "A pregnancy is never a good reason to get married. It is clear that you don't love each other enough to be faithful to one another, and a child in a marriage without love will never be happy. Why are you getting married? Why not just support her and the child...if it is yours."

"Love is never a factored ingredient in marriages of my kind and I still have to tie the knot whether the child is mine or not. I have no choice. The union is good for business and, besides, I want to go into politics and her father will give me a leg up. You see, her father, my father...and I, we are all part of this brotherhood. We help each other to thrive through legal...and sometimes illegal ways. I just cannot go against the pack. That would be suicide."

"You're going against the pack by helping me."

"That's different. They would never know that I helped you. I can trust the captain; he's the only one who knows who you really are. And anyway, it is a risk I just have to take because, had I been free to love whoever I wanted, I would have loved you. I just cannot stand by and let you get hurt...even though deep down I think that you do deserve a good spanking or two. What were you thinking? You were going to let Steve nail you, why him of all people? He is downright mean. And then to add insult to injury you hacked that porn site and demolished it. I adored that site. I lived for it. It made me feel alive in my own dying relationship with my Sophia. I loved that site so much that I had shares in it too and I lost quite a lot of money overnight, thanks to you. But at least I managed to download your footage and I was out of there way before you opened fire."

Alina narrowed her eyes in discomfort, feeling very vulnerable knowing that he was in possession of her compromising footage. She had to somehow find a way to delete it off his system. She gave him a weak smile. "How much money did you lose? Give me your phone; I can always transfer it back to you if you want."

"Nah, it's OK. I heard that the money was siphoned for a good cause. I couldn't stop laughing when my dad told me. You pissed off some really big names, amongst them a very powerful family in Sicily. They called us, and our boys had no choice but to help them. At first they thought that it was Steve's doing but I immediately knew that it was you. The whole thing sounded so *Alina*. I said nothing but I suspected that it was only a matter of time before Steve talked about the one and only computer geek at uni who happened to hold a big grudge against him, and I phoned Max to get you out of there before they came for you. The bottom line is that they really liked what you did and they would do *anything* to have you working for them, believe me when I say *anything,* even murder innocent loved ones. Your gift is more precious than gold to them. Tell me, how do you manage to hack secure stuff?"

"I don't really know. I just do it. I see patterns and stuff and I just go for it. Why don't you give me your phone and I'll try to show you." They lay on the bed, head to head as she fiddled around with his phone, his eyes hardly keeping up with the speed of her flitting fingers. In no time at all she had broken into his phone security code, into his emails, into all his downloads...and then she found what she was looking for....her explicit footage. Before he could even react, she had permanently deleted it from his system.

"Hey, I paid for that thing. Is that why you wanted my phone?"

"Of course, why else would I want it? Did you really think that I wanted to show you how to hack an account? You wouldn't know how to even if I showed you." She smiled wickedly at him.

He calmly smiled back as he rolled on top of her and whispered softly in her ear, "Sorry to disappoint you, my dear, but that's the only footage I bothered backing up, not once, not twice but many many times. I just couldn't risk losing it. It is priceless. I would get to see *my* beautiful naked Alina whenever I want to...and wank all over her too."

"Disgusting pervert, don't you dare. Get off m..." But all her protests were physically blocked by his mouth ramming against hers. It was a brutal kiss, dirty, forceful, demanding and very very painful. It left her feeling cold and numb inside, just as Steve's kiss had made her feel earlier. But by then she had already resigned herself to the fact that she was as frigid as ice. She squeezed her eyes shut and, just as she had let Steve push her around, she let Mark get on with his morbid erotic fantasies. He was expecting her to pay for her fare and there was nothing she could do about it. The only other person on the boat, the captain, would not react to her calls for help.

Even this will eventually pass, even this will eventually pass, she kept saying over and over in her head. She had lost her T-shirt again and she knew that he had lost his shorts and shirt, but still she would not open her eyes. She felt his left hand go down her jeans, his fingers probing, invading, tearing, making her want to scream out in pain. But it was the agonizing feel of his engagement ring against her skin that was tearing her up, emotionally rather than physically. Her mother had always taught her to respect the symbol of the ring, that binding promise of fidelity. Men in a relationship were strictly off limits for her. She would despise herself forever if she ever played the part of *that other girl,* however unwilling she might be. Her strict religious upbringing was screaming at her to do something because Mark was not like Steve. Steve had no ring and she had been prepared to be bullied the whole way for the experience if not for love. Mark was different; he had a ring on his finger and her conscience would never rest if she didn't at least try to stop this.

"Mark, please, please stop. It's hurting me so much," she pleaded.

"It's hurting you because everything is so bloody dry. If you stop being so scared you'll enjoy it." He slipped his hand out of her jeans and grabbed hold of her face, shaking it hard. "Open your eyes, Alina, open your eyes and look at me," he hissed in blinding anger. "I would enjoy it so much better if you would enjoy it too. Help me out here, Alina. The more you give me the more I'll be willing to protect you out there. It's your choice. I can either let you fend for yourself on the shores of Sicily, OR, I can give you names of safe contacts, give you a new identity, a new passport and even set you up permanently in one of my villas. You will be my mistress and you will be safe and happy and want for nothing in this world."

"But will you still marry Sophia?"

"Yes, I will. I can't change that. But I can promise you that you will be my *only* mistress. I love you Alina, and I will need no one else to warm my bed if you are there. Being with you will be everything *else* I would ever need in this world."

"You don't love me; if you did I would be your absolute all, your everything. But I'm not because you need something *else* to make you feel complete. You love power more than you could ever love me. Now, get off me."

"You bitch, you heartless cold bitch. You were going to sleep with Steve but you won't sleep with me after I've risked my all for you."

"Steve had no ring on his finger, you have. Please Mark, I don't want this, let me go."

But he wound one hand around her neck and started to squeeze really hard as he touched himself, deriving all his erotic pleasure from her choking pain. Endless seconds passed, until, finally spent, he looked down on her, giving her a black murderous glare. "Better that than raping you," he hissed close to her face. He unclasped his fingers from around her neck and bounded off the bed, seeking his white shorts and pulling them on with much vengeance.

Halfway to the door, he stopped short and, with great agitation, he started to repeatedly rake his fingers through his dark gelled hair, deeply regretting his rash and vile move. "Shit, shit, shit," he swore. "What the fuck did you make me do?"

"I'm sorry, I'm so sorry." She started to cry, that feeling of inferiority and inadequacy making her want to shoulder all the blame. "I didn't want to push you over the edge. I'm sorry," she sobbed.

"Don't. Don't you dare say you're sorry." And with that he strode out of the room, slamming the door shut behind him.

She knew that she should drag herself out of the bed and clean Mark's filth off her chest, but she was too numb to move.

How had she, a hermit by nature and loving it, allowed herself to be pushed into such a despicable situation? It had all started with that one fatal mistake of befriending Lizzy and trusting her, allowing herself to be poisoned by her. And it had all snowballed so fast from there. This must be her one way ticket to hell, because hell could hardly be any worse than this. She would give anything to undo what she had done. Nothing good could ever come out of all this. Choking in self-disgust, she rolled up in a ball and cried herself to sleep.

*

The sudden silence woke her up with a start. The somnolent purr of the engine had been replaced by the calming lapping sound of the sea. They had docked. It was the end of the boat journey, but the beginning of her daunting challenge in the scary world out there. This was the first time she had ever stepped outside the secure shores of her beloved island of Malta, but this was no holiday, no picnic. A sudden fear gripped her and she found herself strongly wishing that she could overlook Mark's ring on his finger and accept his offer of living the rest of her life under his protective wing in one of his villas in Sicily. She could learn to love him in return. What would she call that kind of love...love for the sake of security, perhaps? It was very tempting, but her mother's voice kept invading her thoughts and wishes...*love for the sake of love itself and for no other reason, not for wealth or sex or beauty. Just don't do what so many others do and settle for anything less than that*...Alina snorted. She no longer believed in that kind of pure love. But she believed in the binding promise of the ring and that was the only reason why she had to reject Mark's tempting offer of security. Soon he would have a wife and a child and she would not be the one to break his family apart.

With determination, she slipped out of the bed and headed for the en suite bathroom. In the next five minutes she was all clean and dressed and ready to go. She opened the door and stepped outside into the lounge area. Mark was there, looking all regal with his open white shirt and white shorts and costly boat shoes. He was sprawled on an armchair, his left ankle on his right knee, his head resting back, his eyes fixed on some spot on the ceiling, the only movement he made being the constant twirling round of the ice in his glass of whiskey. He felt her presence but he didn't want to acknowledge it.

She meekly picked up her rucksack, clutching its shoulder strap for security. "Thank you, Mark, for helping me. I will never forget your kindness," she mumbled out to her worn-out trainers before heading for the stairs.

"Wait, Alina," he said as he sat up and slowly placed his glass of whiskey on the table. "Where are you going from here?"

"I don't know," she said, trying hard to stem the tears going down her cheeks, but failing miserably in her attempt. "I have no choice but to run and run and keep on running."

"I've asked the captain to rent a car and, only if you want to, he can take you to a secure place I have in mind. Don't be alarmed, but I think that the safest place for you right now would be an escort agency...ermm...a brothel I own here in Sicily. It is run by a very good friend of mine, Mara Tucci. Don't worry, you'll be safe with her and she is the one person who will never betray you because she hates the Mafia more than anyone else on this planet. They killed her husband in cold blood and, totally destitute, she was forced to work the streets until I helped her out. Now she will help you. She will give you food and shelter until you get back on your feet and plan your next move. I've asked her to organise fake passports for you and I will pay for anything else you need." He slowly stood up and walked towards her, taking her hand in his. "That's the best I could come up with, but at least it's a plan, much better than running and running. What do you think?"

She wrapped her arms around his neck. "Thank you, Mark," she sobbed. "You are so kind."

"Nah, I'm not. I just hope that these small gestures here and there might compensate for my other sins and buy me that ticket to heaven when my judgement day eventually comes." He unwrapped her arms from around his neck and looked back at her.

"Can I ask for a favour in return? Can you keep in touch? Over all these years I got rather used to seeing you every day and it was your face I sought out from the crowd every single morning from our first day together in fifth grade to the present day. I'm just sorry that I was never strong enough to do anything about it. But this is the life I chose for myself a long time ago and I can't ever back out of it. Perhaps you're right, I do love power above anything else and Sophia's father will help me rise to the very top of the political tree, exactly where I want to be. Only then can I perhaps make a difference to this corrupted world."

"You've got the right heart to lead a nation. I'll vote for you if the Mafia grant me the grace to live beyond a year or two." She smiled at him and touched the ring on his finger. "But, please Mark, if you give Sophia a ring, try to honour the symbol. If you're faithful to her, she might be faithful to you in return. Try it."

"I can promise to try if you promise to keep in touch," he insisted again.

"OK, that's a fair deal."

He smiled broadly at her, happy with his tiny acquisition. She was so stingy with friendships, and keeping in touch was the best he could wring out of her for the time being. "I'll look forward to hearing from you, Alina. Though, I have to warn you to be very careful not to leave any traces which could lead back to you when you contact people you know, be it me, Max or anyone else. Don't ever underestimate the Mafia and don't ever let your guard down. This is your life now, a life on the run. The Mafia never forget."

"I'll be OK. As you probably know by now I thrive in cyberspace. No one can beat me there, not even the mighty Mafia. I'll keep in touch, Mark, and I'll be careful, don't worry."

"How will you make contact? Do you plan on hacking my stuff?"

"Yes, I will. But, trust me, I will not meddle with anything else. I'll just make contact and leave." She leaned against him and gave him a spontaneous brief kiss on his lips. "Goodbye, Mark. Have a good life."

"You too, Alina." He continued to hold her hand as she climbed up the stairs, their fingers interlocked, until the increasing space between them forced them to reluctantly break apart.

She liked Mark, she realised with a start. She didn't love him but she definitely liked him a lot and she wished him cartloads of happiness from the very bottom of her heart. She was pleased that they had parted as friends. As the bright Sicilian summer sun beat down upon her, Alina could not help but feel that burst of optimism. How could she feel otherwise with such a beautiful sun shining above her head?

8. Reaping what was Sown

Luca sat back on a lonely bench overlooking the river Thames, enjoying the heat of the same summer sun. That brilliant glorious ball had finally decided to grace the capital that morning; it was rather stingy with its appearance on the British Isles, but when it did venture out from behind those clouds it more than shone in all its glory, enhancing the natural beauty around him. He absolutely loved London, but he loved it even more when the sun shone on it. A burst of optimism surged through his veins. The sun always made him feel so good.

But it wasn't just the sun that was making his heart soar. He was also basking under that upbeat feel of novelty, the novelty of starting a brand new chapter in his life. The recklessness, the debauchery, the alcohol and the sex had all suddenly lost their brilliant lustre, their challenge, and he could even say that they had started to seriously make him feel bored, overnight...all thanks to that one last crazy fling with Jessica. But if he were to be honest with himself, this transformation of his had germinated before Jessica's arrival and he could pinpoint it to that single second when he had seen *the girl* with her bruised left wrist and smudged eye makeup screaming in pain in her sleep. He was curious to know whether she had got over her trauma. He closed his eyes and once again reached out for her dimension, invading her world at that single point in time, expecting to see her either kneeling down and praying or gazing at the horizon...but...

She was in, what looked like, a splendid lounge of a very luxurious yacht, and she was standing far too close to a man who rather looked like a young and very virile Poseidon with his fierce dark eyebrows and deeply tanned pumped-out chest. She placed her hand on that chest and leaned against him, giving him a spontaneous brief kiss on his lips. "Goodbye, Mark. Have a good life."

"You too, Alina," the god of the sea answered, and he continued to hold her hand as she climbed up the polished stairs,

their fingers interlocked, until the increasing space between them forced them to reluctantly break apart...

Luca opened his eyes. "Bloody peacock," he hissed beneath his breath, his fists clenched tight in blinding anger directed solely at the young man who had dared strut around with that vulgar display of his tanned chest beneath that ostentatious open white shirt of his. Then he burst out laughing loudly in an attempt to play down that initial insane reaction. He was the cool Luca Snell and that emotional response was definitely *not* him. He had never ever experienced jealousy or rivalry, and he never will because he was much too confident in his own skin for that, so very confident so as to seem arrogant. Becca was his if he wanted her and there was nothing *Poseidon* could do to change that. The only way that *god* could ever have her would be if he, Luca Snell, would decide to meddle with destiny and kick her out of his life for good...just as he had heartlessly kicked out his career in law. So far he had never regretted that shift in career, and he never will...or will he? He felt his surroundings spin around him as he was taken to some place in the not-so-far future...

...Luca was sitting at his breakfast table in his father's luxury apartment in London. He was re-reading the card his wife had given him for his twenty-fifth birthday the day before. Her words never failed to touch his heart. He loved her so much. He wanted to give her and his unborn child everything in this world. It was his duty as a husband and as a father-to-be.
He looked around his surroundings and he winced. Soon the place would be too small for his little family of three and eventually four, and besides, the place technically belonged to his father. He should be thinking about moving to a bigger place of his own, but he didn't have the astronomical amount of cash that he would need to upgrade to a bigger house with the same luxurious standing in central London, a location he loved above anywhere else. He didn't want to ask his father for financial help

and neither did he want to use his wife's savings. His pride dictated that he did this all on his own.

And their living quarters was just the tip of the iceberg. All too soon he would have to think about the children's education, their clothing, their needs, their entertainment, priceless family holidays and a gazillion of other things, just as his father had before him. Sitting back and feeding on his father's millions was not something he was prepared to do. Luca shook his head in despair. His pay wasn't quite enough for the standard of living he was accustomed to. His contribution to office intelligence was indispensable and he had rapidly risen through the ranks in name and responsibility but never in salary because his lack of formal certificates prevented any pay rise. His uncle had warned him about this when he had first joined British Intelligence. The fact that he didn't even have a single GCSE to his name would push his salary down, much lower than that of the others who were endowed with postgraduate university degrees. It never bothered him in the past, the pay being generous enough for a bachelor living on his own, but it had started to bother him now that he had a family to maintain. And it would bother him even more when his university-graduated wife eventually went to work after the birth of their child and brought home a pay package twice his size.

He loved his job but he couldn't help thinking about the alternative parallel career that he had chosen to throw away. That big shot law job in a magic law firm in London would have guaranteed financial independence and stability in the form of a large family house in the much-sought-after area of Mayfair, an expensive education for his kids, fun-filled family holidays and...and the perks went on and on and on. Perhaps, at twenty-five years of age he should be thinking about sitting the exams he should have taken when he was still sixteen and very reckless and so short-sighted.

The bedroom door creaked open and a heavily-pregnant Becca slowly staggered out towards him, her hair wild and tousled, her eyes broken and tired.

"Hey, honey, are you OK?" he asked as he took her hand and sat her down on his lap.

She buried her face in his neck. "I'm so tired. I couldn't sleep last night. My back hurt so much. Mmmm, yes that feels sooo good," she cooed softly, approving his cautious attempts to massage her lower back. She lifted her head up and looked back at him, registering his indoor T-shirt and boxers. "Won't you be late for work?"

"I took the day off. I'm staying here with you today. You'll be glad that I did."

"Oh my God," she gasped, "Is it today? Did you see the birth? When will it be?"

"This evening, round about nineish."

"You're so weird. I don't think that I'll ever get used to this thing going on inside your head. But tell me, will the baby be OK?"

"Yes, a gorgeous baby boy, as handsome as his father."

"Will he have your eyes?"

"No, he will have your eyes. Brown is dominant over blue."

"Ooohh, I like your eyes." she sighed in disappointment. "Tell me more, will the birth hurt?"

He pursed his lips, "Ermmm, it will a bit, but I will be there, holding your hand, trying to share the pain. But it will all be over in two or three hours."

"Two or three hours....oh my God!"

"Don't worry, you'll do just fine, honey." He circled his arms around her and gave her a sweet reassuring kiss. He heard her tummy rumble. He lifted her off his knees and gently put her back down on his chair. "The kid is hungry. Let me pamper you today."

"No, it's fine. I can do it," she protested. She liked doing her own meals; her taste buds had always been so fastidious, but even more so during her pregnancy.

He snorted. "I've been living with you for over two years now and I think I have grasped the way you like your piece of bread; crusty buns with NO butter, but with a slice of Gouda cheese and Parma ham, and put the whole lot in the microwave for exactly twenty-five seconds. Not a second more, not a second less. Try me. I think that your fetish taste buds will approve of my work of art." He gave her a small pat on the nose and set to work...

Luca slowly opened his eyes. The glorious sun was still shining brightly upon him, but, after that dip into that alien world, his spirits were somewhat dampened. For starters, he would be celebrating his twenty-third birthday the following month, and that meant that in just over two years' time he would be burdened with fatherhood. Did he want that? Probably not. He was still too irresponsible; he could hardly look after himself, let alone a wife and a kid, and he was not just talking about financial responsibility but also about mental wisdom. He was definitely not mature enough for this; not now and probably not in two years' time. But, on the other hand, that Luca in his dream seemed to be prepared for the challenge. He shrugged.

That Luca had also mentioned that he had been living with her for two years, and so by inference he could conclude that the chance meeting was indeed imminent. Everything would snowball so fast after that; he would ask her to marry him after a mere year and they would have a child the year after. It was scary, very scary, too scary to know that this *girl* would grip his life in such a relentless way. He was beginning to seriously doubt the wisdom of allowing that chance encounter to take place. This was all so confusing. He seemed to be split in half; his heart wanted to get to know her but his logic was rebelling strongly against it.

If he were to let her go, some instinct inside him told him that this *Poseidon* would probably have her. He had seen a *thing* between the two as their intertwined fingers had slowly broken contact. That *thing* had probably caused his initial jolt of envy. That *thing* could probably grow into love if allowed to flourish. What did he know about the guy? She had called him Mark. She had mentioned a Mark and a Steve in his other dream. He smiled to himself; Mark was no competition because she had said that she had hated the feel of his slimy tongue in her mouth despite the fact that he was a campus heartthrob. So, he was a fellow university graduate and he looked very wealthy too. Both attributes would probably make him a better suitor than himself.

And *that* was another thing that had bothered him in that small dip into his future; his lack of formal qualifications and his relatively low pay. It had been an eye opener. He would definitely hate having to rely on his wealthy father to support his family in the lifestyle he wanted, or, even worse, to have a wife who was the main breadwinner. Even if he were to choose to thwart that chance encounter he should probably still think about getting those damned certificates. This world had become too obsessed with that single piece of paper and it had kicked ability aside. When still in his teens, he had strongly rebelled against that mentality, scorning the very idea of structured exams, but he had only damaged his own prospects by taking that immature stance. He should push to take his GCSEs and A levels all in one go during the late sessions offered that coming September. He still had a couple of months to prepare. That would be more than enough. He was not being cocky about it but he would probably get his full set of A stars even if he sat the exams that very week. His photographic memory was infallible and he already had all the information inside his head. All he had to do was to have the patience to sit down and regurgitate it all onto a piece of paper.

After that he might go a bit further and enrol for a law degree on a part-time basis while still performing his duties with British Intelligence, though, from then on, he would rather stick to just office intelligence and strategic advice, an area he excelled in and, more importantly, liked. He would not go undercover again. The university degree would simply be an accessory piece of paper whose only function would be to increase his pay. He would not tell anyone about his intentions, not his mother or father and certainly not his uncle who had so often said to him in that righteous voice of his...*Luca, in this life you will reap what you will sow. One day you will realise that you were wrong and that we were right*...He would hate to see his *I-told-you-so* look in his eyes, and so he would say nothing for the time being and he would only slam the completed degree in his uncle's face when he needed that pay rise.

He stood up and began to walk away, turning his back on the sunlit bench. He had things to do. The first on his list was to apply for his exams online and hope that a kind soul would accept his late applications. Then he had to wrap up the last loose ends of his undercover work which had suddenly started to feel so cumbersome.

9. Stolen Identity

"...Grazie mille, molto apprezzato." Alina pressed the button on the phone and ended the call. She frowned. That was strange, but then again, deep down in her heart she had already suspected that the Bruni sea tragedy was not her story. But it was the only lead available at her disposal, and, even though her mother had warned her not to delve too deep, she grasped onto that precious lead and followed it up by calling Antonio Bruni, Luigi's brother, her alleged uncle, using great caution in her choice of words.

In her broken Italian, she introduced herself as a student investigating past sea tragedies, an absurd explanation for the call, but the unsuspecting man kindly obliged and answered all her questions. He immediately confirmed that the remains of Luigi and Gina Bruni were buried in a local cemetery in Pisa. The body of their daughter Alina was never found, presumed dead. He denied knowing about a fisherman's rescue and a subsequent adoption, and he was very adamant that his niece's body still rested somewhere out there in the Mediterranean. Apparently, he had been the child's legal guardian and he stressed that had she been found alive he would have adopted her himself. He sounded genuine enough and Alina had no reason to doubt him. She quickly apologized for getting her facts wrong and hung up, not wanting to cast any doubts in his mind lest he decided to investigate. All he needed to do was to hack the system of the local Italian registry, like she had done earlier, and there he would quickly get to know that Alina Bruni was still registered amongst the living...though there was no mention of her ever being adopted by a Maltese couple and changing her family name to Spiteri. To the casual eye it would seem as though the girl was still somewhere out there enjoying an Italian citizenship.

She spent her next hour or two delving deep inside all the corners of cyberspace. She found many newspaper articles reporting the tragic shipwreck that had occurred off the coast of Italy but there was no mention of the daughter ever being rescued and offered for adoption some three months later, the story her mother had been fed by the alleged adoption agency. There were many photos showing the happy Bruni family of three, but in all of them the girl's facial features were somewhat obscured, either by her long brown hair or by an overlapping hand. To Alina's trained eye it was obvious that all the girl's images had been photoshopped. Someone had simply hacked the various sites and fiddled around in such a way so that the resulting distorted images would not pique the suspicions of the casual researcher, such as her own parents had they wanted to look up the real story behind the orphaned child. She was sure that if she were to unearth the actual articles in their paper form, the girl's features would be seen in all their finest details. But it was her third day in Sicily and she was still too terrified of venturing outside the safe doors of Mara Tucci's brothel. That trip to the library archives was just not feasible yet.

There had to be some missed unedited photo of the girl tucked away somewhere in cyberspace. She had almost given up on her intensive and illegal search, when, hours later, she happened to invade a facebook private group page which had been highlighted because it contained the name Alina Bruni somewhere inside it. Scrolling down, she eventually encountered a photo of four girls playing together in a kindergarten class and beneath it there was an innocent comment...*Chi e quella ragazza in abito blu?* (*Who is that girl in the blue dress?*). Alina translated a friend's answer...*That girl is Alina Bruni, don't you remember her? She died when her father's boat capsized. God rest her soul...*

So, like the uncle, the friends had been told that Alina Bruni had died at sea because that was nothing but the honest truth. It was immediately evident that the girl in the photo was not her. She shared her colouring, brown hair, brown eyes and a dark Mediterranean complexion, but that was where the similarities ended. The features were not hers. This girl looked so different from her own photo when she was five years old, the photo her mother had proudly displayed on the fireplace in the lounge back home in Malta. The genuine Alina Bruni, daughter of Luigi and Gina Bruni, had in actual fact really died at sea, but the mysterious man with the intense coal-black eyes had, months later, seized the tragic story and stolen the identity of the girl, giving it to her. Selected people within both the Italian and Maltese registry must have helped him to keep the identity theft plausible. The plan had obvious flaws but they were all calculated risks. The dead girl's next of kin would never think of looking her up in any registry, and the new parents in Malta wanted the child too much to risk unearthing the truth. And that was exactly why her mother and father had never approached the sensitive subject of adoption with her. She remembered her mother's plea...*We were cautioned and now I'm cautioning you. You may not like what you uncover if you delve too deep. Please, can you try to let this go?*

But she couldn't ever let it go. She had to unearth the truth, for herself if for nothing else, and she would do that as discreetly as she could. The Bruni sea tragedy had proved to be a dead end, a useless lead, but she was not giving up hope. She thought hard about who her real self could be. If she were to hazard a guess on her true nationality it would be British. There were many clues suggesting that; the language she first spoke when she was adopted, the posh British accent of the man she kept seeing in her flashbacks, the origin of the expensive teddy bear, to name but a few. Now why had the man wanted to erase her previous identity so badly so as to go through all that elaborate plan, even crossing countries to dispel the scent, from the UK to Italy and then onto tiny inconspicuous Malta? Why? It was indeed a clever plan because no one would ever think of looking for a child in Malta of all places, a tiny gem of an island in the middle of the Mediterranean with a population of less than half a million. Few people knew of its sunny existence otherwise known as the best kept secret of the Mediterranean.

A sharp flashback crossed her inner mind...

..."Please Becca, we have to leave before they see us."

"Why? Firemen...the police...they are good people. Our teacher said so."

"They usually are...but not today, I'm afraid. These were far too quick to react. Please Becca, I'm asking you to trust me."...

She did trust him, she had trusted him then and she would continue to trust him because she knew that he had her best interests at heart...even her mother had sensed his genuine soul. The man must have wanted to protect her from something in the UK. Had her life been in danger then as much as it was at that moment in time? Was it something that she or her biological parents had done? It was ironic really; she seemed to be perpetually on the run, being on the wanted list in the UK at the tender age of five, and now thanks to her stupid hacking adventure with the Mafia she was being hunted down in Italy and Malta too. Where should she go next? Despite the potential danger posed by her unknown past, the UK was her obvious choice. She would try to cross the border using one of the two brand new Italian passports Mara Tucci had obtained for her on Mark's insistence.

Her eyes fell on the neat booklets. She had chosen two identities for herself; the first being Alina Bruni because that was the easiest to forge since she already possessed the authentic birth certificate, and the second was a random name of Becca Lenzi chosen for the simple reason that deep down herself she felt like a Becca. She looked closely at her photos. She could so easily pass off as an Italian because she looked like one. Now why did she look Mediterranean when she felt so strongly that her roots were British? Her whole existence was one big enigma. She could only hope to unravel it if she were lucky enough to find the British man with the intense coal-black eyes. She was prepared to comb through every street in the UK to find him. That would be the equivalent of looking for a needle in a haystack but she was determined to go through with it.

With optimistic but naive determination, she went back on her laptop and, using the name of Becca Lenzi, she impulsively booked the first flight out of Sicily to London, leaving in over ten hours' time. She had no choice but to use the funds inside the dodgy Swiss bank account. It was her safest bet since the account itself was highly discreet and it could never be traced back to her. She could always consider this as a loan because she was determined to redeposit the amount back once she earned her own money sometime in the future, whenever that would be.

She closed her laptop and lay back on the bed, feeling very comfortable with her sudden decision to leave. Sicily felt like the lion's den with the hungry Mafia hot on her heels. She didn't feel safe there and she could not imagine herself ever leaving the sanctuary of her room. Malta was out of the question too because they would expect her to go crawling back there for comfort. But no one knew of her connection with the UK. She had outsmarted them all.

She was still smiling with self-satisfaction when Mara knocked on her door. The elegantly dressed and perfumed older lady came bustling in, loaded with five or six shopping bags. "Buongiorno, cara. I buy some nice clothes for you. I guess size," she said in her clipped English as she enthusiastically unloaded all the fine clothes on the bed; sexy lacy slips and underwear and stylishly expensive outfits and shoes that Alina knew she would never be comfortable wearing. "New clothes make you feel happy, cara. Do you like?"

"Oh, Mara, thank you. You are so kind. They are absolutely beautiful," she said, trying to infuse as much delight in her words as she could. She didn't want to offend Mara, she liked her; she was so generous and warm and so very welcoming, just like a loving mother hen. She had been a good shoulder to cry on and Alina would be forever grateful to her for the kindness she had given her in her loneliest and darkest hours. "But I must pay you for these," she insisted.

"No, no, Mark already pay for everything to help you. He likes you, you know. He worried for you and he phone me a lot, asking how you doing. I tell him you cry a lot and he tell me to buy you clothes to make you smile. But you look a bit happier today."

Yes, she did feel happier. After three days of incessant sobbing, that morning she had decided to quit self-pity and retake control of the dire situation she had landed herself in. She had started with investigating her past and that had led to some form of direction in her life. “Yes, Mara, I am happier, and that’s because I have reached a decision. I always feel better when I have a definite plan I can follow. I’m leaving Sicily, this evening. The flight will leave Catania airport in six hours.” She thought it best to lie about her flight, keeping her destination a secret.

“Oh, you leaving, that is sad. I like looking after you. You don’t have to leave so soon.”

“I know, Mara. But I don’t feel safe here with the Mafia all around us. The earlier I leave, the better, before they realise that I’ve escaped from Malta and went to the nearest obvious port, Sicily. They are bound to spot me at some time or other if they start to look for me here.”

“Yes, I see your point. I take you to airport myself. We leave in three hours because you have to check in. Can I suggest that you wear something I buy for you here,” she said, demonstrating with a graceful wave of her hand a beautiful white silk shirt and an elegant navy blue clinging knee-length skirt. “If you wear elegant and sexy it is easier to pass the passport check. Open the first two buttons of shirt and choose a box with a man so he look at your breasts and not at fake passport. And also I do some makeup for you. Mafia are looking for a girl who studies a lot and wears no makeup. Easier to escape them if look like a sexy girl like us...you know.”

Alina burst out laughing. “Thank you, Mara, I never thought of that. You are very clever. Come on, let’s get to work,” and she quickly changed into the elegant outfit and let the older lady doll her up with fine layers of makeup. She couldn’t help thinking about the last time she had let someone dress her up like that. It had ended so badly for her...and for Lizzy. Poor Lizzy; no matter how malicious her intensions had been, she still didn’t deserve to die so young, not like that. Her death would somehow always rest on her conscience because she had selfishly chosen to meddle with that website. She had thought that she was clever enough to punish the evil of this world but she had angered forces so much greater than little insignificant her. She was still brooding in that dark corner of remorse when Mara took her hand and led her in front of a mirror. Alina gasped in surprise. She was virtually unrecognisable.

"Mio Dio!" Mara exclaimed. "You very beautiful, so innocent and pure, just as Mark say. I can see why he is crazy for you. Why you don't like him? He is good man, very kind to me, to everyone."

"I like Mark, but he has chosen to go down the marriage path. He should be with his wife and child, not me."

"He not love her but he likes you. He is sad that he not see you anymore. Very sad. Do you want to talk to him before you leave? That phone is safe," she said nodding at the landline Alina had used earlier to call Antonio Bruni. "Do you want his private secure number? It will make him happy to hear your voice."

Alina sighed sadly as she slowly sat down on her bed. She should make contact, just as she had promised she would, but she won't call him, not on the phone. A verbal conversation was too daunting for her because she lacked people skills. She would prefer to hack his phone and if he happened to be there she would kick-start an impersonal digital conversation and then she would clean out every trace before she leaves. "OK, I'll contact him before I go. But I'll use my laptop. Safer that way."

"OK, I let you talk to him. I go now and come back with suitcase to pack your new things for trip."

As Mara exited the room, Alina took up her laptop and set to work.

Hi, Mark, she was typing a few minutes later.

Wow, this is a surprise, a good surprise...at last. I've been checking this thing every five minutes. I had given up on ever hearing from you, fearing so much that you wouldn't want to have anything to do with me. What took you so long?

It hasn't been that long.

It has for me.

I'm sorry. I've been feeling so battered and bruised and I couldn't do anything else but feel sorry for myself.

I know. Mara said that you cry a lot.

Thank you for the clothes. They were a nice thought and I do feel better now. I just wanted you to know that I'll be leaving soon. Better move on before they start looking for me here.

Good thinking. I can confirm that they are still concentrating on Malta for the time being. But it won't be long before they broaden their search. Please let me know if you need anything from me.

Thank you. You are very kind to me.

That's because I like you. I miss seeing you...a lot, a lot and a lot.

You shouldn't. You're getting married in a couple of days' time. Listen, I have to go, she quickly typed before the conversation got too adulterous for her tastes.

Sorry, I didn't want to scare you. Will you keep in touch?

"I don't know. It depends; will you honour your marriage vows?"

"I will. And if you promise to contact me every single day I can promise you that I will protect your parents. At the moment they are just being watched round the clock by our boys, but I can talk my father out of harassing them should he decide to go down that path. So, tell me, will you drop me a line or two every day?

She gasped. Was he threatening her? Mark was generous and decent but he had a sinister vindictive side too brought on by a very spoilt childhood. He was used to getting his own way too much. She started to type, hoping that her honesty might soften his heart...*This is crazy. Why are you doing this? We can never be together so why are you insisting on keeping in touch? What's the point of doing that?*

Because I know that your presence in my life will keep me sane. Let me tell you a little secret...I have always been so scared of becoming just like my father and when I was a boy I clutched onto the only image of pure innocence I could find around me...and that was you. I used to think that if I could see you every day I would be able to keep walking on straight paths. And that thought stayed with me for all those years. I'm not an obsessive psychopath; I'm just a lost soul trying to break free from the evil I was born into. Our contact together will not be sexual if you don't want it to, but instead it will be that beacon of light that will help me move forward and better myself. Am I making sense or have I lost you?

She was crying with emotion as she quickly typed in her reply. *You're making perfect sense, Mark. I will continue to keep in touch for as long as you need me to, and that I promise. We can talk about anything that's bothering you, anything. And once our conversation is over I'll always remove all traces of it from cyberspace, so feel free to speak your mind with me. And I'll do the same with you. It will be therapeutic for both of us.*

This means a lot to me. Thank you so much.

You're welcome. And, by the way, I like you too, Mark. I'll try to make contact tomorrow evening, round about eightish. Take care xxx

And she wiped the slate clean, fragmenting their entire conversation into a million pieces and dispersing it throughout cyberspace before exiting his privacy. She squeezed her eyes shut, relishing that tender moment. Mark had managed to touch her heart. She felt sorry for him. He was a good man trapped by birth within an evil family, something he had no control over. She would do her utmost to help him emotionally just as much as he had helped her physically over the past few days. She was comfortable with this cyber-arrangement. She smiled as she found herself looking forward to the next day's digital conversation.

10. Playing God

"For fuck's sake, Tom, wake up, man. I need urgent backup...Newbury Park underground station, westbound platform...oh shit, that's too long, I'll be dead in ten minutes." Luca shoved the phone in his jeans pocket as he ran down the flight of steps, two at a time, skidding his rubber soles to a sudden halt at the last step. He drew his gun out from its holster and peered out from behind the concrete column, assessing the collateral damage he was about to cause. He silently thanked the good fortune of the opportune lonely hour of ten o'clock in the evening which had kindly granted an otherwise desolate platform, ensuring no innocent casualties.

Encouraged by that fact alone, he gambled on his life and calmly walked out in full view, his gun aimed at the retreating doctor's head some six metres away from him. At all costs he had to stop him from boarding the coming train due in the next five minutes or so, but at the same time he had to keep him alive long enough to divulge who was controlling him. "Put that bag down, slowly, and back away from it. NOW," he barked, knowing full well that the terrorist scum would rather blast just the two of them on that lonely platform than admit defeat. But, better there than in an overcrowded hospital; his own life in exchange for thousands...a fair deal seeing that he had been the one to spark off this premature assault by exposing his undercover mission, all for the sake of that one very crazy night with Jessica.

The doctor turned round to face him. "All I have to do is press the silver clasp and open the bag, and everything around us will burn. I can do that long before I feel your shot in my head. But the thing is that I don't want to do it here. Too lonely. I prefer an audience. You don't have to die today if you let me go. No one will know."

"I will know."

"Ah, so now you're pretending that you have a conscience. You worthless piece of shit. I welcomed you in my home, I trusted you, and in return you screwed my wife. Oh yes, I know all about that; she came clean after she saw you shagging

that Wills girl on the net. You left me no choice but to beat my cheating wife to her early grave. Her death is on you."

"I have news for you; she isn't dead. She somehow managed to call me, warning me that you've decided to up your game tonight. Hence, this showdown."

The doctor snorted in disdain. "And you actually think that you are able to stop me! You're totally fucked up, a bloody wreck of a secret agent, no discipline, forsaking duty for pleasure. Is this the most British Intelligence has to offer....you? Tell me, was a night with Jessica Wills worth your exposure?"

"Actually, no, it wasn't. Now, put that fucking bag down and tell me who is pulling all your puppet strings, or else..."

"Or else what? I am prepared to die today, but the question is, are you?"

Luca thought that he was but then the lavatory door opened and his Becca stepped out between them, right in the middle, right in his line of fire. She was unaware of what was going on, having been looking down and smoothing the creases of her shirt as she emerged, pulling a small wheeled suitcase behind her.

The doctor was quick to seize the opportunity. "Help me, please," he squealed at her in a timid voice. "He is going to kill me."

She let out a tiny scream of terror as she looked up and realised what she had just walked into. Luca kept his eyes firmly glued to the doctor's, but he could see her in his peripheral field of vision, her head swinging from right to left, assessing them both in seconds; a well dressed doctor clutching an innocent looking medical bag, and a scum of the earth holding a gun and having every intention to use it. He felt her gaze burn through his vicious tattoo snaking high above his tattered T-shirt. That was her single deciding factor, and he saw her inch her way towards fatal danger, exactly what the doctor was banking on. A hostage in his arms would give him more bargaining power.

"You're making the wrong choice, Becca," Luca warned in a steady voice of supreme authority, his eyes never leaving the doctor's. "Or do you prefer that I call you Alina?" He felt her

freeze in mid-step. His words had to compensate for his terrifying appearance, and knowing her so intimately would play in his favour and win her trust. "You once told me that the eyes are the first thing you look at when you meet someone because they are the true reflection of the soul. Becca, I want you to look at our eyes and tell me who is good and who is bad."

"When did I ever tell you that? Who are you?"

But his words had the desired effect. He sighed in relief as she started to walk towards him, drawn to the warm glow of his blazing blue eyes. Unfortunately, that relief was short-lived when he heard the distant rumble of the train at the same time as he saw the doctor's eyes flick up to the red digital light above announcing the imminent arrival. The terrorist's intentions were obvious; he would not get to burn a hospital but at least he would get to burn a train, better that than a lonely platform. In a split of a second, before the doctor had lowered his eyes back down, Luca had nimbly pushed the bewildered girl behind him and shot his quarry bang in the middle of his forehead. The dying body recoiled back with a tremendous force, the lethal bag flying out of his limp hand, the silver clasp remaining untouched.

Luca had managed to save lives; his own life, the girl's and those of the occupants of the train. But he had failed to obtain the name of the puppet master behind the radicalization, and in so doing he had failed the lives of so many others. As he took the hysterically screaming girl inside his protective arms, he couldn't help but reflect on the irresponsible way he had handled his undercover mission. He was indeed everything the doctor had said he was, a bloody wreck of a secret agent, undisciplined, wild and so self-centred...

That was exactly how destiny had re-planned their chance encounter. It had simply replaced the busy street in Mayfair for an underground station, but the events after that would still be the same; they would get to know each other, fall in love, get married, have kids and live happily ever after. Luca scowled; he didn't like this new version of their first encounter. In it he strongly felt like a dirty villain with a heavy conscience, and he had never wanted to play that role in his life. It reeked strongly of failure, failure to complete his undercover mission, and he didn't like failure. He had to find a way to tweak destiny. He shifted around on his narrow lumpy bed and thought hard.

It had all started with that regrettable encounter with Jessica more than two weeks back. She didn't take kindly to rejection and after he failed to make contact with her the following week, she called Tom herself and casually mentioned something about intimate images Mel had taken with her phone, images that would cash in thousands for the simple reason that they would smear the Prime Minister's daughter, especially it being so close to a general election. He cursed his recklessness, having been too intoxicated that night to notice what Mel had been doing; a fatal mistake. Nonetheless, he brushed the threat aside, taking a gamble on the fact that Jessica, in spite of her wild nature, would never risk exposing herself in such a way. After he failed once again to make contact the second week, Tom was kindly sent the image in question and asked to forward it to him. Jessica was captured face-on but he wasn't, however the distinctive henna tattoo on his neck would easily single him out as the dirty lover. Again, he brushed the second threat aside.

But apparently, according to his dream, Jessica would have the audacity to expose both of them if he failed to show up on the third week, just to prove the point that she was prepared to play havoc if she didn't get what she wanted. He had underestimated her, thinking that she was unaware of his true role, but she must have known that the change in appearance could only mean undercover work commissioned by her father who she happened to despise. Giving Mel the permission to post that image on the net would be her sweet revenge for both men. And after that, he could easily predict how the rest of the events would unfold. It would be safe to assume that the posting would go viral in minutes and the doctor's wife would see it, recognise the tattoo, and in a moment of panic she would confess everything to her husband. He would beat her to near death and up his game, opting for an instant killing spree before British Intelligence closed in on him and the lethal toy he had been building for months. Severely wounded, the wife would manage to call Luca, her former lover, and warn him, and he would immediately give chase, confronting the doctor on the station platform.

Luca had the advantage of foresight, and, having seen the time and date on the station board in his dream, he knew that he still had four days before disaster would strike. He had enough time to tweak that dream. The easiest option would be to preserve the secrecy of his undercover work and give in to Jessica's demands, thus stopping that image from going viral. But he would rather die than sleep with that vicious girl again. The other much more complex option would be to wrap up the case and obtain the name of the doctor's puppet master in the next day or two. If he could do that he would transform himself from a villain to an ultimate hero, from failure to success. British Intelligence would have all the information they need to close down the undercover mission and convict the doctor and his controller, and in so doing preserve the lives of many potential victims. The lurid image of his adventure with Jessica would still be leaked out on the net, eventually, but he didn't care about people gaping at his nude arse; all he cared about was the success of his undercover mission.

He smiled widely. He could turn this around. He knew he could. He was Luca Snell with the gift of the gab and he would work relentlessly for two days to persuade the doctor to give him all the fine details. He had achieved a lot in the past two weeks, having already been determined to close the case as quickly as he could. In fact the doctor had already started to trust him more and more; he just needed him to trust him that tiny bit more before that image hit the net, because after that he would instantly lose all that accumulated trust.

*

Two days later Luca had a wide cocky smile on his face as he strutted towards his uncle's office. He briefly knocked on the door and, without waiting for an invitation, he barged inside and rudely slapped a file down on the desk. The sun had once again shone upon him and he had the case all tidily sealed and wrapped up with a pretty red bow. He was a winner, which was much more than he could say for some other agents who were enjoying fatter pay packages just because they happened to possess some very useless paper certificates with their names printed on them. In his view, his uncle more than deserved this arrogant attitude because he had been the one to freeze his pay to that minimum level, saying that he wanted to be transparent as far as qualifications and wages were concerned so as to fend off any accusation of nepotism.

Ben Blake leaned back on his chair and narrowed his coal-black eyes in disapproval. “It is against protocol for an active undercover agent to step inside this building. There are no exceptions. You should know that by now.”

“The undercover mission is over,” Luca brusquely responded as he slumped down on an armchair and looked him straight in the eye.

The nephew and uncle were physically similar, except for the colour of their eyes. They also shared the same psychic ability, a high IQ and an incredibly sharp acumen. Both were on the very top of their game. The older man fully recognised the unique potential in his protégé but he also knew that it could so easily get lost if that youthful energy remained unharnessed. Through the years he had reined in a lot of frustration provoked by the reckless paths Luca had chosen to follow again and again, and he had closed an eye or two on quite a number of occasions, but arrogance was not something he was prepared to tolerate.

“I am Chief of this institution and the mission will only be over when I say it’s over. Do you understand that?” The intense black gaze met the blazing blue, both unmoving, both unflinching.

“Well, I beg to differ. If you care to read my report you’ll quickly get to know that there is nothing more I can do. You’ve got all the names there...yes the puppet master too, the ghost you’ve been hunting down for more than a decade without success, until I came along and did what all of your other agents failed to do. I would strongly suggest that you read that report before you pass any form of judgement."

Ben pursed his lips but said nothing. He was much too dignified to engage in a heated argument with the immature and rebellious youth. That was definitely beneath him. He calmly broke all eye contact and started to read through the contents of the file. It did not take long for him to grasp the enormity of what had been revealed and he quickly reached for his phone. "Harry, I want you to drop everything you're doing and come in here, now, please."

The door opened within seconds. When the Chief called, no one dared loiter, not out of fear, but out of deep respect. Luca was probably the only person in the entire intelligence department who ever clashed with the much loved Chief. His tall dark frame, stern gaze and firm but fair rule demanded reverence from all who knew him. "Thank you, Harry," he said. "I want you to quickly read through this report and assemble a team ASAP. We should be ready to close in on our targets in the next hour or so. I'll be with you shortly after I've had a word with my nephew."

"Yes, Chief." Harry exited the room and a flurry of activity was immediately sparked off beyond the closed door of the office.

Luca tapped his fingers on the arm of his chair. "See, I told you so. I cleaned up everything and all you have to do is send in your boys and claim the final glory to your name, all thanks to *MY* cunning hard work."

Again, the uncle chose to brush the conceited arrogance aside, wanting to tackle it with clever words rather than a headstrong battle. "Well done, Luca, a brilliant piece of work, I have to grant you that much. Though, I couldn't help notice that you failed to log in the real reason behind your sudden and desperate endeavour to expose the puppet master in these last few days. I am of course referring to your little illegal adventure you had a while back, you know, *The Jessica Incident*, the very incident that would have brought about the near-fatal disaster in Newbury Park underground station, the disaster you foresaw and wanted to prevent at all costs."

"Shit." That was a very sharp stab at his over-inflated ego.

"Did you honestly think that I didn't know about that night with Jessica? I knew what you were going to do way before you even thought of it. My psychic abilities are so much more developed than yours because I embrace them and I can see further than just my own little selfish circle."

"Then why the hell didn't you try to stop me?"

"Because I try to refrain from playing God, unless I really have too. Changing the natural course of events could prove fatal because you never know which way the domino pieces will fall."

"Bla bla, bla bla, I've heard that lecture a thousand times before. You're full of bullshit, Uncle. Are you saying that you were actually going to allow that to happen? What if he had managed to open that bag and detonate the device?"

"The device was harmless because as soon as you uncovered its location in that derelict house I sent someone in to finely alter the chemical composition of the components, just in case you impulsively chose to take a different path and ended up with an even bigger disaster."

Luca clenched his teeth in anger. "And you didn't even bother to tell me about it. I would have killed that man on the assumption that the device he had was lethal. Fuck you. Tell me, how could your conscience allow you to accept the premature abortion of the mission just for the sake of preserving destiny? What about the puppet master? Had destiny prevailed his identity would still be a secret today."

"Now, I admit, that was my mistake. I underestimated you and I never thought that you would ever be able to wring that information out of the doctor, so why prolong the mission unnecessarily especially when you were becoming so dangerous, a liability to the establishment, a liability to yourself and to your own wingman and the backup team he so often had to rouse on a moment's notice just to satisfy your adrenaline surge. You were a ticking bomb, a disaster waiting to happen. The Jessica incident proves my point. Your actions there were reckless, irresponsible and self-centred with a complete disregard to the secrecy of the mission. In all my years with British Intelligence, and that's many years, way before you were born, I can tell you that no one has ever behaved in such a despicable way. They may not achieve half of what you do but they are loyal to their mission. It really hurts me to say this, but Luca you give me no choice but to suspend you. In actual fact you deserve to be fired, rather than just suspended, but because of your brilliant execution of the mission in the last two days, I am prepared to give you a second chance."

Luca shrugged. "Fair enough," he conceded, his anger somewhat diminished by the clever way his uncle had presented the dire but true facts relating to his disaster-seeking personality. "I deserve that much. Suspended for how long?"

"For as long as it takes for you to grow up and behave in a responsible manner. I'll be the judge of that. In the meantime I can promise that I'll clean up your mess and your explicit image will not be plastered on the net."

"I don't really care about that."

"You should. If Larry Wills gets to know about this you'll be fired on the spot, he won't sugar-coat it with any suspension, and you know that the Prime Minister's decision immediately overrules any of mine. And Luca, one more thing...the girl, Becca, she is good for you. She is the only reason I allowed an irresponsible agent such as yourself to go undercover because I knew that without that step you wouldn't have met her. You already thwarted the first chance destiny gave you to meet her. You're lucky enough to be given a second chance. Grab it. This time you happen to know the date, the time and the place you were meant to meet. Honour it."

"Shit, do you know about Becca too? Jeez, Uncle, get a life." Luca narrowed his eyes as all the complicated equations started to add up in his mind. "Since you knew about the first destined meeting, am I right to assume that, besides being the reason I went undercover, she is also the reason why you lured me to London when you first offered me a job?"

"Yes, she is. She is also the reason I got this," he said as he waved his badly scarred left hand which had undergone its fair share of reconstructive operations to bring it to its present barely functional state. "I knew her mother well. There was a house fire, a long time ago, when the girl was five. I happened to foresee it because I felt the girl's connection with you. You see, almost all of my premonitions seem to be linked with members of my family. I don't see everything but what little I see I try to piece together and form as solid a picture as I possibly could. Had I not intervened with that fire, the girl would have died and your life would be forever void, directionless and out of control, exactly as it stands at this point in time. She is the only one who could neutralise that wild and reckless streak you inherited from your father, just as my sister neutralised his a very long time ago."

"You bloody hypocrite. How many times have you cautioned me about disrupting the natural course of events, and yet the whole time you were playing God and planning my life when I was just a mere boy. How dare you," he boomed on top of his voice as he stood up tall and banged his fist on the desk. His anger had by then reached uncontrollable levels. This was a nasty revelation to him. Apparently, his whole life had always been moulded in the direction his uncle wanted it to go, starting with saving the little girl's life, onto his job offer in London and lastly the planning of his undercover mission. Along the way he himself had attempted to veer off course just to flavour the unknown, but his uncle had always been one step ahead of him, pushing him back onto the path he thought was right. "How dare you," he boomed again.

Ben stood up and leaned across the desk, matching the ferocity of the youth's stare. "Yes, I do challenge destiny sometimes, BUT ONLY IF I ABSOLUTLY HAVE TO. You wouldn't be here today hadn't I played God with your father's life. He should have died when he was twenty but I changed that and he met my sister and that was the best thing that could ever have happened to him. He was a total wreck before that, lost and headless, just like you. Listen to me, Luca, please; Becca is good for you, without her you'll just be flitting along from one bed to another, nothing anchoring you down. You need her. Don't throw away this second chance to get to know her because you might reach the point of no return as far as she is concerned, and after that she will never belong to you."

"I don't care, at least it would be my choice...NOT YOURS."

"This is what you don't understand; everything you see in that future is your choice, not mine, not destiny's, not anyone's, but yours. It is everything you're intrinsically inclined to do. Take law for instance, you would have chosen that career because you are naturally gifted in speech and you're a fast thinker, smart and creative. Law would have made you tick, but, because you foresaw it, you chose to throw it away before you even tried it. Don't do the same with the girl. Meet her, talk to her and you'll see how she'll touch your life."

"Fuck you, Uncle. Don't you ever dare meddle with my life again." He turned round and exited the room, banging the door shut behind him.

Ben sank down on his chair, feeling exhausted. He should have handled that better, but he couldn't always foretell how Luca would react because the kid was constantly disrupting every single fibre of what should happen. During that past year as he followed the progress of the undercover mission, he had had several scares as the young rebel constantly chose paths that should never have been chosen, paths that could so easily have ended with his demise, but the kid seemed to have a knack for landing on his own two feet every single time. The exposure of the identity of the puppet master showed just how brilliantly able he was. Perhaps he should cut him some slack and trust him with whatever decision he chose to take with the girl.

Ben slowly stood up and headed for the door. He had a lot of things to coordinate. Thanks to Luca's sharp wit they had the name of the ghost that had eluded them for years. British Intelligence would be celebrating hard that night.

11. The Man on the Train

Alina stepped out of Harveils, the top-end toy shop in the very heart of Mayfair. Her shoulders sagged down in utter defeat. Her expensive teddy bear was just another dead end. What was she thinking going in there? The condescending man behind the till had given her such a hard time, making her feel so inadequate and naïve. And perhaps she was so, having stupidly assumed that he would just hand over the names of who had purchased a teddy bear similar to hers some sixteen or seventeen years ago. Looking back, that had been a really dumb move, but it had been the only desperate move she had on offer after more than two weeks in the UK achieving nothing as far as her investigation into her ancestry was concerned. The mathematical probability of her ever knowing the names of her biological parents was next to zero. Besides, who was she kidding, they were probably both dead and the sliver of hope of having a family to belong to in the UK was just that, a hope, an unrealistic hope. And equally as unrealistic was the chance of her ever bumping into the man with the coal-black eyes. She wasn't even sure whether she would recognise him if he were to walk past her. She saw no point in staying there. But where else should she go?

She stopped in the middle of the busy pavement, people jostling her about. But she didn't care. She had just reached her checkmate; trapped, suffocating, scared and lonely, just like a condemned man with a noose around his neck. She thought of her sunny island in the middle of the Mediterranean with that warm tight-knit family atmosphere that had always made her feel so secure. She so desperately wanted to go back there inside her parents' loving arms. She was tired of running and running and hiding. That was not her. She couldn't even sustain it for a month, let alone the years and years that were yet to come. Perhaps she should go back and face the music. Let the baddies find her and exploit her and her skills. She had no energy left inside her to fight them off.

She looked up at the sky and sent out a little prayer for help. "Please, dear God, help me choose the right path. I'm feeling so lost," she murmured beneath her breath. Going back to her parents' home seemed like the best option available. She squared her shoulders and started to walk away. She would pack her small bag and leave the two-bedded terraced house she had just rented in Newbury Park, an area in the north-east side of London. Being a fair distance away from central London it had been the least expensive property she could find, price being an important determining factor since she did not want to withdraw too much funds from her Swiss bank accounts, too conscious of the fact that she would one day have to redeposit everything she had used. Unfortunately she would get to waste what she had just withdrawn, having paid beforehand for a whole year's rent because at the time she had thought that she was strong enough to stay that much, but she was obviously made of much softer stuff.

*

Hours later Alina was going down the stairs of Newbury Park underground station, dragging her small wheeled suitcase behind her. Desperate tears were streaming down her face and she was thankful for the desolate lonely hour of the evening which would have otherwise sparked off a lot of curious stares her way. She hated drawing any kind of attention to herself but she just couldn't stop crying. She had booked a very late night flight back home, but she was dead scared, especially as Mark's earlier dire warning kept echoing deep inside the dark recesses of her mind. She quickly sought the sanctuary of the lavatory, just to pull herself together before boarding the next train.

She splashed cold water all over her face and leaned back against the wall, trying to control the rapid sobs that were wrecking her breath apart. She was trapped; staying was futile but going was fatal. She closed her eyes and recalled the digital conversation she had just had with Mark before leaving her rented terraced house....

...It all started with good uplifting news on his part. Sophia had given birth to a healthy and beautiful baby girl the night before. Even though the couple had already tied the knot, the new mother insisted on a paternity test and Mark was confirmed as the biological father. He was ecstatic with the news, uploading several photographs of himself proudly holding his daughter. Alina was pleased to see him looking so happy and, for the first time ever in his life, responsible and mature. The birth of the child seemed to have changed him overnight.

I don't love my wife and she doesn't love me, he typed in confidence. Over the past weeks he had quickly settled into the habit of pouring all his honest thoughts onto that digital conversation, sparing nothing. It was the only period of the day when he stripped off all pretence and was himself. *But we both love the child,* he continued to type, *and we pledged to try to make it work for her sake. However, being a father will never change the feelings I have for you and please don't let this news break up our daily conversations. I desperately need your presence in my life to help me walk on solid paths. I would be so lost without you. Talking to you, even in this way, completes me.*

It was during instances like these, when the conversation steered on inappropriate emotional grounds, that Alina often questioned the wisdom of allowing this to happen. He had a wife and a child and this affectionate attachment to herself was not healthy. But he always seemed to realise when he had crossed the line and he would quickly move on to other topics before she had a chance to abort the conversation.

I saw Steve in hospital this morning, he wrote. *He is out of intensive care and doing relatively well. I thought that you would be pleased to know that.*

Oh yes, thank you. I feel so bad about what happened to him and to Lizzy. I will forever feel that guilt. It should have been me lying six feet under, not Lizzy...which brings me to my news. She paused for a while but then, with steadfast determination, she started to type again. *Mark, I can't keep running forever. I am already exhausted. I have decided to come back. I will not let them hurt my parents and I am prepared to do whatever they ask of me. That will be my punishment, my just desert for meddling with other people's affairs.*

No, no, no, no, that's a big mistake. You don't know what it feels like having to live by their rules, having no option but to play dirty or perish. One thing will lead to another and another and another until you find yourself soulless and drowning in deep shit, unable to escape. It is a life sentence, hell on earth, and I know exactly what I'm talking about, why else would I have married someone I don't love? Please, please I'm begging you, don't come back. I cannot bear to see you get hurt in that way. You don't have to keep on running. I can help you. I can set you up in one of my villas in Sicily, not as a mistress as I once proposed, but as a good friend. You will be safe with me because no one will suspect that I am helping you. Please think about this option before you immerse yourself in irreversible corruption.

I will think about it. Listen, I have to go now. Goodbye, Mark, take care, xxx. And she fragmented their conversation before hastily exiting his hacked account. She had lied to him because she was never going to think about it. She would rather immerse herself in irreversible corruption than in irreversible adultery with a married man. This digital conversation was the furthest she would ever go with him, the physical space between them giving her some comfort. If she were to live in his villa, he would visit regularly and that would inevitably lead to only one thing. She had already started harbouring fond feelings for him, and she knew that if she let him in her bed he would have no qualms whatsoever with cheating on his wife with her, if anything he would encourage it. But she had already promised herself that she would never play the part of *that other girl* who broke a family apart, so Mark's tempting offer of security was strictly off the table.

However, his dire warning about living soulless within the Mafia ring had deeply rattled her and she had not stopped crying ever since. She looked up at the lavatory ceiling and shot a little prayer once again as she put her hand in her jeans pocket, fingering the key to her rented house. She had not given it up, not after reading Mark's plea. She had already paid for a year's rent and she might as well keep it just in case she needed sanctuary again; she had escaped once and she could always escape again if she needed to. Encouraged by that thought, she quickly wiped her face dry, knowing that she was already running late. If she were to miss that train she would eventually miss her flight.

She opened the lavatory door. Having been looking down and smoothing the creases of her shirt as she emerged, she walked straight into an elegantly dressed young man in a dark blue suit, her old trainers treading heavily on his spotless leather shoes in the process. The first to hit her senses was the musky but subtle smell of costly masculine perfume permeating out of his immaculately white shirt collar just inches from her nose. His jawline, at eye level, was chiselled and strong, covered with a stylishly groomed stubble. Polished sophistication was the clear signal she received in those initial few moments.

"I'm sorry," she mumbled. Her eyes travelled up to his cocky and rather cheeky lop-sided grin which matched the mischievous twinkle in the bluest pair of eyes she had ever seen, the colour of which sharply reminded her of the deep blue Mediterranean Sea that she loved so much. She felt a sharp pang of nostalgia. His eyes were actually making her feel really homesick. The decision to go back home to her beloved Malta had to be the right one if a random man's eyes could provoke such an intense yearning for the place. A ghost of a smile touched her lips for the first time in weeks.

The man turned his head, offering his cheeky grin to his friend a few paces to his right. "Hey, Tom. Cough it up. Twenty quid. I won the bet fair and square; a dark-haired beauty walking straight into my arms before the train arrives." He looked back at her, "Now for the second part of the bet," and before she realised what he was on about, he slid his right hand through her silken brown hair, jerking her head towards him. He went straight for his instant kill, gently stroking his lips against hers, his tongue slowly teasing its way in, performing its tender erotic play.

She blushed deep red, feeling strangely aroused, but the mere knowledge that the kiss was part of a bet instantly killed that initial burst of passion, and her hand flew up to his face, slapping him hard. She recognised his type. He was the Steves and the Marks of the UK, a member of the Campus Populars had such an organisation existed there too. They were all the same all over the world, easily recognised by their expensive attire and the aura of arrogant self-confidence they carried around them, as well as the appalling way they treated the girls who swooned around their feet. She had had her fair bitter taste of such men that fateful night she dated Steve and she would never get sucked into that situation ever again. Her initial assumption that this man had a decent soul behind those vividly blue eyes was deeply flawed. She pushed away from him and deliberately rode her small suitcase over his pristine shoes before moving down the deserted platform.

"Sorry, mate," she heard the friend say as the first distant rumble of the approaching train hit the night air. "I don't think that you managed to knock her socks off, not even close. I definitely won the second part of the bet, so let's call it even."

She looked away and pursed her lips together, trying to stop the catastrophic flow of tears. *I must not let them see me cry. I must not let them see me cry...*she whispered to herself over and over again. She could do this for just a few more seconds. The train rambled in sight and slowly halted to a stop. She quickly jumped on, seeking comfort from the presence of a middle-aged woman inside the carriage, hoping that her company would prevent any further abusive behaviour. To her relief, both men steered away from her carriage and boarded the adjacent one, but seconds later she saw *Blue Eyes* jump off again.

"Sorry, Tom, I'm not in the mood for partying tonight," she heard him say.

"Oh, come on, Luca, don't bail out on me. It's your last night in London, the chicks here need you to pay your last respects," the friend called across the open doors.

A whistle sounded and the doors started to close. "Goodbye, Tom. Enjoy tonight. I'll call you when or if I ever come back here," and he quickly moved down the platform alongside her carriage and he tapped on her window. "I'm sorry," he mouthed while the train started to move away, and it looked as though he had genuinely meant it.

An inexplicable dark cloud of grief descended heavily upon her as his lone figure on the platform faded out of sight. She covered her face with her hands and the long overdue tears gushed out. It felt as if she was deeply mourning something, surely not that arrogant idiot with his sensual kiss, more likely mourning the end of her morally good life as she knew it. Mark's words kept dancing before her eyes... *One thing will lead to another and another and another until you find yourself soulless and drowning in deep shit, unable to escape. It is a life sentence, hell on earth...*Her heart went out for Mark. He was as trapped as much as she would be one day.

She was still sobbing when the train slowed down to a halt in its next station. The women inside her carriage disembarked. She was left alone with her misery, but before the doors closed again, the friend, apparently called Tom, exited his own carriage and nimbly slid inside hers. Fear replaced grief and her first instinct was to dash for the doors, but they were already closed. She looked up at the red emergency button and he immediately read her intentions.

"Hey, I'm not gggoing to bite," he stammered uncomfortably as he fidgeted with his hands. "My jjjob is to put bad guys behind bars, so you're pretty safe with me. I could see you crying from the other carriage, and I jjust wanted to see if you're OK."

She looked up at him through her veil of tears. He was a good-looking guy in his own right, tall, well-built, dark hair and strong rugged features, but he had been somewhat diminished standing next to his friend who had that overpowering ethereal charm. As was typical of her, she looked deep into his pale blue eyes, and she saw a lot of herself in them. Despite his good looks, this guy was self-conscious, shy and awkward, and his previous boisterous remarks were made through the presence of his dominant friend who seemed to boost his confidence. His body language as he stood in front of her was proof enough that he had made a tremendous effort to crawl out of his comfort zone and approach her, just to offer his compassion. She valued that, knowing how daunting it could be.

"Thank you so much for asking. I appreciate your kindness. I'm fine." She was obviously not fine because no matter how hard she tried the tears would not stop running, but she did manage a very weak smile for his benefit.

Relieved by her gracious response, he lost his awkward pose and stammer and he sat down on the seat opposite hers, leaning forward and speaking softly. "We didn't mean to make you cry. We were just goofing around. Luca is always doing that, he is loud and unruly and spontaneous and totally crazy, but harmless and great fun to be with. Girls go nuts for him and they let him get away with murder. He probably thought that you'll welcome his dirty kiss, girls usually do, but he obviously went a bit too far this time."

"Hey, it's OK. I'm not crying over that idiot. I'm crying because...because I've reached my crossroads and I just don't know where to go next. I came to England looking for some answers, but everyone here is so cold, everything is so cold. I can't live here," she sniffed. She thought of the condescending man behind the till in Harveils; he had made her feel so insignificant at a point in her life when she desperately needed a kind word. And the incident with *Blue Eyes* hadn't helped her fragile mental state either. And neither did the woman in her carriage who had seen her cry but hadn't even offered a sympathetic smile, not that she wanted one, but it would have made her feel less insignificant. She felt so foreign and out of place, so numb, so frightened and lost in such a huge country. She wanted to have a reason to stay but she couldn't find one. On the other hand, the act of leaving was just as menacing.

Tom leaned back on his seat. "Oh, come on," he said with a teasing smile. "We are not *that* cold here in England. You could well warm up to us, eventually, if you give us a chance. What answers are you looking for? I might be able to help you."

"I doubt that." She too leaned back on her seat and looked at him. It finally dawned on her that she had found a warm heart in that vast place after all, and she clasped onto it as if all her life depended on it. She wiped her tears away and, before she could stop herself, she blurted it out to this random man on a train. "I was adopted. My birth certificate says that I'm Italian but deep down my heart I know that I'm British."

"Why? You don't look British, but you certainly look Italian," he said, stating the obvious.

"I know, but I had a British accent when I was first adopted. I gradually lost that over the years, I guess, but I also have some fragmented flashbacks and a ridiculously expensive teddy bear from Harveils to prove the point. I've been living here in London for quite some time now, trying to unearth my past, but I've had no success. I just don't know how to go about it. I've given up and so I've booked the first flight back home."

"You could try comparing your DNA with the database we have here in the UK. You might be lucky enough to have a blood relative somewhere out there who had a brush with the law and his DNA is on our system. If you find a close match, an uncle or cousin or whatever, you could easily try to trace it from there."

"Mmmm, yes, very clever, I never thought of that. All I have to do is get in trouble with the law and have my DNA sample taken, then I can hack their system and compare to my heart's content," she said with a big smile on her face.

"Whoa, stop there. Who said anything about hacking?" he responded with an equally big smile on his face.

"I was only joking." But she wasn't.

"Why get in trouble with the law if you could bribe a secret agent to compare your DNA for you? He could so cheaply be bought for a mere dinner date…say tomorrow evening?"

"You?"

"I wasn't lying when I told you that I put bad guys behind bars. By the way, what I do for a living is confidential information, but you look like a sensible kind of girl, different, different enough to slap the irresistible Luca Snell on his face. That alone makes you trustworthy in my eyes. Let's hope that my gamble with you doesn't backfire and I'll end up on a job-seekers allowance."

"No, of course not. Your secret is safe with me."

"Good. Listen, I have to get off at the next stop; meeting some friends, you know. If you decide to jilt your flight back home, call me tomorrow morning and we will discuss this further over dinner." He took out his pen from his breast pocket and, taking her hand, he quickly scribbled a number on her palm. "I'm Tom Clark, by the way, and you are?"

"Alina Bruni," she answered, remembering the family name on the passport she was travelling on that day.

"Really pleased to meet you, Alina Bruni," he said as they shook hands. The train rambled to a stop. "See, I told you that we are not that cold here and we do like to help from time to time." He patted her cheek with his finger and stood up, heading straight for the open door and disappearing into the night.

She sat back and looked at the phone number scribbled on her palm. She had been granted a reason to stay. Unearthing her roots was such an attractive lure, though not without its perils. She once again remembered her mother's final plea...*We were cautioned and now I'm cautioning you. You may not like what you uncover if you delve too deep. Please, can you try to let this go?*

She sighed as she fingered the handle of her small suitcase. The crossroads were hers for the taking. Should she go or should she stay?

12. The Accent and the Island

Luca sat back on his chair and sipped his scalding cup of coffee. It was the first day of autumn, a pleasant afternoon, and the sun was decent and enticing enough for him to seek his favourite spot in the cafe, the table in the corner of an open terrace overlooking the River Cam. Lacking interest but having nothing better to do, his eyes lazily followed the crowds of tourists punting by as they absorbed the awe-inspiring architecture of the timeless colleges of Cambridge. The tranquil beauty of the atmosphere around him was astounding...but it wasn't for him. He sorely missed the sounds and the smells and the fast-paced energy of his vibrant London.

A bit over two months had passed from that fateful day when he chose to turn his back on the city and *the girl.* To say that he regretted it would be a gross understatement. After that disrupted encounter, his life turned all tasteless, bland and sombre. Something inside him shattered; blasted and broken into tiny invisible pieces, never destined to be whole again. Why did he choose that for himself? Why? The reason was simple enough; at that time he was desperate to desecrate what his uncle had started to build when Luca himself was but a mere boy.

Despite the big row and the heavy words exchanged with his uncle, that night he couldn't stop himself from wanting to meet *her* in the flesh, but at the same time he was overwhelmed by that steadfast determination to fracture destiny. He had to reach a compromise with his torn self. He somehow managed to manipulate Tom into accompanying him on that platform. His friend's unsuspecting presence and the associated macho banter were meant to extinguish any romantic ideas he himself might develop after seeing her. He had decided beforehand on an arrogant and vulgar approach, just to see how desperate destiny was to see them together, and as it turned out it was not that desperate after all, and the girl simply slipped out of his life for good. Her tearful face framed by the train's window would forever haunt him.

After that, he immersed himself in this new future he was trying to build for himself, a future well away from his uncle. The headmaster of his former school in Cambridge was more than aware of his impeccable memory and exceptionally high IQ, and he accepted his late application to sit fifteen GCSEs and five A Levels all in one special session in early September. His original intention had been to do his exams in secret, but he couldn't do that anymore. His suspension from British Intelligence meant that he was once again financially dependent on his father. He didn't like it but he had no other choice. He refused to go back to living with his parents in their mansion but he accepted the offer to move in his father's bachelor apartment in the heart of the city centre of Cambridge. Out of six siblings he was the only one still living off his father's wealth. His two older brothers and three sisters were all doing very well for themselves. Ironically, his intellect had always exceeded theirs by a million miles, but he had managed to achieve the least, turning his whole life into one big tangled mess. But at least he was now trying to piece it back together.

He put his hand in his breast pocket and took out the piece of paper he had received that morning, his examination results, A stars across the board. But he felt no jubilation. He crunched the paper up in a ball and aimed, throwing it right inside the half open bin a few paces away. Nothing in his life gave him any pleasure anymore. He had even stopped socializing altogether, no late night clubbing, no pub crawls, no wild dancing, no dating, no girls, no sex, nothing...because suddenly everything tasted so dry.

Luca took another sip from his cup of coffee and grimaced, not at its taste, but at his chosen life. He knew that his future with Becca was truly and definitely erased forever because he no longer had those unconscious dreams depicting their happy life together. He had even lost his ability to consciously dip into her world at any chosen moment in time. He had tried it several times, just to see her and lift that shrouding depression he was under, but he had failed in every attempt. It was as if his link with her had been irreversibly severed. Now that she was gone, he wanted her more than ever before. He closed his eyes and once again tried to reach out for her dimension, and he concentrated hard, and hard...but nothing happened. He wondered if his uncle could still see her. He remembered Ben saying that his abilities were far more developed. He could always swallow his pride and ask for his help. He took out his phone and was about to call him when he heard something.

It was the distinctive accent, Becca's accent, hard and elongated, not quite guttural but putting a lot of emphasis on all consonants, an accent not quite Italian or Spanish nor Greek, an accent he had never heard before and could never place. He looked over his shoulder and saw five girls sitting and laughing around a table at the other end of the terrace. Two were British with a northern accent, one was Scottish, one was Canadian, and the fifth had Becca's elusive accent. He looked closely at the girl. She had Becca's characteristics too; sun-kissed Mediterranean complexion, brown hair, brown eyes. He picked up his cup of coffee and walked up to the table, taking up the sixth vacant seat, too confident that he would be more than welcomed amongst this pride.

"Sorry to interrupt you, ladies, but do you mind me asking, where are you from?" he asked as he looked straight at the girl. "I couldn't quite place your accent."

The girl smiled widely, flattered by his attention. "Malta," she said.

"Malta? Oh....Malta, oh yes, I forgot all about that." He had completely overlooked that tiny island in the Mediterranean sixty miles south of Sicily. It all made sense now; Italian and British cultures all mixed in one, the former due to proximity and the latter due to it having been a territory of the British Empire in the distant past. Nowadays, the island itself had its own distinct autonomy. He remembered reading something about the place and its people; English was a strong second language, spoken fluently by most, and that was why it had lost the typical clipped Italian accent and evolved, adapting itself with a unique accent of its own, spoken only by less than half a million people who inhabited the island. With a population that small, this girl could easily know Becca. She certainly looked the right age group, and she seemed to have the same social class and academic background. He got all that from the way she dressed and the books that were peeping out of her bag. He gave her a charming smile.

"So, what brings you here to the UK? Holiday?"

"No. I'm a student. I did my undergraduate in Malta but chose to do my postgrad in English here in Cambridge."

Perfect, he thought. Becca was definitely a university graduate, having mentioned a campus heartthrob in one of his dreams. It was getting closer and closer. "How many universities do you have in Malta?"

"Just one."

His heart started to beat faster and faster. He needed a full name and preferably an address. Instinct told him that Becca had probably gone back to her homeland that day he met her at the station. She had a wheeled suitcase and he also remembered her saying something about going home in that dream depicting their first destined meeting on a busy street in Mayfair...*Good bye Luca Snell. Wish me luck. I'm going home*...she would have said had that dream materialised. The obvious suddenly dawned on him and he started to sweat beneath his collar as an alien kind of intense fear gripped him. If she had indeed gone back, had the people she was trying to avoid managed to hunt her down? Was that the reason why he had ceased to be able to dip into her world, because her world didn't exist anymore? He felt sick. By letting her go he had brought about the demise of the only girl he would ever love.

He looked at the girl before him, and he shed his entire act, exposing all his desperate trepidation in his vividly blue eyes. "I am looking for a girl. She has your accent. She is tall, about five foot tenish, slim built, long brown straight hair and brown eyes. I think that you might know her by the name of Alina. I don't know her family name. I am almost certain that she went to your university in Malta and she probably studied maths or a maths related subject. Do you know her?"

"Oh...you must be talking about Alina Spiteri. No one really knows her except by name. She speaks to no one, a complete loner, never socializes. All I know is that she is very bright, a maths geek, but a lot of people say that she is crazy, violently crazy. Her only friend, Lizzy, was stabbed to death, and her boyfriend-for-one-night, Steve, was beaten to near death the day he went out with her. There were some rumours circulating around her but as far as I know there were no arrests."

It was amazing the way facts were so easily distorted giving rise to cruel rumours. Whatever happened, Luca knew that the gentle and God-conscious Becca was definitely not violent and certainly not crazy. "Do you know where she lives? Please, it would help me a lot. I really need to talk to her."

"I don't know her that well. But I know that her cousin, Max Borg, is a lawyer, graduated two years ago, I think. He lives in a village in the centre of Malta, H'Attard. It is a small village and everybody knows everybody. Malta is not like the UK; it is very small and compact and it would be very easy to find him."

"Thank you so much. You were very helpful." He gave her a grateful smile and left the table. He felt that vitality surging through his veins again, something he had ceased to feel ever since he had turned his back on *his girl*. He knew what he had to do. He had to find her at all costs and pray hard that she was still walking amongst the living.

*

Twenty-four hours later Luca was sitting patiently in a waiting room, listening to the hypnotic drone of the rotating fan above his head. He was the last client on Max Borg's list for the day. The girl in the cafe had been right; it had been so easy to locate the lawyer and make an urgent last minute appointment. Everything in Malta was so compact and the people were so friendly, so eager to help a tourist, some going out of their way just to point him in the right direction. There was this warm ease about the island and its people. He liked it. He was comfortable there.

The door opened and the previous client left. Max's large frame came though the doorway. He extended his hand and gave him a wide welcoming smile. "You are Luca Snell, I believe, come in, please take a seat. What can I do for you today?" he said as he ushered him in his tiny office and took his place behind his desk.

Luca leaned back on his chair and looked deep into his chocolate brown eyes, wanting to scrutinize his every move. He went straight to the point. "I am looking for your cousin, Alina Spiteri."

The brown eyes narrowed, immediately shedding their warmth. "Good luck with that. If you find her, please let me and her parents know."

Luca felt the ground beneath his feet shatter and he was thrown into that cold abyss of deep remorse. He saw no trace of a lie, no trace of any hesitation in the cousin's curt response. It was obvious that she had never made it back home. His previous high hopes of finding her alive and safe within her family's arms had just been brutally crushed. He leaned forward on the desk and clasped his head in his hands, not even trying to hide his devastation. "Some two months ago I met her on a train. She had every intention of coming back here even though she knew that it was risky. She was scared, she was lonely, she was lost. I could have helped her. I had the skills to help her. But I did nothing. And now I have reason to believe that she might be in deep trouble...even..." He stopped, he could not bring himself to say the word dead. He looked up at the man before him; he too was scared, as scared as he was.

"What makes you think that she is de…that something bad happened to her?"

Luca pursed his lips. He could hardly tell him that he had ceased to be able to invade her private world. In truth, that was the only flimsy evidence supporting his claim. "I just feel it. I have to know what happened to her after I left her on that train. I need you to tell me everything you know. Who was hunting her down?"

Max looked at him, his eyes now as cold as a Siberian winter. "If you didn't help her then, why do you want to help her now? Listen, I don't have time for this." He quickly scribbled something on the back of a small business card. "Please call me only if you have a legal problem I can help you with. Goodbye, Mr Snell," he said as he pushed the card in his hand and ushered him out, firmly closing the door behind him.

Luca stepped outside under the scorching Mediterranean sun which was still blazing hard despite being early autumn. It was so hot and humid and he was too warmly dressed in a stupid suit and tie. He started to fan himself with the business card, deliberating his next move, and his eyes fell on the scribbled message on the back...*Golden Bay 8 o'clock. Take a taxi and make sure that no one is following you...*Max had written. Jeez, someone was spying on the lawyer in his own office, restricting his conversations. This was far more serious than he had expected from a small tranquil island and he hoped that he had not triggered anything nasty by his visit. What kind of deep trouble did the shy Becca land herself in?

He spent the next three or four hours going around in circles, retracing his steps, being meticulous about it, but by the time he stepped onto the sandy beach he was positive that his somewhat carelessly planned visit to the lawyer's office had not piqued anyone's interest...yet. He recognised the splendid beach as one of her favourite spots and, like her, he found himself lusting for the horizon and the deep blue colour of the Mediterranean. It was indeed infectious being so peaceful and quiet. At that time of day there was no one on the beach and he sat down on the golden sand and waited and waited, but eventually he saw Max's huge frame trudge the sand as he made his way towards him.

"You obviously care about my cousin, enough to come all this way to look for her, but not enough to help her on the spot when she needed you," he said in a less than friendly tone as he sat down beside him.

"I'm sorry. I shouldn't have turned my back on her. Believe me, I will regret that mistake for the rest of my life. But I can do nothing about the past, and all I can do is try to find her, hopefully alive, and help her. I need you to trust me and give me all the details. What can you tell me about..."

"No, no," Max interrupted, "You answer my questions before I answer yours. Who are you, Luca Snell, and what did you mean by saying that you have the skills to help her?"

"I work in a special police unit in the UK," he said, not wanting to go into any specifics. "I can offer her protection so that she does not have to live in fear."

"Ah, so *your people* have their eye on her too. What will she have to do in return for that protection? Will you exploit her skills too?"

"Oh please, for goodness' sake, she simply hacked an account! We have plenty of hackers of our own, we don't need amateurs."

"Alina is no amateur. She didn't simply hack an account. She wreaked complete havoc. Her skills are unique. Whoever has her first will have a free pass inside every corner of cyberspace, and believe me when I say *EVERY* corner. Why else would the Sicilian Mafia want her so bad?"

"Fucking hell, really?" Luca sat up straight. He had somehow assumed that some local gang was hunting her down for retribution on account of some petty hacking crime she had committed. However the involvement of an organisation such as the Mafia was huge, but it was nothing that he couldn't handle, that is if she were still alive. "My interest in Alina is personal and it has nothing to do with her computer skills. I can assure you that no one will exploit her for them if she is under my care."

It was Max's turn to scoff. "Oh please, yeah personal, as if. Are you seriously suggesting that you fell in love with her after one meeting on a train?"

"It was a very intense life-changing encounter."

"Alina is the biggest self-conscious introvert on earth. I couldn't ever imagine her stringing more than two words in a conversation with anyone, let alone with someone as daunting-looking as you. Go on, talk me through this encounter. Tell me something that only she would have told you."

Luca smiled as he prepared to divulge everything he would have known about her throughout the course of their lifetime together. "She strongly believes that the eyes are the true reflection of the soul and she happened to see something in mine. She spoke of a special kind of love, a love for the sake of love itself, something her mother told her. Or would you like me to tell you about her fastidious taste buds, the exact way she likes her piece of bread; Parma ham and Gouda cheese, no butter, and stick everything in the microwave for twenty-five seconds, not a second more, not a second less," he finished with a twinkle in his eye.

"Wow, OK. She must really like you if she told you all that on a train journey. Either that or she must have reached the end of her road that day. But anyway, after hearing that I think that I can trust you enough to put your mind at ease and tell you that she is alive and well, at least she definitely was up to three days ago. So, you needn't worry about her."

"How do you know that?"

"I must admit that I panicked after hearing your news this afternoon, thinking that something had indeed happened to her. She used to hack my phone and make contact from time to time, but after the Mafia increased their surveillance on my stuff she decided to back off, not wanting to rock the boat. But I knew that she had developed this friendship with a friend of mine and I called him. Apparently, she still manages to contact him on most days and they exchange information in the form of a digital conversation. It is her way of keeping in touch with what is going on here."

Luca let out a small sigh of relief. His inability to dip into her private world had nothing to do with that world not existing anymore. She was still alive and he was prepared to go through hell to find her. "I need to see these conversations she's been having. There will be clues to her whereabouts. May I speak with this friend?"

"No. He wouldn't want to. It's complicated."

"Trust me, Max, I CAN HELP HER. She does not have the stamina to keep on running forever. They will eventually catch up on her and kill her."

"They will not. This friend happens to have links with *The Family* in Sicily and he has access to inside information. He will warn her if they are closing in. Besides, even if they do find her, he reassured me that they will not harm her because she is no use to them dead. She would be coerced and intimidated, but not murdered if she cooperates. I have no reason to mistrust this guy because he was the one who risked his all and smuggled her out of here in the first place. God knows where she would be without him."

Luca scowled. He knew who this friend was...*Poseidon,* otherwise known as Mark, the terrible kisser, the bloody peacock with his open shirt and tanned chest. This *god* somehow had a thing for the shy girl and he was prepared to go to great lengths to help her, even betray *The Family*. "Does he have any idea where she's living right now?"

"No. He has offered her asylum in one of his many properties but, so far, she has refused his offer and he doesn't want to pressure her into anything lest she terminates all communications. At least this way we still know that she is doing well. She might still be in the UK or she might have moved on, I don't know. But I guess, when she is tired and broken she will go crawling to that offer he made her."

Not if I can help it, Luca thought. There was obviously nothing more he could do there on the island. His best bet would be to go back to the UK and try to retrace her steps from there. He would recruit his uncle's help and use all the resources British Intelligence had to offer. After all, it looked as though Becca was a dangerous weapon in the hands of the enemy and Britain would want to keep such a weapon close to its heart.

He gave Max a casual shrug, wanting to convey a message of indifference. "OK, that's fine. Thank you for letting me know that she's well. If there is anything I can do to help her, please do not hesitate to call me, at any time of day or night." And he gave him his phone number before parting with a warm handshake.

*

The next morning Luca was on the first early flight back to London. He looked with interest at the local Maltese newspaper he had been offered by the Air Malta flight attendant. He couldn't help smiling to himself. He now had a full name to the face of *Poseidon*...Mark Deliri, a rising star in the local political scene. The front page photo couldn't have been any clearer; the dark eyes, gelled hair, polished appearance, calculated smile and a wife and a baby girl to reinforce that wholesome credible look. Mr Deliri looked exactly like someone who had everything in life, except that one girl who warmed his heart.

13. Caged

Alina prowled the perimeter of her small fenced garden, trying to enjoy those last few weak rays of sunshine of that first day of autumn. But nothing could lift her flagging spirits. She felt as trapped as that wretched lioness on display at a zoo. Those solid iron bars caging her inside represented all the tiny choices she had ever made, all painful mistakes, one after the other. Her naive perception of the world around her combined with her deep-seated insecurities had all culminated up to that impossible point in time.

"Oh God, give me a break," she snarled at the pale blue sky of that pleasant afternoon.

She had originally considered Tom's chance meeting on that train as a lucky godsend and she had embraced his offer of help with open arms. How could she not? The prospect of discovering her roots was too enticing to throw away. But there she was, more than two months on, as clueless as she had started out. She was seriously beginning to think that her DNA had matched no one's on the database but Tom had decided to keep stringing her along, dishing out false hopes and promises that should have materialised by then. It was his way of keeping their relationship alive, and that relationship was the exact reason why that chance meeting was anything but a godsend.

It had all started with the simple innocent concept of a boy helping a girl. The girl was grateful and the boy exploited those feelings of gratitude and quickly changed the terms of the friendship, turning it into a relationship. Alina was not assertive enough to stop herself from being pushed into something she would never have chosen for herself, and Tom quickly recognised that flaw in her personality. He saw in her a much weaker character than his own, someone he could easily dominate and at times even intimidate. All the subtle signs were there in the way he kissed and in the way he tried to touch her. She had not slept with him yet but that was only because she had used all the cunning she possessed to avoid intimate places. Crowds were her biggest comfort. But she knew that she couldn't avoid it forever.

He was getting impatient and too possessive. The wisest thing to do would be to pack her bags and continue the homeward journey she should have taken two months back. She had never told Tom about her Maltese connection and the cyber-crime she had committed there. To him she was just Alina Bruni from Pisa looking for her biological parents in the UK. He would never think of looking for her in Malta. Running away from him was feasible and very tempting, but that would only expose her to a different kind of intimidation at the hands of the Mafia.

Something inside her told her that she shouldn't be running away from every problem. She had to tackle Tom and firmly end the relationship before his feelings ran any deeper. She was never going to fall in love with him. She hated it when they kissed and this time she knew that it was not just a question of her being frigid. That very notion was totally laughable after the way she had been strangely aroused by a stranger's sensual kiss on that station platform. It was just a pity that it had been marred with the malicious background of an immature bet. Perhaps she had been too quick to slap the kisser's face...another mistake of hers. She touched her lips and smiled as she always did when she thought about *Blue Eyes* and his cheeky grin, which happened quite a lot those days, so much so that she finally had to admit to herself that she was infatuated with him, as infatuated as any schoolgirl would be with an actor or a pop-star, something she had never experienced before. There was this kind of magnetism around him, a force she couldn't understand or resist, and the more she heard of his wild escapades the more intriguing he became.

The name Luca Snell cropped up way too often in Tom's conversations because he seemed to think that an association with the loud and crazy fun-loving devil would somehow raise his status in her eyes. She quickly learnt that the privileged Luca was the son of an Earl and a Hollywood actress. He was a bright but reckless secret agent, constantly seeking a life on the edge and often getting himself and others into precarious life or death situations, but he somehow always triumphed in the end. He had one big weakness, a voracious sexual appetite, a weakness that eventually brought about his downfall. An illicit affair with the infamous Jessica Wills while he was still undercover earned him an indefinite suspension from British Intelligence, though the whole thing was hushed up by his uncle, chief of the institution. Alina often wondered how many codes of ethics Tom had broken by divulging such highly secure information. She suspected that he only did that to impress her with his cool lifestyle and thus reinforce his superiority over her. Whatever the reason, she didn't mind sitting back and listening to all the dirty gossip about the captivating Luca Snell.

But in all truth, *Blue Eyes* was everything she was not, a complete opposite, if she were the North Pole he would be the South, if she liked white he would like black. He wouldn't like her and she shouldn't like him, but she sure liked thinking about him. She was smiling to herself as she left her garden and went inside. The weak sun hadn't lifted her spirits but the memory of Luca Snell and his erotic kiss had.

She was tying her hair up as she stepped in the shower when she saw her phone lying on the bathroom windowsill. *Ah, there it is,* she thought. She was always misplacing her phone. She picked it up and gasped. Over the space of five hours she had had no less than forty missed calls from Tom. She frowned. She was tempted to delete them all but her docile disposition gave him the benefit of the doubt, and, with a shrug, she listened to one of the many voice messages he had left.

Alina, please, pick up the phone. I need to talk to you. I need to talk to someone. My mother just passed away. The pain is killing me. Please Alina, return my call. I need you.

His voice was all broken with tears. She had never heard a grown man cry and it touched her heart. She immediately called him back. His voice was by then slurred and somewhat incomprehensible but she managed to gather that he was at his place. She quickly had her shower and left for the twenty minute tube journey to his home.

Tom managed to answer his door after the fourth ring. He was in a complete mess, clothes half undone, wild tousled hair, red sore eyes, reeking of alcohol and quite unsteady on his feet.

He wrapped his arms around her shoulders and sobbed on her hair. "I loved my mum but dad took her away and I will never see her again. He's hurting her, he's hurting her so badly. I have to help her," he slurred, drool sliding down the corners of his mouth.

His words made no sense. Alina knew that his father had died a long time ago and his mother had been in a care home for years after suffering from several stokes. From what she gathered, it had not been a happy marriage and Tom's drunken state, induced by the death of the mother he loved, seemed to have taken him back to a childhood he never wanted to remember.

"Your mum will be OK. She finally found her peace," she said, trying to soothe him, but not really knowing how to do that. She took his hand and gently led him inside his bedroom where he slumped down on his bed.

"Please, Alina, stay with me tonight. I don't want to be on my own."

"I will not leave until you're feeling better, I promise. Now, go to sleep. It will be fine in the morning, you'll see," and she patiently held his hand until he closed his eyes and drifted off into a restless drunken sleep. There was that childlike vulnerability around him and she didn't feel as scared as she should have been, seeing that she was alone in a house with a man under the strong influence of alcohol. She slowly stood up and looked around the room which was in a similar wrecked state as the man himself. She had nothing better to do and she set to work, trying to put things in order.

She was halfway through her clearing frenzy when she saw his laptop on the floor beneath his bed and she remembered that she had not made contact with Mark that day, or the day before, and he was bound to get jittery. Borrowing the laptop for a quick digital chat seemed like a logical and innocent thing to do. Tom was still mumbling in his intoxicated sleep and she sneaked the gadget out of the room and booted it up on the kitchen table, taking less than ten minutes to break through his security code. Once inside his personal cyber-world, she was overwhelmed by the temptation to snoop around and she quickly got sidetracked from what she had originally set out to do. She knew the name of the geneticist, Alan Scott, who was illicitly handling her DNA as a personal favour to Tom. She wondered if the two had corresponded in any way. After more than an hour she came across a faint trace of a deleted email sent more than a month ago. She worked on it and finally retrieved it in its original form.

We have a strong match, Tessa Bell, definitely the mother, but it doesn't make sense. We also have another match, paternal side. It's huge, too huge to put down in writing. Come and talk to me after office hours.

Tom had been lying to her all this time. She ground her teeth in anger and, using his access code, she ruthlessly invaded all the highly secure intelligence files he had at his disposal, completely disregarding the rights of privacy. She was looking for only one thing, Tessa Bell. It didn't take long to uproot the name and she quickly read through the gist of the contents of the file. Tessa Bell, nee Mifsud, Maltese origin but living in the UK, married at the tender age of sixteen to a wealthy British businessman, Oliver Bell then aged fifty-five. That initial burst of love and passion quickly faded away and the considerable age gap started to cause a fair degree of friction in the marriage, culminating with the teenage wife murdering the husband some two years later, allegedly in cold blood. However, Tessa maintained that the marriage was abusive and the killing was done in self-defence. Her claim was overturned and she was sentenced to life imprisonment. Of particular interest to Alina was the fact that Tessa was also accused of embezzling her dead husband's four million pound trust fund. However, it was never proven because the money was never found.

Alina gasped; the four million in her Swiss bank accounts, the very money she was presently living on. With trembling hands, she went back to the text, scrolling down, skimming through. Tessa was aged twenty-one when she was found dead in her cell just three years after her incarceration in a prison on the outskirts of London. Her post-mortem stated that she died of fulminant viral myocarditis. Alina looked at the date of the post-mortem report...and that was the reason why all this didn't make sense...Tessa had died a good eight years before Alina was born.

She couldn't be her mother. But then she scrolled down and encountered the face-on photo of the eighteen-year-old Tessa. Alina screamed and stood back, toppling over the kitchen chair with a big bang. The resemblance was there, same eyes, same cheekbones, same smile. Alina had apparently inherited very little from her biological father as far as her facial features were concerned.

The sound of shuffling footsteps diffused through her shattered world, and she looked up. Tom came staggering through the doorway. Her scream must have disturbed his semi-conscious state, but she didn't care.

"You lied to me," she hollered at him. "You've known about Tessa Bell for this past month, and still you said nothing to me. How could you? I trusted you."

His glazed eyes travelled to his laptop now proudly displaying all his secure files. His mouth narrowed in a thin line as he sprang forward, hitting her across her face. "How dare you look into my personal things, you bitch, you fucking bitch." And he continued to advance on her and hit her, and hit her. The last thing she remembered was falling over and smashing the back of her head against a chair.

14. Twisted

Luca opened the door to his father's luxury apartment in London. It felt so good to be back in the city and his spirits were high. He was well on his way to getting his life back in order, claiming what was originally destined for him; a successful career path and, more importantly, his girl and the happy family life they would share together. Human nature was indeed twisted; he only got to appreciate what he had after he had completely lost it.

He looked at the time on his watch and he quickly put away the groceries he had bought after his return from the airport. His uncle had graciously cleared half an hour from his very busy schedule in order to hear what he had to say, and Luca didn't want to be late for that meeting. In less than fifteen minutes he was all showered and elegantly dressed in his best suit and out of the apartment again, steadily making his way towards the agency.

He knocked very gently on his uncle's office door and this time he waited for the invitation to go in before stepping inside. He adjusted the knot of his tie and cleared his throat as he looked straight into his uncle's coal-black eyes.

"I'm sorry, Uncle, for being so rude to you last time. I was way out of order."

"It's OK, Luca, things were said in the heat of the moment, so, let's forget the past and look ahead. Please take a seat. Your mother told me that you've done all your exams over the summer and apparently you aced every single one of them. Well done. Are you thinking about university too?"

"Yes. I want to read Law here in London. I will eventually put in my application for the coming academic year. Staying in the city would enable me to study but at the same time keep on working with British Intelligence. I'm sure that I can handle doing both together...that is, if my job here is still available."

His uncle smiled warmly, "Yes, of course it is. You were suspended, not fired. Everybody here knows that your contribution is priceless and we all miss your input. It was just your reckless actions that were getting on our nerves, but I gather that you are willing to tone it down from now on. If that is the case, then you can start working with us again as of today, with a pay increase in line with your new qualifications."

"Thank you, I appreciate the second chance. Ermmm...I just wanted to ask you one more thing." Luca hooked his index finger beneath his neck collar, loosening it, feeling very uncomfortable about approaching the mental topic of the psychic ability they both shared. He took in a deep breath and plunged ahead. "Uncle, I used to be able to see what the girl, Becca, was doing at any moment in time...but I can't anymore."

"That is because she no longer forms part of your future."

But Luca was determined to remake her part of his future again, and he was prepared to die trying. "Uncle, you said that your abilities are far better developed than mine. Would you be able to see her?"

"I don't know. I generally sense situations that are closely connected to a family member, and if she isn't part of your future it would be difficult for me to invade her world. But I can try if there is a valid reason to do so."

"She is in deep trouble. I have to help her."

"What kind of trouble?"

"Deep shit with the Sicilian Mafia," and he sat back and poured out everything he had gleaned from his encounter with Max Borg. "As you see," he concluded, "Her computer skills are unique and if the word leaks out she will have other organisations, some far more dangerous than the Mafia, hunting her down. She is a lethal weapon in the hands of the enemy and it is within our interest to keep her close to our hearts. British Intelligence should intervene, not to exploit her skills, I will definitely not allow that, but just to keep her safe and out of the enemy's grasp."

"Wow, OK, you definitely have a point there. I knew that she was a bright kid, but not to this extent."

"I need to know what happened to her after I left her on that train. She might still be here or she might..."

"Luca, she's still here in London. I didn't want to be the one to break the news, especially now that I see that you've developed feelings for her, but...she's with Tom, your wingman Tom. I'm sorry."

"Tom? Are you sure?"

"I'm pretty sure. His mother passed away two days ago. He was utterly devastated and I went into his office to offer my condolences and shift his work onto another colleague, just to give him time to get back on his feet. I happened to see the girl's photo on his phone. I asked him about her and he said that they were an item and that they were going very strong, his ray of sunshine as he called her."

"Ahhhh," Luca moaned as he clutched his chest in agony, feeling as though someone had rammed a knife in his heart and twisted it hard. Why did he do this to himself? He had never factored in Tom who usually never had the balls to approach girls and, even so, that night he had steered him onto another carriage after he himself had decided to ditch the planned crazy night of clubbing. But, despite that move, the two must have met just the same. What a cruel twist of fate! He would have tried to win her back from anyone on earth, except Tom. He couldn't do that to his best mate, his wingman, the shy and helpful and conscientious Tom who adored the very ground Luca walked upon. He was like a brother to him. He couldn't do that to a brother. Or could he? He could if she was unhappy.

"Luca, are you OK?"

"No," he gasped through clenched teeth. But he tried to pull himself together in the best way he could before asking his all-important pivotal question. "Is she happy with him?"

"I don't know. But he is happy with her, really happy. Luca, I'm sorry, but I did warn you about this some time ago, and you knowingly made your choice. You shouldn't play with other people's emotions, definitely not with Tom's. The fact that you can't see her in any of your dreams indicates that it is probably too late for you two. You have to let her go."

"I will try. But I still stand by what I said. We have an interest, a duty, to protect her from coercion. I think that she will eventually need a new and robust identity. We, as an intelligence organisation, have to help her with that."

"I will help her, but I will do it independently. I cannot involve the agency in this because I don't want anyone to make the link between the present day Alina and the little girl I rescued from the fire. I strongly believe that someone here wanted the mother and child dead that night and they authorized that tragedy. I don't know why and I never found out who, and that was why I had to send the child to Malta and protect her with a new identity. But it seems as though she screwed that up and she is now being hunted down under that name too. And you screwed it up even more. Living the life of Mrs Snell would have been the best possible identity for her, keeping it within the family, but now that's been abolished, and as always I have to be the one to clean up all your shit." Ben was rapidly losing his temper, something he rarely did, but he should have predicted it by now because every private meeting he had ever had with Luca always seemed to end with a nasty display of fireworks.

"I'm sorry, Uncle. It was my mistake and I shouldn't be asking you for help. I will work on this myself and help Tom to give her the new life she deserves. I promise, I won't get emotionally involved with her. It will be just business."

Ben looked up in surprise. Now that was something he hadn't expected, a subdued response from the fiery Luca. The poor kid was in pain, he could see that in his eyes. He had learnt his lesson the bitter way. "No, I don't want you involved in this. It is not fair on her, on Tom, and on you. I will handle it. Though, I'm still not sure whether I can trust Tom with all the details of her past, especially my involvement with her rescue from that fire, so I don't want you telling him anything for now until I think this through."

"That's fine. I'll do anything you tell me to and I will not let you down again."

"That's good to hear." Ben sighed, saddened by the cruel fate the boy had paved for himself, but it had been his choice and his alone. There was nothing else he could do for him. "I'm sorry, Luca, I wish that I had more time to talk to you but I've got some urgent meetings to attend this morning and I need to crack on now. You can take the rest of the day off, and tomorrow I'll get someone to brief you on the projects we're tackling at the moment. Welcome back on board, Luca." Ben stood up and shook his hand, silently dismissing him.

Luca made his way to his former office and locked the door behind him. He sank down on a chair and buried his face in his hands and, for the first time in his life, he cried. On top of losing everything, he would also have to go through life seeing his best friend with a wife and kids that should have been his in the first place. That would be brutal to his soul. He would be forever locked inside that limbo, never able to move on because deep down his heart he knew that he could never stop loving his Becca. But he had realised that two months too late.

The ring of his phone pierced through his misery. He wiped his tears and cleared his throat, and somehow managed a distorted Hello.

"Hi Luca, it's Max Borg."

Luca sat up straight. "Oh, hello Max. Is something wrong?" He could hear the background noise of a crowd. Max was probably phoning from a public booth, difficult for the Mafia to bug or trace, good thinking on his part.

"I don't know. I might be overreacting. ***She*** *usually makes contact with my friend on most days, very rarely skips a day, never two in a row. She has now skipped three, and my friend called me this morning after waiting all night for her to make contact yesterday. Your unexpected visit alerted him to potential danger and he didn't want to dismiss this silence on her part as a coincidence. He definitely knows that the people on his end are still clueless to her whereabouts, so something else must have happened to her, if anything at all. Anyway, I just thought that I'll let you know just in case you can do anything from your end."*

"I have already made big progress here and I think I know where I can find her. I will try to talk to her and ask her to make contact with *your friend*."

After a further exchange of a few pleasantries, he hung up, deep in thought. He had this uncomfortable feeling in the pit of his stomach. He too didn't want to dismiss it as a coincidence. He had the day off and he might as well conduct his own little investigation and perhaps try to make contact with her. His uncle won't object to that just as long as Tom remains clueless for the time being. He would of course keep his conversation with her on a professional level, just business, just passing on her cousin's concerns, nothing more. Obtaining her address would be child's play. All he had to do was to charm one of the ladies downstairs into taping Tom's phone and extracting the landline number he had started calling in the past two months.

*

That afternoon, Luca drove at a leisurely pace along Tavern Street, his eyes darting to and fro, trying to absorb his surroundings. It was a middle-class residential area, fairly quiet, fairly safe, nothing remarkable, nothing scary. She had made a wise choice.

He parked his car on a narrow side street a few metres away and he set off on foot. Number 53 was the end terraced house in a block of six. The two-storey house itself was plain and compact, not more than five metres wide and six metres long, with no front garden and, what looked like, a very small back garden. He crouched down and did his shoe laces in front of the property. Through the frosted glass of the door, he could see the reflection of accumulated mail on the doormat. She was not in, and she had probably not been in for a couple of days judging by the amount of junk mail behind her door. The curtains of the window beside the door were not drawn and he could see right through a small living area and a kitchen at the back, both lacking any sign of life inside. He casually looked up. There were two front windows on the upper floor. One was ajar; probably the bathroom window, it being opaque. Evidently, she had not bothered securing her house before leaving.

He looked up and down the quiet neighbourhood. The two or three pedestrians at the far side of the street seemed to be minding their own business and he turned the corner onto the narrow footpath between the two end terraced houses. The wooden fencing around her back garden came up to his chest, but he didn't even have to leap over it because the gate was not padlocked and all he had to do was to lift the iron latch and calmly walk in. The small patch of green lawn was overgrown and wild, clearly not maintained at all that summer; she was not the gardening type. He looked up. On the upper floor there was just one window, again ajar with curtains not drawn. His eyes travelled down to the glass back door leading into the kitchen. Simple lock, piece of cake; he had been trained to pick any kind of lock and he confidently walked up to it. But he didn't even have to sweat it out, because, to his utter amazement, not even that door was locked. He had never before seen such complete disregard to simple security measures. She had this aura of naive innocence about her, a blind trust in the world that could only be the result of growing up in the pious security of a small island. She had no chance in hell of ever surviving the onslaught of any malicious organisation on her own.

The kitchen and the living area were clean and well-ordered, nothing out of place, nothing meddled with or missing, not even her laptop which was lying comfortably on the kitchen table. Apparently, no thief had taken advantage of the blatantly open house to all. He drew the front curtains together and went through her mail, all junk mail except for a single house bill addressed to Alina Bruni. She had not even thought of changing her first name, an amateur's mistake and eventual ruin. It was nothing short of a miracle that she had survived this long.

He went up the stairs. The larger of the two bedrooms overlooked the back garden. Again, the room was in perfect order with her brown teddy bear proudly propped on her neatly made bed. He immediately spotted two passports bearing the names of Becca Lenzi and Alina Bruni, obviously fake. They were ostentatiously lying side by side on her dressing table, graciously inviting the casual intruder to take a look. Luca shook his head in despair; she had not even tried to hide the incriminating evidence of her crime.

He started to sift through her few personal belongings. There were the usual bunch of plain and practical jeans and shirts and sweaters like the ones he had so often seen her wearing in his dreams, but to his surprise, interspersed amongst them, there were also some delicately fine silk blouses and skirts as well as lacy underwear and revealing slips and lingerie, all Italian labelled, all designer wear, all very costly. A tremendous force of blinding jealousy gripped him and he ground his teeth in anger; he loathed the thought of her wearing such mouth-watering outfits for Tom's benefit. The very concept made him feel sick.

"Argh," he growled, flinging aside the black lacy slip he had found neatly folded beneath her pillow. "Serves me right, it was my choice, my fucking choice," he hissed to himself. He sat down on the side of the bed, consciously trying to remind himself about the purpose of that visit. It was business, purely business. He could do this and he had better learn fast because he had a lifetime of seeing the two lovers together, and there was absolutely nothing he could do about it. Feeling shattered but still determined to shield her from harm in the best way he could, he continued his tour of the house.

The smaller front room was bare of all personal belongings and it just contained an empty bedside table and a bed stripped off all bedclothes. This was the room she never used.

Adjacent to it was the bathroom with its opaque window ajar. Unlike the other rooms it lacked that orderly feel, having a bath towel and a plain black cotton thong and matching bra scattered across the floor. Her phone was lying in the midst of bottles of shampoo and deodorant on the windowsill; a strange place for a phone to be, but he subconsciously knew of her absent-minded tendency to misplace things. He picked it up and listened to a couple of the many voice messages Tom had left two days ago. He fiddled with the phone and quickly got to know that her last call had been to Tom. This was the room where all her last activities in the house took place. He could just picture it all; she stripping off her clothes to take a bath, then spotting her phone and discovering Tom's desperate calls for help over many hours, she returning the call and then quickly having her shower before dashing to her lover's place to offer her much-needed gentle comfort. She must have been too absorbed in her caring role to bother contacting her cyber-lover, Mark Deliri, who was apparently tearing his gelled hair out with worry.

Luca turned on the ball of his heel and marched straight out of the bathroom and into the bare front bedroom, desperately needing to be in a room untainted by her painful presence. He sat on the side of the bed and took out his phone, deciding to call Tom for completeness' sake.

His friend answered after the fifth ring. *"Jeez, Luca, good to hear from you at last. How are you, man? Are you back in London?"*

"Yes, I am. My suspension has been lifted as of today. Tom, I heard the news about your mother. I'm sorry. How are you keeping?"

"OK I guess. I'm hoping that time will heal all wounds."

"I'm sure it will. But hey, I heard that you've also got a girl to help you heal those wounds." Luca waited, his heart beating fast. He had managed to ease the girl into their conversation; now all he needed was Tom's confirmation that she had been with him those past two days.

Tom took his time to answer and Luca could hear the opening and closing of a door. *"News travels fast!"* Tom finally said. *"But yes, I'm lucky to have her."*

"Is she with you right now...healing those wounds?"

"Yeah, she's in the other room."

"Great, I'm so happy for you," Luca lied. "So, is it serious, has she moved in with you?"

"No, not yet. She's different, very old school, like a delicate flower too fragile to tarnish." Tom lowered his voice to a barely audible level. *"I think that I have to ask her to marry me if I ever want to have sex with her,"* he snorted out. *"She's such a bloody prude...but she's a great girl, and I love her, so we'll just have to see where all this goes, I guess. Anyway, Luca, I've got to go, but we definitely have to get together to celebrate your return big time, I get the booze and you get the chicks, just like old times. You know what I mean, I'm in a relationship but I'm not hanged, dead and buried yet. I still want to enjoy life. We'll talk about it next week when I return to work, yeah?"*

"Yes, sure. See you, Tom. Take care." Luca hung up, a shadow of a smile touching his face. Tom was not in love with her, despite his claims. He had every intention of cheating on her and he had even instigated the idea of a sex party. And neither was she in love with Tom because she had turned all frigid on him, something he knew would never happen with himself. It seemed as though he was the only one who could thaw her icy covering and touch her heart. After all, they had once been destined to share a life together, and, even though that had been disrupted, the intrinsic predilection to fall in love with each other must still be there.

He lay down on the bed, waiting for her return. Tom didn't sound as devastated as he had been two days ago and she would almost certainly crawl back home that night because she had this compulsion for systematic behaviour, making her predictable, unlike Luca himself whose actions were often erratic and spontaneous. He just couldn't wait to see her again and this time talk to her in a mature and civilized manner as opposed to what he had done on that station platform. Perhaps after a humble apology she would start viewing him under a different light. However, he was determined not to charm her that night. He would keep their meeting on a professional level, just asking her to make contact with Mark and then he would take his leave. He didn't want to be the one to break up her relationship with Tom because he was certain that it would eventually wither away and reach its natural death on its own. All he had to do was to wait patiently in the sidelines until that happens, and in the meantime he would subtly assume the role of her bodyguard, just to steer her away from trouble because Tom didn't love her enough to do that.

He yawned and turned on his side. He hadn't slept at all the night before and he was dead tired. As he drifted off to sleep a thought kept nagging his logic. If it were that simple to win her back, then why couldn't he see her in any of his dreams?

15. That Other Girl

Her head hurt, it hurt so badly. It was making her feel sick. She needed to go to the bathroom before she made a mess. But where was she? Where was the bathroom? She rolled over the side of the bed and fell face down on the plush green carpet and she retched and retched, unable to stop the acidic bile from pouring out of her. Through her thumping pain, she heard the door open and he came running by her side, one hand holding her hair back, and the other soothing her arm.

"It's OK, honey, you'll get better, you'll see."

She coughed and spluttered. She had nothing else left inside her to throw up but her head still hurt. He pulled her away from her vile mess and he cradled her in his arms as he gently wiped her face with a wet towel. Who was he? She blinked once, twice, but the blurred image couldn't get any sharper. She gave up and closed her eyes. She felt him lift her back up on the bed. Her head hurt, her head hurt...that was all she could think of...her head hurt, her head hurt. She moaned in agony and drifted away to some other place far far away...

*

She floated up to the surface of sanity. The pain in her head had receded to a faint nagging ache behind her eyeballs and the associated nausea had dwindled. The storm had passed and she had survived. Alina opened her eyes and the space around her slowly formed a solid image. Where was she? What had happened to her? Her eyes roamed the room, desperately seeking something to cling on to, something familiar, something logical. She saw the black silhouette of a man, his tall frame blocking the morning sunlight streaming through the window. But who was he?

He started to move towards her and he sat down on the side of her bed. "Good morning, honey. Welcome back to earth," he said as he gently caressed her cheek.

In that single split of a second everything came flooding back, drowning her. *Tom*. She had to get away from him, from his softly burning touch, and she forced herself to sit up. The sheet covering her fell down to her waist. She was stark naked. Panic gripped her and she pulled the sheet back up across her chest. What had he done to her?

"I didn't rape you, if that's what you're thinking. Sex isn't much fun if the girl is puking all over the place. I had to take your clothes off because you soiled them. There they are, thongs and all, all washed and clean," and he nodded towards the pile of freshly laundered clothes on top of the bedside table.

"Thank you," she whispered, not knowing what else to say in her vulnerable naked state.

He threw back his head and laughed. "Only *you* could say a polite *thank you* in these circumstances. Anyone else would have hit me back. And that's exactly why I love you." He leaned across her and started to kiss her lips.

Get away from me, she wanted to scream, but she couldn't, she was too petrified to protest and too petrified to pretend to reciprocate the kiss.

He pulled back, perceiving her numbing fear. "Alina, honey, I'm really sorry."

"Sorry for what? For hitting me, or for lying to me about Tessa Bell?" She looked up, summoning enough courage to meet his cold blue gaze.

"For both. Come on, Alina, be reasonable, I was drunk and I didn't know what I was doing. You've got to forgive me." He moved back, his shoulders sloping down in defeat. "My father used to hit my mother and I used to watch the massacre from the top stair, crying my heart out, wanting to do something but feeling too scared to intervene. Oh God, how I wish I had helped her then." A few tears rolled down his cheeks, tears of sorrow, tears of regret. "I used to pray so hard that I would never grow up to be my father, but it seems as though a few drinks was all it took to become him. But I swear, this will never happen again."

She found it embarrassing to witness a grown man's tears, and, besides, she was much too generous and docile to scoff his pitiful excuses. "It's OK. Don't worry about it. I survived, so no harm done." She couldn't help wondering how long she had stayed in bed; he was well dressed and groomed, certainly not looking like someone who had just recovered from the drunken stupor of the night before. "I'm a bit confused. When did it happen? Yesterday?"

"The day before. You were unconscious for the better part of thirty-six hours with very few lucid intervals...that's how bad it was. I'm sorry." He wiped his tears away. Apparently they had served their purpose now that he had her absolution. "I did look after you well, you know. I even got a doctor to see you, a good friend of mine, very discreet. You have a couple of stitches on the back of your head and he did advise hospital admission for observation, but I figured that you would want to avoid that at all costs, seeing that you're travelling on a fake passport under the name of Alina Bruni, a girl from Pisa who died at sea many years ago." He gave her a knowing look. "I'm not the only one who has been lying. Isn't that so, Alina *Spiteri*?"

She gasped, shocked to the core. But, thinking about it, his revelation was not that surprising; he was a secret agent, a British Intelligence secret agent, the cream of the crop, and he was bound to see right through any clumsy act of hers. Her hands started to tremble as she was once more thrown back behind the bars of that cage of suffocation. The more he knew about her and her cyber-crime, the tighter their relationship would get. She neither had the knowledge nor the stamina to outrun the Mafia as well as someone like Tom, and he was well aware of that. He had been taking advantage of her vulnerability ever since that first day he had met her, completely taking over her life, not because he loved her but because he had finally found someone he could easily suppress. It was just a question of one weak character feeling the need to dominate another even weaker character. What she needed was a strong person who would be secure enough in himself to encourage her to blossom from an awkward bud into a beautiful confident rose. But such a selfless person didn't exist and her blossom would be stunted, forever trapped in Tom's tyrannical cage.

If she had to endure his close presence, she might as well demand to know the results of her DNA testing. She looked him straight in the eye. "Who is Tessa Bell?"

"Not your mother," he answered smoothly.

"Bullshit. She looks like me."

"She died eight years before you were born. She can't be your mother. It was a false positive result."

"What about the paternal part? That thing that was too huge to mention in an email?"

"Another false positive result."

"Liar."

"The science behind DNA testing is never accurate. We get a lot of erroneous results all the time, and that's why I didn't tell you anything about it. I actually proved that Tessa's link was invalid. I took a trip to the prison where she died and I had a word with Rita King, her cellmate who found her dead. She confirmed everything, date and all. It all matched perfectly with the post-mortem report. There's nothing more to say. Case closed."

"Deep down inside my heart I know that Tessa was my mother. The date of that report must be wrong, it has to be wrong. I want to speak to Rita King myself. Will you take me, please?"

"Will you let this go if I take you?"

"Yes."

"Fine, get dressed." He put the pile of clothes in front of her and he lowered his tall frame onto an armchair opposite the bed. He sat back and watched her closely, deriving a quasi-sadistic pleasure from her obvious discomfort.

"Can I have some privacy, please?" she asked meekly, clutching the sheet tighter against her chest.

"No need for that. I've seen everything there is to see. I don't want any more awkward *secrets* between us and we can consider this thing as our symbol of trust, that first step towards our life together. Go on, get dressed." She didn't move but neither did he. "Listen," he finally said after minutes of silence, "Do you want to go and talk to Rita King, or do you want to stay naked in bed all day? I can join you if you want me to. It's your choice."

She lowered her gaze and slipped out of the bed, silently putting on her clothes under his watchful eye. It was his way of reinforcing his dominance over her. He liked doing that and he would never stop doing that. He had this knack for making her feel so small and insignificant. She hated him for it.

*

Tom opened the car door and firmly took hold of her elbow, helping her out. He turned her round to face him and he slipped over her eyes the pair of dark sunglasses he had bought from a store on the way there, their purpose being to hide the nasty black bruise around her left eye.

"If someone asks, you were involved in a car accident. Do you understand that Alina *Spiteri*?" he cautioned, subtly threatening her by stressing out her surname.

"Yes, yes, whatever you say, Tom." Her self-esteem was nonexistent and she was just too exhausted, mentally and physically, to fight back. She let him propel her through doors and rooms and security checks, averting her gaze from everyone, letting him do all the clever talking and requests. She only looked up when Rita King sat at the other end of the small wooden table.

"Hello again, Rita," Tom said with a big confident smile. "I'm Tom Clark. Do you remember me? I came to ask some questions about Tessa Bell some time ago. This is Alina Bruni, a friend of mine. Would you be so kind to tell her everything you told me?"

Rita's half closed eyes slowly travelled from Tom's face, to his silk tie and down to his hands resting on the table, stopping their journey on his bruised knuckles. She then turned her apathetic gaze onto Alina, fixing it on her dark sunglasses in that dim lighted room. She raised one eyebrow but said nothing. She then leaned back on her chair, taking her time to answer; she was in no hurry to leave, any company was good company.

"There's nothing to say really. We were both in for life, having committed similar crimes, both killing our abusive husbands with no one believing the abusive part of our lives.

Tessa and I shared a cell for three years. She was a good kid, a good friend. That day she died was a day like any other. I remember it well. After supper we all went back to our cell. We were just talking, and then she collapsed on me, forehead burning, her mouth foaming, her eyes rolling up to the ceiling. I called for help, but she was long dead by the time the guard arrived."

"Was she definitely dead? Are you sure about that?" Alina asked, her voice shaking with timid emotion.

"Yeah, stone dead."

"Did you go to her funeral?"

"Yeah, we all did. She was cremated. It was a beautiful service."

"Did she ever mention having a child? Perhaps in confidence? Please, it is very important to me. I think that she's my mother...or grandmother," Alina blurted out, throwing all caution to the wind and exposing her desperation. She was clutching at straws. The concept of a grandmother would be conceivable if Tessa had a child at fifteen years of age and that child in turn had another child at fifteen.

"No, she had no children. That brute she was married to didn't want any...that's what she told me."

"But she must have had a child," Alina insisted again, tears in her eyes, not wanting to leave empty-handed without a ray of hope to clutch onto. But Rita had nothing more to say and the silence stretched on.

Tom's phone started ringing, suddenly shattering that awkward silence. He smiled broadly as he identified the caller. "Excuse me, ladies, I've got to take this. I won't be long." He stood up and walked to the other end of the room before answering. "Jeez, Luca, good to hear from you at last. How are you, man? Are you back in London?"

Luca was back in London! Alina could not understand why her heart had started to beat so fast. She consciously reminded herself that he was Tom's best friend, and Tom was a big jerk, and Luca must be an even bigger one.

"Take off your glasses," Rita was hissing at her. "Go on, girl, take them off."

Alina was taken aback by the aggressive tone in the command, but, being Alina, she did what she was asked to do.

"A bloody punchbag, just as I thought," Rita growled in a half whisper. "It takes one to know one. You have to leave him before it's too late. They all promise never to do it again, but they inevitably will, it's in their blood. Tessa wouldn't want to see her only daughter with the likes of him."

"Her daughter?" she mouthed.

"Yeah, honey. You are her daughter. You look like her, same eyes. I didn't want to tell you anything in front of that bastard." She aborted her hushed speech and waited for a few seconds as Tom left the room. "Tessa didn't die that day. Some six months before her faked *death,* two men in nice suits came to see her..."

"What did they look like?" Alina quickly asked, trying to grab as much information as she could before Tom came back inside the room.

"It was a long time ago and I didn't get to see them that well because the two or three official meetings they had with her were all held inside the private room. Now, Tessa was a stunning girl and one of them seemed to appreciate her looks. He got in the habit of calling her out of her cell in the dead of the night and, hours later, she would come back smelling of sex. This went on for months, on most nights; he just couldn't get enough of her. She told me that she had fallen in love with him, and he with her. He was a rich and powerful man and eventually he faked her death. I helped with the illusion. She didn't have to thank me but she did, funding my boy's education. Because of her my baby is a doctor today, you know. I will never forget her kindness. She did manage to come to see me years later, in disguise, and she showed me a picture of her little girl, you. That was the last time I saw her."

"Can you tell me anything about my father?"

"I'm sorry, she was very secretive about him, very protective, him being an important man and married too..."

Alina felt faint. The binding promise of the ring was sacred to her, something that should never be tampered with. But, apparently, her mother had played the part of *that other girl*, breaking up a family blessed with the union of marriage. Alina herself was the vile product of that deception, a daughter of a mistress. She felt so dirty, so foul, so worthless. This would not help with her self-esteem.

She heard the door open and Tom's imposing presence was towering over her again, smothering her once more with dread and fear. She looked deep into Rita's half closed eyes which seemed to be radiating a fair amount of encouragement for what she had to do later that day...somehow find a way to leave Tom before it was too late.

*

She hated him with a passion. He was hurting her. He was gagging her, choking her, suffocating her with his forced presence. It was brutal. It was demeaning. She had to get away from him. She had to get away from him…somehow. She waited and waited, patiently enduring the painful humiliation. At the opportune moment she reached out for his empty bottle of wine, her fingertips slowly teasing it her way until she was able to grab hold of its neck. It was a question of survival. It was either him or her. And the bottle came crashing down on his head…

16. Trust

His phone started to ring. Luca turned on the bed and mumbled, too intoxicated with sleep to bother answering the call. It continued to ring and ring. He finally prised his eyelids open, feeling disoriented. He was in a tiny dark room bathed only by the faint blue glow of the moon. *Oh yes*, everything came flooding back, he was in Becca's house.

He heard the water running in the adjacent room. "Bloody hell," he swore beneath his breath as he rubbed away the exhaustion out of his eyes. He had slept right through her return and she was probably in the bathroom having a nice hot shower, blissfully unaware of the intruder who was sleeping away the night in her spare room. He heard the tap turning and the gurgle of gushing water stopped. The ensuing hushed silence amplified the sound of his persistently ringing phone. He quickly extracted it from his pocket and squinted at it. It was his uncle. Jeez, had that hawk dipped into his world and seen him disregarding all the rules again? Was he about to fire him? He prodded the answer button, hoping against hope that the girl hadn't heard the incriminating ring.

"Hello," he whispered into the phone. He could hear heavy breaths on the other end of the line, just as if someone was writhing in deep pain. "Uncle, are you there? What's up?"

"Luca...you've got to get out of there," his uncle gasped in agony. *"Get out of there, now...don't let her answer the door...take her with you and escape through the back window, her bedroom...it's the only way I see succeeding...don't be tempted to go down the stairs to escape through the kitchen door...you will be right in their line of fire when they open the front door...and avoid turning on Tavern Street....walk through the backstreets to your car...did you get all that?"*

"Uncle, what's wrong with you? Are you in pain?"

"I just saw you ***die*** *in many different ways, that's what's wrong with me,"* he hollered, *"And it hurt like hell."*

Luca sat up straight. His mother had warned him about the excruciating pain Ben had to go through whenever his psychic abilities chose to take him through the death of a loved one. Apparently, it was an intense brutal pain ripping him inside, viciously shredding him to pieces. His mother had wanted to prepare him for it when it eventually came, but, so far, Luca had never experienced that kind of pain and he hoped that he never would, knowing that his abilities were rudimentary compared with his uncle's. He just had the ability to see Becca and nothing more, and lately even that ability had been lost. The sanity genes he had inherited from his father must have diluted the full blast of the Blake madness. He didn't envy his uncle at all.

"It's OK, Uncle. Don't worry about it. I'll get us both out of here alive..." He looked up. Becca had just walked into the moonlit room, bravely but naively investigating the sound of his hushed whispers emanating from her spare bedroom. She was wearing a scanty black lacy slip that barely covered two inches of her thighs, the same slip he had tossed aside after finding it neatly folded beneath her pillow. He was completely lost for words, stunned by her magnetic sexual appeal. He saw her turn on her heel and dash for the stairs. He sprang into action, grabbing hold of her wrist and dragging her back inside the room while he continued to talk with his uncle. "Thank you, Uncle. I'll call you as soon as we're safely out of here," and he hung up.

"Let me go, let me go," she screamed as she tried to wriggle out of his tight grasp.

"This is not how it looks. Please, stop struggling and listen to me. I'm Tom's friend, I wouldn't hurt you. You can trust me. My name is..."

"I know exactly who you are, Luca Snell. You're the guy who tried to kiss me at the station."

He couldn't stop that cheeky grin from spreading across his face. "I'm flattered that you remembered that kiss."

"And I'm flattered that you even remembered giving it. Please, let me go."

He caught sight of the black bruise beneath her left eye. "Fucking hell," he swore. He quickly looked her up and down, the light of the moon showing up the brutal patches splodged across her arms and legs and neck. He remembered what Jessica had told him a long time ago, about Tom's sadistic tendencies and his manhandling of Mel during their sexual encounter together. He had so easily brushed that aside and forgotten it. "Did Tom do this to you?" he gasped in horror.

"Yes."

"I'll fucking kill him. Did he rape you?"

"No."

"Then, did you consent to his sadistic play?"

"Of course not. Are you crazy?"

He rattled her arm, bitter frustration and guilt blackening all his thoughts. It was important for him to know how far the two had gone together. "Did you have sex with him at all?"

"We didn't sleep together, if that's what you're asking." She started to cry, confused and scared by his dark anger. "He wanted to and he was hurting me so badly but I managed to smash a bottle of wine on his head. That stopped his intentions long enough for me to dash out of the front door amidst his profane threats. I was so scared that he would follow me out and drag me back inside, but he didn't, instead he must have sent you here. Please, don't make me go back to him, please don't hurt me."

"No, no, no, you're mistaken. I'm not in league with Tom over this, and I've never hit a girl in my life. Please believe me. In fact Tom doesn't even know that I'm here. I've been looking for you because your cousin in Malta was worried that something happened to you. Why haven't you made contact with Mark Deliri in these past few days?"

"Because I was unconscious on Tom's bed."

"Fucking hell. Was it that bad? I'm so sorry. I'm so sorry. All this is my fault," he moaned in agony, knowing that he was solely responsible for the way her destiny had penned out. She shouldn't have met Tom, and she shouldn't have been beaten into unconsciousness because he should have been the one to take her home with him that night he met her at the station. But like a spineless coward, afraid of commitment, he had chosen to turn his back on her. "Please forgive me, Becca."

"Becca? Why are you calling me Becca? And how do you know about Mark Deliri?"

The doorbell rang. With much stealth, he moved to the side of the window, pulling her along. He tentatively peered out. There was a pizza delivery van outside her door. "Did you order pizza?" he asked.

"No."

Was that Tom's backup team? Were they ordered to shoot first, think later? Probably. His uncle had been right. They were about to die unless he acted fast and she trusted him. His heart started pumping, urged by that sudden burst of adrenaline. This was his world, a world on the very edge, and he always thrived in his world. Now, what had his uncle suggested? Avoid the stairs and go through her bedroom window. But first he needed her to cooperate. He would gain precious minutes if she were to do that. He lifted her chin up and looked her in the eye. "I won't hurt you but those people down there will. Becca, honey, the eyes are the true reflection of the soul, and I want you to look into my eyes and trust me. We are both going to die unless you do that. Please, Becca, work with me and we will survive this."

"OK."

Good. There wasn't even a hint of resistance from her end. Still holding her wrist, he moved out of the room and into the bathroom, turning on the light as well as the extractor fan and the shower to their maximum strength. The loud noise made by the fan and the gurgling water would mask their own. He then pulled the shower curtain around the bath and exited the room, firmly locking the door and putting the key in his pocket. It would be safe to assume that the assassin's attention would shift to the bathroom and that would hopefully buy them some time. He crossed the landing and went inside her bedroom.

"Can I quickly put something on before we go?" she asked.

They both heard the front door open. The team had been quick to pick the flimsy lock...or perhaps, more likely, she hadn't even bothered locking it. "I'm sorry, we don't have time," he whispered as he locked the bedroom door with soundless precision. He tiptoed across the room towards the open window and he leaned against her, whispering in her ear.

"I'm going first. You have to jump down from the far right corner. Don't worry I'll catch you. Trust me, I'm trained to do this." He let go of her hand and climbed over the windowsill. He moved to the far right to avoid falling in line with the glass kitchen door, and he took the plunge. With all the nimble agility of an athletic field agent, he landed squarely on his feet, squatting down on his haunches, the thick unkempt lawn softening his impact. He stood up and looked back at the window. He saw her turn her back on him and move away. She had not trusted him, opting to walk into mortal danger. But he was prepared to die for her. He was about to scale up the drain pipe when she reappeared, her teddy in her hand.

"Seriously? Your teddy?" he mouthed up to her.

She pursed her lips and threw it down at him, aiming at his face, and then she climbed over the windowsill and moved to the right. She stood there, her back to him, still clinging on, unable to take the plunge.

"Come on," he hissed. He couldn't stop his eyes from looking up her short slip and admiring the rounded curve of her backside graciously unhindered by the tiny black thong she wore. "Take your time. Nice view from here." He grinned. He was about to die a happy man.

"Seriously?" she whispered down to him. "Thinking about sex at this dire moment?"

"I might as well die with a smile on my face," he whispered back.

She must have found that funny because she too was smiling as she let go of the windowsill and jumped off, landing smartly in his arms.

"See, that was not so difficult. I told you that I was well trained in the art of catching beautiful girls falling from the sky," he teased as he put her down and gave her the teddy. He took her hand and led her out of the garden and onto the footpath. His uncle had told him to avoid Tavern Street. He had to make his way to his car via the backstreets. He set off, seeking the shadows, him leading, she tottering behind him barefoot. They must have made a curious picture; a man in a suit and tie pulling along a girl scantily dressed in Italian labelled sexy lingerie but innocently holding her small brown teddy bear in her other hand. But the shrouding night must have spared them from that casual stare and he was soon safely ushering her onto the passenger seat of his car.

He slipped in the driver's seat, fastening his seat belt and turning on the ignition. He glanced at her, expecting her to react and secure herself before setting off, but she was all rigid and obtunded, her eyes staring vacantly out of the windscreen. He gently shook her shoulder. "Hey, you can relax. You're safe now."

She turned her big brown eyes on him. "I don't know about that. Every decision I've made so far has ended in disaster...all mistakes...from start to finish...running away from home, refusing Mark's offer of security, trusting Tom, and now this. Why do things keep happening to me? I'm so tired of running. This is not me."

"It will be fine from now on because you're with me. I will look after you."

"That's exactly what Tom said, and look how that ended. And anyway, why do you want to help me? There must be something in it for you. Mark helped me because he wanted emotional support, Tom helped me because he wanted someone to bully around...and you, what do you want from me?"

"Nothing."

"No one does anything for nothing."

"I do." He leaned across her and fastened her seat belt because he had to drive off and she seemed too emotional to think about basic mundane needs. He tucked in her teddy behind her seat belt and he smiled at her, "There, teddy is all safe and strapped up too," he joked, wanting to lift her mood.

To his relief, she gave him a weak smile. "That teddy has sentimental value, you know," she said, trying to explain her childish obsession with the toy. "Besides, I hid my bank stuff in it. I didn't want anyone finding them because they are not actually mine. You see, I've just found out that I've been living off this money that my biological mother stole from her husband before she murdered him...and the husband isn't my father, so technically I shouldn't be using that money. My father is some other married guy that my mother chose to sleep with...yes, that's how messed up my life is. Are you sure you want to get involved in all this twisted mess?"

He burst out laughing. That honest confession was the pinnacle of her innocence; she couldn't get any more naive than that. "Thank you for letting me know. But it won't change anything as far as I'm concerned. If anything it makes you more intriguing," and still chuckling to himself, he put the car in gear and drove off. When he was a safe distance away, he took out his phone, put on his earpiece and called his uncle as he continued to drive.

"We're in the car. I'm taking her home. Thank you, Uncle, I owe you one."

"I bet that you're glad that I played God tonight, eh?"

"Sure am. What exactly did you see?"

"Well, I think that she was destined to die alone today, hence the reason why she no longer formed part of your future. But you impulsively decided to sleep over at her house and that shifted destiny and I was able to see it clearly because it affected you. Hadn't I phoned, you would have been woken up by the doorbell and she would have answered the door. They would have shot her and then you and set everything on fire. That was the picture in its raw form. Then I tried playing around, twisting destiny by putting in external factors such as calling and telling you to escape via the kitchen door or to do this or do that, but in every scenario I saw you die again and again, until I came up with the solution of you escaping through the back window and backstreets."

Luca looked at the girl sitting beside him. He was sure glad that she couldn't hear his uncle's side of the conversation. She would have thought that they were complete nutters. "That's awesome, the way you can play around and cheat fate."

"Yes, but it's not easy to do. I had to see you die time and time again, and that hurt a lot. I do care about you, you know." He paused. *"Luca, I have to be honest with you, you're not out of the woods yet; she is but you're not. In this new future you just created, I see her having your child but I can't see you there with her. I want you to go to your place and stay there until I figure this out. Don't even think of doing anything daring or eccentric, and that's an order that you have to obey if you want to live to see your son."*

"OK, will try to. Listen, Uncle, Tom is probably behind that assault tonight. She is all battered and bruised and she has been lying unconscious on his bed for two days. From what I could gather she managed to smash a bottle of wine on his head and escape from his house this evening. He might have sent his backup team to silence her. They used a pizza delivery van and Tom likes using that decoy."

"No. Those men were not professionals, definitely not our boys. For starters, they didn't cover the back of the property; our boys would have because they are trained to be meticulous. Besides, I saw them well in my dream and I didn't recognise them. I tracked down the van and it is indeed a delivery van, probably stolen for the job. I think that one of them is a paid hit man and the other his sidekick. They would probably be clueless as to who contracted them through a series of middlemen in the underworld. Bringing them in would achieve nothing. I made the decision not to send anyone after them for the time being because that would expose my connection with the girl which in turn would expose you and the fact that she would probably be spending some time at your place. As it stands, no one knows where she is, safer that way. That girl has a lot of enemies."

"She sure does, but I don't think that the Mafia are behind this. They want her alive, not dead."

"Then it must be her other demons from the past. Tom might have unwittingly done something to unleash them. I'll come down to your place in the morning and I'll explain things. Perhaps I should have had that chat with her a long time ago, my

mistake, but I was always under the impression that you would be by her side, keeping things under control."

"Yeah, I know, I messed up. But anyway, I'll see you in the morning. And thanks again, Uncle."

He took off the earpiece and flicked his phone on her lap. "Here, you had better try to contact your cyber-lover, *Mark*. The poor guy is tearing his gelled hair out with worry. Tell him that you're fine but don't mention me in the conversation."

"He is not my lover. He is married with a kid and I don't meddle with that stuff."

"Hadn't he been married, would you have fallen head over heels in love with him?"

"I don't know...maybe. He is pretty genuine. Why do you ask? Are you jealous?" She must have heard the edge in the tone of voice he used.

"Maybe. But, on the other hand, I happen to know that he is no competition. He is a bad kisser and you really hated the feel of his slimy tongue in your mouth. Go on, correct me if I'm wrong." He gave her one of his cheekiest grins. Judging by the look of utter bewilderment on her flushed face, he had hit the nail right on the head. Well, of course he had, she had told him so herself in one of his dreams.

He sat back, driving on in silence as she dived in headfirst into the security of his phone, shredding his privacy apart. Most men, Tom amongst them, would have found her intellect intimidating, scary, forcing them to resort to tactics of physical suffocation just to maintain that position of supremacy. He, in contrast, found her intellect appealing, rather sexy and even arousing. He was secure enough in himself to encourage her to share his step of dominance rather than try to push her down on the one below. That way their relationship would be truly symbiotic, both needing each other to grow and flourish.

17. Bouncing Ball of Uncontained Energy

He opened the door to his apartment for her, and, with that cheeky grin she loved so much, he theatrically waved her in with a sweeping flourish of his hand. Alina couldn't help smiling to herself. He had such an easy-going jovial character, maintaining his confident cheer even in the face of mortal danger. His optimism was infectious. He was this ball of fiery energy that couldn't be contained, restlessly bouncing around all over the place, bubbly, wild and spontaneously entertaining. She could see why he was so popular with the girls; even Tom seemed to harbour feelings for him. She recalled Tom's face lighting up as he answered his call at the prison rooms; *Jeez, Luca, good to hear from you at last,* Tom had said with genuine enthusiasm. And she also remembered the staggering number of times he had idolized him in all of his conversations with her. Yes, she suddenly realised with a shock, Tom definitely had deep feelings for the reckless rogue, feelings that could never be reciprocated because Luca had eyes only for women.

And she could feel his eyes on her swaying hips as she crossed his expensively furnished lounge. She did not find his lustful stares and sexual innuendos offensive; coming from anyone else would have made her clam up in fear, but not Luca. He made her feel confident enough in herself to want to tease him and she took her time with her walk, acutely aware of the hem of her short black slip swinging in with every step she took. She sent a silent *thank you* across the miles to Mara Tucci for her tasteful gifts. She had slipped into the habit of wearing them at night instead of her usual frumpy T-shirts. As Mara had promised they did make her feel good, and they were making her feel even better knowing that Luca was closely watching her backside.

She flung her teddy bear on his couch and slowly turned round to face him. His blazing blue eyes lazily travelled up to the contours of her breasts tantalizingly revealed beneath the fine lacy material. He didn't even try to hide his lust and his gaze remained fixed on her chest. She instinctively knew that she was going to sleep with him that night. The act would mean the world to her, but to him it would probably be just another entertaining night with a random girl. Perhaps she should recoup her dignity and play a bit harder to get, just to be a little bit different from the many girls who stripped for him and begged to share his bed. That way she would at least gain an ounce of respect from him and he would vaguely remember her in the years to come.

She flicked her long brown hair forward, covering her delicately laced breasts. "Hey, will you stop looking at me that way?"

"What way?"

"That way...your lustful stare. It makes me feel so..."

"Wet and horny," he finished for her, his eyes now travelling down her thighs.

"No, of course not," she responded, blushing deep red, knowing that those were the exact words she would have truthfully said had she known him a bit better. "I was going to say uncomfortable. But, seriously, stop looking at my body and start looking at my face instead."

There they came again, his cheeky grin combined with that impish twinkle in his teasing eye as he dragged his gaze up to her face. "I thought that you liked it when I looked at you that way. You said so yourself," he responded, trying to defend his actions.

"When did I ever say that?"

"Once, in one of my dreams. We had just exchanged our vows and I was looking at you across the sea of guests, thinking what a lucky man I was to have such a beautiful bride. And then you turned round and saw me looking at you and you beckoned me over, saying those exact words...wet and horny."

"Oh my God, you really have an over-fertile imagination and the biggest ego ever created on earth." But she couldn't stop herself from laughing out loud. "Though, I must give it to you, that was a witty chat-up line, a perfect ice-breaker, which would have made me weak in the knees had I been gullible. Yes, I can definitely see why you're such a hit with the ladies. You see, you can stop acting around me because I know all about those *other* gullible girls you bed. Tom told me everything, sparing no detail."

"Really? Everything? OK, that untimely disclosure must have relieved the burden of some very awkward confessions on my part when you and I eventually hook up. That's one silver lining to Tom's betrayal." Looking very uncomfortable, he loosened the knot in his tie and prepared for the deluge. "What exactly did he tell you?"

"He spoke of clubbing and booze and...beautiful nude girls and wild sex parties. He said that you are this confident handsome womaniser with a string of stunning girls all viciously fighting for your attention. And, shockingly, you actually encourage their behaviour because you need a large pool to choose from, just to satisfy your voracious sexual appetite. He said that you've slept with some really high profile celebrities, your latest conquest being Jessica Wills, that politician's daughter. An affair with her whilst you were undercover earned you your suspension from British Intelligence..."

"What? Come again. Did Tom tell you about our undercover work, the agency, what we really do? That is classified information, a sacred code of conduct that was never meant to be broken. If this ever comes to light there will be hell to pay. Believe me...huh... I wouldn't want to be in Tom's shoes. My suspension would look significantly pale sitting next to the thrashing he would get. Fucking hell, he must have been really keen to get into your lacy thongs." He was seething with anger at what he considered an act of ultimate treachery.

It was her turn to feel uncomfortable. What had come over her? She very rarely talked so much. She started to fidget with her hands, fingering the lace on the hem of her scanty slip, her big brown eyes boring into his, pleading, fearing his wrath. "I'm sorry. I won't tell a single soul about it, I promise."

"Relax, we're not going to kill you just because you know our secrets. We might lock you up in a dark dungeon, but we will not let you starve to death." He must have sensed that hint of terror in her voice and he had quickly diffused the situation, turning it into a joke, his cheeky smile surfacing again.

Apparently, his cheery nature forbade him to brood too long in anger and his bursts of rage never lasted that long. She liked that in a man.

"Thank you," she said, giving him a grateful smile.

"Great, so let's move away from the agency and go back to my *voracious sexual appetite*, as you or Tom choose to call it. Would you believe me if I told you that I have changed? Not the appetite bit, that is still going very strong, but the fact that I need only one girl in my life. What I'm trying to say is that I REALLY like you and I want to start on a fresh new page. If we get together I will need no one else but you, trust me, I will never cheat on you or leave you because I know that this thing I feel for you is genuine."

"You are a very smooth talker...Tom did say that you've got this wonderful gift of the gab," she snapped, giving him a sceptical frown, wanting nothing more than to shove his beautiful lying words down his throat again.

"I'm not lying, please, believe me."

"I can't. Your reputation precedes you." She didn't mind his flirting, she liked that, but she couldn't tolerate his outright lies. She knew too many of his filthy stories with women to ever believe his vow of fidelity to a random girl he had just met. What was he trying to do? Make her fall in love with him and break her heart just for the sake of it, just for fun? She was too vulnerable and fragile for that, so easily broken and never fixed. Then something dawned on her; just as his first kiss at the station had been a bet, this could also be an elaborate hoax, the aim being to drag her out of her house and seduce her. After all, what proof did she have that the men ringing her doorbell had indeed been murderers? The whole thing was looking more and more like something Luca and Tom hatched up for a laugh, another malicious bet. She was as gullible as those other girls he had slept with. She had to get away from him before she added yet another mistake to her long list of mistakes. But she couldn't make her way back home wearing just her sexy lingerie.

“May I borrow one of your shirts, please,” she asked in a hushed timid voice, her previously gained confidence now crushed into tiny pieces.

“No, you may not,” he answered sweetly.

“Why not?”

“Because I have nothing that could possibly fit you any better than that transparent black cloth draping your heavenly form.”

She no longer found his sexual innuendos acceptable because she was suddenly seeing him through a different shade of light, perceiving him as a manipulative liar and a cheat rather than a harmless sex-loving womaniser. Flicking back her dark brown hair, she turned on her heel, walking purposely towards the open door of his bedroom, her bare feet treading the plush thick carpet. She jerked open his wardrobe door and flicked a random shirt off its hanger.

“Do you mind?” he said from somewhere too close behind her. “I don’t recall giving you my permission to borrow anything that belongs to me. That shirt is one of my favourites. Can you put that away, please?”

She turned round to face him and looked him in the eye, flinging his precious shirt on the floor before viciously kicking it out of her way. “You’re vile. Forget it, you’re not going to sleep with me tonight. And stop looking at me. I’m not some tasty piece of meat you feel inclined to devour just to appease that appetite of yours.”

“Hey, I’m only human. I can’t help looking if you wear something as sexy as that black thing. You must have worn it for only one reason...to be admired. And admiring is what I’m doing,” he tried to tease to deflate her sudden change in the mood.

But nothing he said could appease her burst of bitter resentment. “I was going to bed when I found you lurking in my house,” she hollered. “What do you expect me to wear in bed? There was no one there to admire me, except perhaps some mute pictures on the wall.” She reeled backwards, feeling faint, and she leaned heavily against his bedside table. What was she doing there, arguing and standing half naked in a stranger’s bedroom?

This was not where she wanted to be. She wanted to go home, to her real home, her home in Malta, to her mother's love and her father's protection. She had never said a proper goodbye to her father, the man who had lovingly raised her in so much security. Only Mark had the ability to help her go back home and perhaps try to minimize that Mafia threat to an insignificant level. She had to call Mark. She grabbed the phone on the bedside table and started punching in his private number.

But Luca quickly stepped forward, cornering her, one hand around her waist and the other roughly prising the phone out of her clenched fingers. At that moment in time she was aware of just three things; his muscular chest pressing hard against her, the futile struggle and the final shattering sound as he flung the phone across the room; the first thrilled her; the last two angered her.

"What now," she screamed at his face, now mere inches from her own. "Can't I even borrow your phone?" She could feel herself breaking down into pieces. Fresh tears started streaming down her face. "Please," she begged, "Please, I have to go back home to Malta. I don't belong here. Mark can help me; all I have to do is call him and he will come for me and take me home. Please, can I call him?"

"No, I'm really sorry, but you can't, not yet." And he held her tight in his arms, desperately trying to restrain her hysterical struggles as he repeatedly passed his fingers through the long soft brown hair flowing down her back, wanting nothing but to soothe her. It somehow worked and her struggles eventually gave way to grief and she sagged against him, crying her heart out.

"Please, I want to call Mark, I want to call Mark," she sobbed on his shoulder.

With one swift movement, Luca lifted her off her feet and carried her to his bed, gently sitting her down on the edge. He knelt before her and cupped her trembling hands in his, giving her a reassuring squeeze. "Honey, are you in love with Mark? If you tell me that you are then I'll take you to him myself, now, this very second. Are you?"

"No, I'm not."

"Then calling him and staying with him just for the sake of security is a very bad idea."

"I just want to go back home. I miss my mum and dad so much," she continued to sob, heartbroken.

He wiped her tears away. "Honey, I can take you to see your mum and dad."

"Really? Can you?"

"Sure, I can, but we will have to plan this carefully so that it is safe for both you and them. We will have to start off by giving you a new identity, a new life, and in that way you won't have to live in fear. After that, any dip into your old life will have to be weighed and carefully calculated. You can't just walk up to them. You have too many enemies. Remember, someone tried to kill you tonight."

She slipped her hands out of his reassuring grasp. "You can stop pretending. I'm not stupid; that was a hoax, a bet that you and your best mate Tom must have made. Tell me, how much will he have to fork out if you win the bet and manage to seduce the naive girl tonight? Ten quid, twenty, thirty perhaps?"

"It was NOT a bet. It was real," he responded with a passion. "And Tom and I are no longer mates, not after what he did to you. Right now I want nothing more than to go to his place and beat the shit out of him, but I can't do that, not just yet. My first priority has to be your safety."

She saw his knuckles turn white as he clenched both of his fists in tight balls, a reflex action that couldn't have been staged. She looked straight into his eyes and there she saw the fiery rage that matched the anger in his fists. He looked authentic enough. "So the guy you were speaking to on the phone in the car was indeed your uncle, and not Tom pretending to be him."

"Yes, it was really my uncle, and like me he is genuinely concerned for your welfare."

"Tom told me that your uncle is Chief of British Intelligence. Did he lift your suspension and am I your next assignment?" She desperately wanted to have a logical reason behind his interest in her. There had to be something in it for him and being part of a paid job was logical enough for her to trust him.

"Ermm," he pursed his lips and shrugged his shoulders. "Not exactly, but you can look at it that way if it makes you happy."

"What other way is there to look at it?"

"I am not actually being paid to babysit you but I am doing it because I want to, because I like you. Listen, honey, I'm sorry I was being so obnoxious earlier. I was only teasing, only flirting, because I was conceited enough to think that we were on the same page and that you liked me too. I was obviously wrong, so, from now on, you won't get any more trouble from me," and to prove his point he bounced back up on his feet and moved away from her, creating a safe respectable distance between them. "You can have one of my shirts to cover up, but that doesn't mean that you can leave this apartment. I suspect that that was the main reason why you wanted to borrow one. But if you think about it, staying here is your safest option. No one knows that I have picked you up and no one will think about looking for you here. Don't worry, you won't have to stay with me forever, only until my uncle and I can figure out what to do to help you. Please, can you give me your word that you won't try to escape from here? Otherwise I will have to go looking for you and that could be life-threatening for both of us."

"OK, I can see your point. It seems as though I've got nowhere else to go, so I might as well stay here for now."

"Fine." He was smiling again, not the cheeky smile, but the wide heartwarming smile that lifted all gloom out of any dreary space. He was that bouncing ball again, full of energy as he paced the room, dishing out orders she was expected to obey. "And in the meantime you are not to make contact with anyone. Well, you can talk to Mark over the internet if you want to, but don't mention my name and don't ever ask him to take you back home. I think that it is best if I read through your conversation, just to sanction anything that might be unsafe for you to say. Are you OK with that?" He saw her nod. "That's great. Now, make yourself at home. You are welcome to take my bed; I'll sleep on the couch out in the lounge. You can lock the door too, just in case you are still concerned about my *voracious sexual appetite*," he finished with a loud laugh.

Hey, hey, hey, she thought to herself. This was not how she had originally thought the evening would end. More importantly, she didn't want it to end that way, sleeping alone in his bed. How on earth had she managed to spoil it all for herself? She had set out to play *hard* to get, not *impossible* to get. She sighed sadly. She was destined to die a virgin because if he wouldn't sleep with her, she wanted no one else to, and she was too conservative and shy to beg him to reconsider. She dragged her miserable thoughts back to what he was saying to her. The playful cheek had crept back in his smile. He must have seen the disappointment in her eyes. She looked away in embarrassment, but he remained standing in front of her, his hands in his pockets, apparently waiting for an answer.

"I'm sorry, I didn't quite get that last bit," she mumbled.

"I said are you hungry? I can fix us a light snack and then we can both call it a night."

She wasn't hungry. She was still suffering from the after-effects of the concussion caused by Tom's fists of anger, and her stomach still felt queasy after the bucketloads she had thrown up over the past two days. But a snack seemed like a good idea to try to recoup the opportunity she had just stupidly kicked aside.

"I'm famished," she smiled up at him.

"Fantastic," he smiled back, his jocular mindset now restored to its former radiant glory. It seemed as though he too didn't want the evening to end just yet. With another theatrical and lighthearted wave of his hand, he ushered her out into the dining area.

18. The Child

"...Everything you see in that future is your choice, not mine, not destiny's, not anyone's, but yours. It is everything you're intrinsically inclined to do..." Those were the exact words his uncle had told him some time ago, which seemed like a century ago. And the irksome but wise old owl had been absolutely right. Loving Becca was something intrinsic to his being, just as if it had been woven in his very inner core. He would instinctively choose only her in a crowded room full of beautiful girls, and he would choose her over and over and a million times over again, and that choice would be made not on the basis of her dark Mediterranean beauty but on her innocent charm. The fact that she would probably be the only one to shyly step back and try to blend within the walls of the room would make her stand out even more in his eyes.

They were complete opposites, he realised that, but those differences that had made him cringe so much in the past had only strengthened the attraction after having met her in the flesh. He liked everything about her, flaws and perfections, physical and otherwise. He liked the way her big brown eyes constantly sought his for a glimpse into his soul. He liked the way she smiled, so shyly, so self-consciously, so innocent, so pure. He liked her morals and principles and goodness, the building blocks that made her who she was, and he even liked her naive inexperience with men and sex; it made him feel that she was truly his and he respected her for it. She was someone he would want to keep and cherish and one day ask to marry.

The same intangible force of the universe that was attracting him to her was most probably working on her too. But he was receiving mixed messages from her, which wasn't so surprising seeing the vulnerable state she was in, and he knew that he shouldn't be taking advantage of her in her current state of mind. After she had broken down crying in his arms, he had vowed to himself that he would not sleep with her that night, despite every fibre inside him wanting to.

With that in mind he followed her into the dining area, diverting his gaze away from her finely laced backside and onto her delicate ankles. But he found the movement of her bare feet treading his plush thick carpet to be equally as erogenous. Jeez, he was even lusting for her ankles. How on earth was he going to survive the night with her sleeping in the next room with only a door separating them? He tore his eyes away from her ankles and concentrated hard on the simple task of offering her a chair at the small circular breakfast table, but again he found himself unable to stop his eyes from caressing her exposed legs. The act of sitting down had made her black slip ride high, too high, compelling him to look hard between her legs, wishing he could catch a glimpse of her black thong again. Just thinking about it made his heart rate rise a notch. Damn, Tom had been right to say that he had a voracious sexual appetite. He shouldn't be thinking about sex after he had just promised her that he would behave. He made a conscious effort to drag his eyes away and his heart skipped a second beat as he met her knowing look. She had caught him red-handed in his lustful act...but she said nothing and neither did she try to pull down her slip and cover herself up.

He stepped back and cleared his dry throat, feeling that an apology was probably in order. "I'm sorry," he mumbled. "Do you want to borrow one of my shirts?"

"I'm all right, if you're all right," she mocked, and she elegantly crossed her legs, giving him a glimpse of the delicate curve of her backside against the seat of her chair.

Why was she teasing him? Why was she testing him? Perhaps she was trying to prove a point, that he was nothing but an animal, a lustful stag hunting down a mate, driven only by sex. He just had to show her that he was in fact made of stronger stuff and that he was not the dirty scoundrel Tom had painted him out to be. "Yeah, I'm all right," he croaked. He took in a deep breath and passed his fingers through his jet-black hair. "Right, where was I? Ah yes, I had to prepare a snack."

He turned his back on her, busying himself at the kitchen end, turning on the kettle. This was his one chance to redeem himself and amaze her, and he knew exactly how to do it. All thanks to the many images he had had of her over the years, he was aware of all her tiniest likes and dislikes, her fastidious taste buds and her tendency to systematic behaviour which resulted in a diet limited to a few ingredients. He had bought some of those ingredients that very morning after his flight back from Malta; perhaps bringing her home with him that night had always been his subconscious intention, and he had somehow succeeded. He placed on the table some crusty buns, Parma ham and Gouda cheese, all her favourites. He sat down beside her and he set to work, grinning widely, knowing that she was scrutinizing his every move. He sliced open the buns. *And now, dear Becca, wait for the magical touch*, he thought to himself. She didn't like butter. She just liked ham and cheese in her bread and she reckoned that twenty-five seconds in the microwave added just the right touch to the snack, leaving the cheese in its semi-melted state. So, in the microwave it all went for twenty-five seconds, not a second more, not a second less. He had a crooked smile on his face as he placed the plate before her.

She kept staring at him, open-mouthed.

"Is something wrong?" he asked with an innocent twinkle in his eyes.

"Ermm, no. That's perfect, exactly how I would make my bread...no butter."

"Yes, I thought so. You don't look like the *butter* kind of girl," he taunted as he proceeded to layer his own bun with butter, heaps of butter, just the way he liked it. "Go on, eat up while it's still warm. Tell me, do your fastidious taste buds approve of my culinary skills?"

"It's really good, excellent , but it's just a piece of bread and one could hardly call those skills to prepare it *culinary*."

The kettle hissed. He stood up for the second elaborate performance of the evening, clowning around whilst preparing a simple hot drink for both of them. She liked her coffee strong with half a teaspoon of sugar, he himself took three. And the milk in her cup had to be carefully measured too, four teaspoons.

She stared at the cup before her, the half eaten bun in her hand. "Oh, come on, this is not a coincidence. You seem to know me inside out. OK, I get it now, you're a secret agent and you must have been spying on me. How long have you been doing that?"

"For as long as I could remember," he grinned. "Years and years. Though, I wouldn't call it spying. Your image just randomly invaded my space and I used to see you go about your daily activities. Do you know how many times I've seen you kneeling down at the altar of your local cathedral shooting prayers up to the sky? Or lusting for the horizon at Golden Bay? Or curled up in bed with your teddy? You used to wear T-shirts in bed and this is the first time I've seen you draped in black lace. You look good in it...oh well, let's not go down that path again."

"Why is an institution as big as British Intelligence interested in little boring me?"

That was the second time he had hinted at his weird dreams and premonitions but once again she had brushed it aside, preferring the logical explanation of him physically spying on her on account of some mission assigned to him by his agency. He was about to tell her that British Intelligence were not the ones interested in her, he was, the reason behind that being the simple fact that their destinies were closely intertwined, but then he looked into her eyes and he knew that she was not prepared for the truth, and perhaps she would never be. He wasn't even sure that he ever wanted her to know about that insane side of him, and he took the decision to drift along with the lie...or rather, half truth. "Your IT skills piqued the interest of our agency. You are a dangerous weapon in the hands of an enemy and we want to keep you close to our hearts, offering you sanctuary in the form of a new identity and a whole new life. That way no one will exploit you for your skills."

"Was Tom in on this too?"

"No, it was just myself and my uncle, a highly covert mission," he lied. "Tom shouldn't have come in the picture at all. That night at the station was my mistake, a bloody fatal mistake on my part. You two shouldn't have met and dated, and you shouldn't have been knocked into unconsciousness...I'm so sorry for making you go through that, I really messed up big time." He pushed his plate away from him and he leaned his elbows against the table, clasping his head between his hands as a tidal wave of remorse washed over him...and that wave started to whirl around him, round and round, and he was taken to some other place in another dimension...

...He was in the middle of a beautiful Mediterranean garden full of fresh-scented orange and lemon trees and busy bees buzzing around him under that scorching midday sun. Why had he been transported there? Then he saw her, his Becca, his beautiful Becca, walking amongst the trees, plodding along in the heat, her heavily pregnant belly turning every step into a chore. She stopped to catch her breath and she leaned her back against the trunk of a tree, her hands slowly stroking her unborn child. He moved towards her and he leaned in on her, his lips seeking hers, wanting to kiss her discomfort away, but he was nothing but a ghost in that dimension and she walked right through him as she resumed her slow walk. He followed her out beyond the trees and onto a clearing, the colossal back garden of a luxurious villa with its white rich splendour glistening in the sun.

The carefree loud laughter seeping through the heat of that day immediately grabbed his entire attention. He turned his head towards the happy noise, finding its sheer merriment highly infectious, and a smile spread across his face. There was a man and a young boy splashing around and having bucketfuls of fun in a lavish open-air swimming pool. He looked closely at the man easily identified by his perfectly chiselled chest and strong arms and deeply tanned face...Mark Deliri, otherwise known as Poseidon, that day the god of the swimming pool rather than the god of the sea. Luca shifted his attention onto the boy, a handsome boy of around four years of age, who was evidently deeply fond of Mark as he wrapped his tiny arms around his neck and planted a big kiss on his cheek.

"I love you, Uncle Mark," the boy said with heartfelt childish passion. "I love you with all my heart."

"I love you too, Luca," Mark responded as he ruffled the boy's jet-black hair.

"I don't like it when you have to go away and I don't want to call you Uncle Mark, I want to call you daddy."

"You know that I would like that very much. Let's just ask mummy what she thinks about that today, she might have changed her mind," Mark answered as he looked up at Becca now standing by the edge of the swimming pool. There was a hint of bitterness in the man's voice; the boy seemed to have touched on a sensitive issue between the two adults, an issue that seemed to have caused a fair amount of friction between them.

"Luca, honey," the mother explained patiently to the young boy. "We've been over this a lot of times now, and my answer hasn't changed and it will never change. You have a father and his name is Luca Snell, and he told me to tell you that he loves you very very much."

"Then why isn't he here with me?"

"Honey, he really wants to be here, playing with you, but he can't. He's in heaven up in the sky, watching over you and loving you."

"Will the new baby call Uncle Mark his daddy?" the boy asked, going back to the very root of his problem.

"Yes, honey, but Mark is his real father..."

"That's not fair, if the baby can call him daddy, then I can call him daddy too. I hate you mummy, I hate you," the boy screamed, throwing a terrible tantrum as he splashed around.

"Hey, hey, it's OK, Luca," Mark said as he wrapped his arms around the boy, trying to calm his childish anger. "What's in a name? I'll still love you whatever you call me, and that's a promise. OK?" and he swam with him to the other side of the pool, away from his mother, and he stayed with him, playing with the new boat he had just bought for him until his good humour was restored and all was forgotten.

"This is not fair on him, you know," Mark hissed at her after tactfully leaving the boy with his toy and making his way out of the pool for some serious adult talk. "He is but a boy and he doesn't understand this. All he sees is the imminent arrival of a new baby, another boy, who could easily steal away my affection from him. You should be building bridges between the brothers

and not give cause for resentment. You know that I love him as my own, so why not let him call me daddy if wants to? Why is this so important to you?"

"I don't want the memory of his real father to die with him. Do you know what his last words were...Tell our son that I'll always love him...that's what he said to me as he touched my belly....I don't know how he knew that I was pregnant...but he somehow did." She had started to cry now.

"I can't understand your allegiance to a guy you barely knew, a guy who was irresponsible enough to knock you up and get you pregnant and leave you destitute."

"He didn't leave me, he died to save my life," she hissed back with a vengeance.

"Fucking hell, isn't it high time you stopped loving that ghost, Alina? I can accept the unpalatable fact that you only came to me because you were tired of running, but after giving you everything I expect a little love in return. Is that too much to ask? Can't you see that this is hurting me?"

"I'm having your child, what else do you want from me?"

"I want you to love me at least half as much as I love you."

"I'm sorry, Mark. I never wanted this for myself, living the life of a secret mistress of a wealthy and successful politician...just like my mother...how very ironic," she finished through clenched teeth.

"I spend more time with you than I do with my wife."

"And I hate myself for it. I'm breaking your marriage apart, and that thought is slowly killing me inside."

"You, more than anyone else, know that my marriage is just a beautiful facade with nothing but empty space behind it. I don't love her, I don't sleep with her, and she doesn't love me, but we can't stop the charade, we just can't, she knows it and I know it, and you should know it too. You are not breaking a marriage apart because there was nothing to break in the first place; it was in ruins before it had even started. Please Alina, I really need you to give me just a little bit of love right now, just a little bit, I really need that, please, Alina."

She wrapped her arms around his neck. "I do love you, Mark, I love you more than just a little." She could not abolish the tiny tremor in her little lie, but she tried to bury that beneath a sensual kiss...

That tidal wave ebbed away and Luca was left lying broken on the shore of his tangible world of sanity, his logical world, his true dimension in the present. He had not moved; he was still sitting at the table, still clutching his head in despair, but she had by then leaned against him and was caressing his jet-black hair, deep concern in her voice as she repeatedly tried to call him out of his misery.

"...Hey, it's OK, please stop beating yourself up over it. None of that was your fault. You were not the one to deliver those blows. Luca, are you crying? Please stop. It's OK. Please look at me..."

What was she talking about? What blows? He tried to think back and he recalled the last bit of their conversation. Ah yes, they had been discussing Tom and his iron fist, and he had been overwhelmed with remorse. She was now trying to absolve him of all his sins, but she didn't know the whole extent of all his crimes, how he had viciously torn apart their happy life together, and the life of the children they had always been destined to share. Tom's blows were just the tip of the iceberg of his litany of mortal sins committed against their love. He rubbed his hands across his face, wiping his tears away before roughly flicking her caressing hand out of his hair, knowing that he didn't deserve her compassion.

"Stop trying to make me feel better. It WAS my fucking fault. You were always my responsibility but I was too immature to..."

"I am no one's responsibility."

He banged his fist on the table. "You ARE my responsibility. End of discussion. Now drink up your coffee and go to bed," he barked, his frustration with himself getting the better of him. He stood up, almost knocking his chair over, and he strode towards the sofa and roughly flicked her teddy to the ground. He then viciously kicked off his shoes before slumping down in self-disgust, closing his eyes, feigning exhaustion.

He heard the clink of china as she wordlessly started to gather the plates and cups and cutlery they had used, intending to wash up before leaving him alone with his angry thoughts. "Leave them there, I'll do them myself tomorrow," he snapped again, keeping his eyes closed, not wanting another tempting glimpse of her scanty lingerie. "I thought that I told you to go to bed."

"OK," she whispered, and he felt her silently cross the room. Then she stopped short. "Can I please use your bathroom first?"

Her timid response to his irrational anger put him to shame. He sighed and sat up. "Yes, of course, no need to ask. Feel free to do whatever you want, just as long as it's in here. Don't even think of going outside these walls, OK? And I'm really, really sorry I snapped. I am being such an arsehole today." He grinned at her.

"Yes, you are when you're angry, but I see that you never brood for long. I like that....and I like your wild spirit and effervescent personality too. It is bouncing all over the place and it lifts my mood. And oh, before I forget, I like your cheeky smile too." She gave him one of her fantastic exotic smiles that sent thrills all down his spine.

"Great, so now we're exchanging *likes*. I am going to make this simple, I like everything about you, personality and physically...as well as your scanty lingerie," he teased.

"Yes, I gathered that much; you like the lingerie and you like your women all perfumed and sophisticated and sexy."

"No, you're wrong. I used to like those things but now I like just you, whatever you're wearing." He stopped. He could see exactly where this flirting game would eventually lead. He had to slam on his brakes because he knew that he couldn't go the whole way that night. "Go on, go to the bathroom and stop teasing me. Your presence is wreaking complete havoc to my wretched imagination." He dismissed her with a playful wave of his hand and slumped back down on the sofa. He heard the bathroom door close, but she chose not to lock it, a sign of trust perhaps?

He sighed. Window shopping was all he could do that night. His uncle had been right; as it stood at that moment in time he was destined to die and, as Mark had pointed out in his dream, it would be extremely irresponsible of him to sleep with her and get her pregnant, knowing that she would have to raise the child by herself. True, he could always avoid the pregnancy and still sleep with her, after all he had been doing just that to all the other girls he had slept with in the past, but the act itself would still have consequences on her soul, and those very consequences greatly troubled him. He just didn't want her to get emotionally attached to him to the extent that she would be unable to let go and move on after his death, just as he had seen her do in his dream. He loved her too much to condemn her to a life of perpetual emptiness. If he were to die, he wanted her to live a full and happy life with someone who would love her and cherish her, someone like Mark. For that reason alone, he had to sit tight and do nothing that night, hoping that his uncle would play God and change destiny once again. Ben had done that plenty of times, and he would do it yet again. Luca was positive that he would not die and the dream he had just had would never come to pass...but he was not taking any chances.

With that in mind, he stood up and took off his suit jacket, flinging it carelessly on the ground beside her teddy. Then he proceeded to turn the sofa into a bed, conjuring up his guest pillows and duvet. He was stripping off his tie when she emerged from the bathroom, all groomed up with her hair all fluffed up to the side, making her look both sexy and vulnerable. The rest of her pose made her intentions obvious.

No, no, no, don't do that to me. I'm too weak to refuse an offer, he thought to himself.

"Ermm," she began as she started to fidget with the lace on the hem of her slip, "You don't have to sleep on the sofa tonight. I don't mind if you want to..."

Shit, shit, shit, he thought. She had set her propriety aside and was about to invite him into her bed. He didn't want to have to turn her down and he quickly cut through her proposal. "Don't worry about it, I'll be fine here. I'll see you in the morning. Goodnight," and with that he slumped down once again on the sofa and covered his head beneath the duvet, shielding himself from his overwhelming instincts.

"Ermm OK. Goodnight then," she said, unable to hide neither her surprise nor her disappointment.

He heard her walk to his bedroom but she didn't even close the door and he was able to hear his bed creak as she lay down. She tossed and turned for quite some time but he eventually heard the regular even breaths of deep sleep. He soundlessly slipped out from beneath his duvet and stripped down to his boxers, wanting to make himself comfortable enough to fade into that restful slumber. But he couldn't no matter how hard he tried; he tossed and turned and tossed and turned for hours on end until he heard her scream...

19. Destiny Prevails

...The touch of a sticky hand broke through that slipping state of bewildering numbness. The man...he had survived the second blast. He'll get them out of there. He had promised. She believed in him. He could be trusted...but was she dreaming?

"Becca, honey, please open your eyes. Oh, please dear God, let her be alive," the man prayed. "Becca, honey, please, look at me."

She forced her eyelids apart and she stared deep into his coal-black eyes, just inches above her, the dancing grey smoke giving them that ethereal feel...

Her voice finally broke through the restraining chains of her nightmare and she started to scream and scream and scream, her whole body trembling with fear, writhing in pain, rocking the bed, her eyes open wide with terror as they stared vacantly up at the darkened ceiling.

"Becca, honey, it's OK, it's only a dream. Wake up, honey."

Alina blinked, once, twice, and a thread of life started to diffuse through that vacant look. Slowly, her big brown eyes started welling up with tears as they stared at the deep blueness of the eyes above her, just inches from her own. *Oh my God, oh my God*, she thought to herself as she was flung down the perplexing lane of déjà vu. It had suddenly dawned on her that Luca really looked like the man who had rescued her from the fire; his jet-black straight hair, his jawline, his everything...except the colour of the eyes which was all wrong...and the age. But otherwise, everything else tallied. He was even calling her *Becca,* just like the man had called her in her dreams. Was she going crazy? She squeezed her eyes shut and she felt the odd tears trickling down the side of her face. He gently wiped them away.

"Becca, it's only a dream. It's not real. Open your eyes and talk to me, honey."

She swallowed hard and opened her eyes. He was sitting on the side of her bed, holding her tight, his face too close to hers, his powerful aura embracing her. "Why do you call me Becca?" she whispered.

"You would have asked me to call you Becca...*new life, new beginning, new name...*that's what you would have said, and because of that I've known you as a Becca all my life. But I can start to call you Alina if you want me to."

He spoke in riddles she didn't want to understand. Her logic raked her brain for an alternate explanation. She had left two fake passports back in her rented house in Newbury Park; Alina Bruni and Becca Lenzi. He must have liked the sound of Becca better. It was odd because she did indeed want him to call her Becca. "Becca is fine."

"Great, that's settled then, Becca it is," he said with a grin. "Are you OK now, are you back with us on planet earth?"

"I'm sorry I woke you up. I've been having these nightmares ever..."

"Since you could remember," he finished for her. "I know about them, and your mother usually comes to your room and calms you down. Today, you've got me instead. Did that work well for you?"

"Yes, it did." He knew so much about her, some really intimate stuff that only she should know. Should she be scared? She didn't want to be. He made her feel so secure, physically and emotionally, and his presence gave her the confidence in herself to ask, "Will you stay with me tonight, please?" She flicked down the edge of the duvet.

"I shouldn't," he said as he shook his head, "but I really want to." He finally shrugged and slipped in beside her, pulling her close to him, the length of their half naked bodies basking in the warmth, their legs intertwined. She was overwhelmed by that strong comfortable feeling of belonging there in his arms, just as if it had been written in the stars above from the very beginning of time. She thought that he felt it too, or rather she hoped that he did. He had buried his face in her neck, drinking in her sweet scent, his lips brushing against her skin, his stubble softly grazing her making her burn with blinding lust. Why had she ever thought that she was frigid? Her mother had been right all along; back then she just hadn't met her other half, the only man on earth who could spark off her slumbering flames. Was she his other half as much as he was hers? He was deeply aroused too; she could definitely feel him against her. However, he was probably aroused by every other decent looking female and the concept of the other half did not exist in his world. But she consoled herself with the fact that that night he belonged to her, to her alone. She ran her finger down the length of his spine.

"Ahhhh," he moaned against her neck, "Stop doing that."

"Why?"

"It excites me, and I was kind of hoping that I'll be strong enough to keep this pure and innocent, just a boy hugging a girl for comfort."

"That's admirable and highly ambitious, but don't you think that it's a little bit too late for that now?" she teased as she pressed her thigh hard against his groin which seemed to have a mind of its own, completely disregarding the words pure and innocent. "Go on, kiss me." And she ran her finger down the length of his spine again, this time her brazen confidence making her go that little bit further down his boxers.

"Oh well, what the hell! You and I were always meant to be and destiny will have to prevail tonight. I'm too weak to go against it." He smiled down at her. "Becca, honey, perhaps now is a good time to tell you that I don't just *like* you, but I *love* you, I always have and I always will," and he brushed his lips against hers, his movements slow and sensual as his tongue teased its way in, performing its tender erotic play all in tune to his skilfully wandering hands...

20. Tom

Luca opened his eyes just as the first beams of light streamed in through the gaps in the curtain. He felt so good in himself. This was exactly where he wanted to be, waking up in bed with his soul mate, his other half, their naked bodies intertwined in their restful sleep. The night before had been mind-blowing, out of this world, something he had never experienced before in his life. Sex was so much better when love played a part. It enhanced the passion and gave great flavour to the act, and once he had sampled them both together he would never ever settle for less. He thought back on his many sexual experiences with Jessica and a whole bunch of other girls, and he remembered that cold empty feeling of the morning-after that had made him scuttle out of their bed and out of their lives. He now knew that love was the only ingredient that would make him want to stay.

And staying with her forever was all he wanted to do. He just hoped that his uncle would be able to tweak the way destiny stood at that moment in time. Bits of that *swimming pool* dream had potentially already come into play, namely the conception of the child. The passion between them had risen so dangerously high that he had completely disregarded the basic rule of contraception. He had once again acted irresponsibly, but, in his defence, so did she, as she egged him on and on, inflaming all his thoughts and obliterating his rationality. *It takes two to tango*, he thought to himself.

He looked at the girl sleeping in his arms and he shifted the long brown strands of hair away from her face. He bent down and kissed her lips, softly, wanting to wake her up and make the most of their short time together.

She opened her eyes. "Oh!" she exclaimed in genuine surprise. "You're still here. Tom said that you never last the morning and your girls almost always wake up to an empty bed."

"Really? Did he say that to you?"

"Yes, he absolutely loved bringing you up in his conversations, and the intimate details he gave were unnecessary, inappropriate and highly embarrassing...but I never stopped his colourful tales because I enjoyed listening to all the gossip about the virile Luca Snell and the beautiful women who shared his bed at night."

"Damn Tom, I see that he told you a lot of things that he shouldn't have. I am not the dirty scumbag he told you I was..." He stopped, he didn't want to lie to her. "Oh well, perhaps I was indeed a dirty scumbag but you've got to believe me when I tell you that I've changed...*you* have changed me." The last time he had told her that, she had clamped down in disbelief, wanting to protect herself from what she thought were flattering lies. He racked his brain, trying to think of anything that would make her believe his sudden urge to turn over a new leaf. He had an earth-shattering inspiration and he smiled widely at her. "The feelings I have for you are intense and genuine. It is this kind of pure love, an unselfish kind of love, a love untainted by monetary gain or sexual intentions, a love for the sake of love itself," he finished off, using the exact words she would have said during her wedding vows. He heard her gasp in surprise. He felt a sharp pang of guilt for cheating and he added something of his own in the end, "I would die a thousand times for you, Becca." And that was the absolute truth and ironically something he was about to literally do some time very soon unless his uncle defied destiny.

"My mother used to speak of that kind of love, but I never thought that I would ever find it. That was just beautiful, Luca, thank you," she said, her voice trembling with the emotion evoked by his words.

The level of guilt went up a notch and he didn't want to take the credit for something she would have told him herself had he not cheated and stolen her lines. He quickly deflated the importance of his tender declaration of love. "Nah, that was not beautiful, last night was. In fact it was more than just beautiful, it was divine, like nothing I've ever experienced before. Tell me, was it just as good for you too? Yeah, OK, it must have been a little bit painful seeing that it was your first, but other than that did I do it for you?"

She blushed deep red, "I had been really hoping that you wouldn't have noticed my lack of experience, that I was a complete novice."

"It was hard to miss. But I'm curious, why didn't you want me to know?"

"A twenty-one year old virgin must be the uncoolest title in your book."

"You don't know my book at all. I respect you all the more for your moral values. You are someone I would want to keep and treasure and that is the exact reason why I stayed in your bed this morning."

"You are so gifted with words and you are making me feel so good. I think that I am falling head over heels in love with you, Luca Snell." She flashed her exotic smile and wrapped her arms around his neck, drawing him down on her. They started to kiss and touch, passions riding high again, now so much higher after those beautiful heartfelt words of his.

Shit, shit, shit, Luca rebuked himself as a thought invaded his carnal craving. His tender words could only cement her emotional attachment to him, and he had already decided that he didn't want that, not if it meant that she would be unable to move on after his death. Everything he had seen in that damned *swimming pool* dream was slowly coming to fruition, all by his own making. He was *irresponsibility* itself. Damned him and his wonderful gift of the gab!

Perhaps now was a good time to start pushing her away, but he didn't want to do that. He settled for honesty instead. He broke away from her. "Becca, honey, I want you to promise me that if something happens to me, you won't shed tears over me and you'll open your heart to other men."

"What made you say that?"

"In my line of work I've stared at the face of death plenty of times now, and I love you too much to see you live the empty life, perpetually attached to the memory of a ghost."

"You're so...intense...and so crazy and so unpredictable. Whatever will you say next?"

"Promise me."

"I can't. Can we move away from this morbid subject and go back to what we were doing?"

He was saved from declining her tempting offer by the ring of his phone somewhere out there in his lounge. His uncle had promised to call. "That is probably my uncle with his next set of directives. I had better take that call. Hold on, don't move from there, I'll be back soon. This discussion is far from over." He sprang out of the bed and made his way to the lounge, knowing only too well that she was ogling his stark naked backside. He scrambled around his haphazardly discarded clothes on the ground before finally finding his phone in his jacket pocket. It was indeed his uncle. He pressed the call button.

"Good morning, Uncle, and what a fantastic morning it is today," he said in his chirpy jokey voice, wondering if that wise old hawk knew what he had been up to all night.

"Luca, I've got some terrible news."

Luca slowly sat down on the sofa, his uncle's sombre tone chilling his inner core. He listened carefully to what he was saying on the other end of the line. It was one blow after the other, leaving him numb and lifeless inside. "Uncle," he finally responded with passionate conviction. "Her soul is too pure to do something like that, not even in self-defence. I went into her bathroom after she had her shower and before we escaped from the house, and her discarded clothes were not bloodstained. I can vouch for that. She didn't do it."

"I know, Luca. I need to have a serious talk with her. I'll be there in ten minutes."

"Yeah, OK. See you soon." He felt his phone slowly slip to the ground. What kind of twisted fate had he instigated that day he had turned his back on her at the station? He had merely flicked over the first domino piece and now they had all started to fall, one after the other, in rapid succession, and it seemed as though he couldn't stop them, no matter how hard he and his uncle tried. It was Lady Destiny's vengeful retribution for repeatedly meddling with her preordained affairs.

"Luca, what's wrong?" Becca had come to stand before him, clothed again in her black lacy slip, too proper and demure to walk about naked even after that beautiful night they had shared together.

He took her hand and pulled her down on his lap, circling his arms around her, wanting to sustain her for what was to come. "Tom is dead, murdered, stabbed through the heart with a kitchen knife." He looked closely at her, studying her every subconscious move. He saw nothing but utter devastation and shock and disbelief. "And they are saying that you did it." He saw all her blood drain out to her feet as she continued to stare at him, too distraught to deny. "Honey, they found the shards of a broken bottle of wine with your fingerprints on it, the same fingerprints that were on the kitchen knife that killed Tom. Witnesses have come forward, saying they saw you run out of the house. They said that you looked distraught and one even testified to seeing the bruise you have around your left eye. The police raided your house and found your white shirt and jeans in your bathroom, all splattered with Tom's blood. They are now looking for you and your face is plastered all over the net and TV news channels."

"Luca, please, you've got to believe me," she whispered, too drained out of energy to properly vocalize. "He was alive and bellowing with anger when I ran out of his house. I did smash the bottle of wine on his head but I didn't stab him through the heart. I need you to believe me, even though no one else will."

"I believe you, honey. I went into your bathroom before we left your house, to switch on the stuff and distract those thugs, remember, and I can definitely vouch that your discarded clothes were not splattered with blood. Red blood on a white shirt would have been very hard to miss. I have a photographic memory, an infallible photographic memory, and I am positive about everything I saw."

She wrapped her arms around his neck and started to cry on his shoulder. "Thank you, thank you for believing me. It is very important to me that you do. Oh God, how did I manage to get myself in this mess? What do I do now? Should I go to the police and try to explain?"

"No, honey, no, that's a bad idea. Whoever wanted to kill you last night is doing this to force you out of hiding and corner you and perhaps finish the job he had started. He will manage to get to you even in the deepest prison cell. But you'll be safe here with me. Don't worry about it, my uncle and I will figure this out, eventually. Trust us. Which reminds me; my uncle will be here in the next minute or so. He is a really kind soul, stern and sombre but really kind and just, you'll like him. Everyone at the agency does. He is the best loved Chief of all time," he said with that great sense of pride. "Here, put on my shirt," and he leaned against her and picked his discarded shirt off the ground, covering her with it and even buttoning it up for her because she was too traumatized to think for herself. Then he gently lifted her off his lap and sat her down on the sofa as he proceeded to clothe himself. He had just zipped up his trousers when the doorbell rang.

21. The Needle in the Haystack

Alina huddled against his shirt, comforted by its masculine smell, his smell. The irony of life; the beautiful ecstasy of the night before followed so closely by the hideous desolation of the morning. Happiness had to be followed by sadness just to maintain that balance of life. How very cruel. But in all truth, she wouldn't swap that night with Luca for anything in the world. Everything she had done so far, all her painful mistakes, had been worthwhile since they had all led up to that divine encounter, and if she were given a choice to go back in time she would change nothing if that would compromise meeting him. She hung down her head, hiding her face behind her flowing dark hair, and she squeezed her eyes shut as she listened to the friendly exchange between uncle and nephew at the door.

"Are you showing off those abs again, Luca?" the uncle teased, "Don't you have any shirts?"

"Sorry, Uncle, but I had to act the part of the gallant gentleman and give my only shirt to the beautiful lady...though I did that very grudgingly, I might add," the nephew responded with the flippant, light-hearted attitude that was so typical of him. It seemed as though all the natural disasters in the world could never dampen the bounce of that sparkling ball of uncontained energy.

His confident strides crossed the room and he took his place beside her, wrapping his arm around her shoulders. She responded to his touch and she buried her face in his bare chest, unable to look the daunting Chief of British Intelligence in the eye, greatly fearing the aggressive grilling she was about to get from him. Unlike Luca who had just slept with her and was inclined to be lenient, the Chief was bound to assume that she was guilty of Tom's murder, seeing that all the circumstantial evidence pointed that way.

"Hey, Becca, it's OK. He is not going to bite," Luca whispered against her hair.

She heard the older man's small sigh of exhaustion as he sank into the armchair opposite them. "Hello, again, Becca. It's been a long time. Do you remember me at all?"

There was something familiar in the way he had uttered her name, *Becca.* She would recognise that intonation any day; after all she had been hearing him calling her in her dreams for as long as she could remember...

...Becca, honey, please open your eyes. Oh, please dear God, let her be alive. Becca, honey...

Her heart started to beat fast and faster and faster still. Could she have found the needle in the haystack? This man was the only reason behind her choice to seek asylum in the UK after the Mafia fiasco, and against all odds she had found him when she least expected to. She lifted up her head and she met his coal-black eyes, all kind and fair but too stern, just the way she remembered them. Her eyes roamed the rest of him. He looked so much like an older version of Luca. Her wandering gaze finally settled on his badly scarred left hand.

"I'm sorry about your hand," she said in a half whisper. "You were badly injured that day, all because of me. I remember just snippets of what happened but I definitely know that you saved my life. Thank you."

"Don't mention it. It was my duty and my pleasure to help you that night."

"You are my father...aren't you?" It was a statement turned into a question all for the sake of diplomacy. She felt Luca sit up straight, too straight, and she saw the coal-black eyes shift onto the young man who was about to swear out loud.

"Don't be daft, Luca, why would I allow my nephew to fall in love with my daughter?" He then turned his powerful gaze back on her. "No, I am definitely not your father. I am proud to say that in my entire lifetime I have never slept with anyone but my wife, my soul mate. I have nothing to hide and I am willing to go through a paternity test if you insist on disbelieving me."

"No, no, I'm sorry, I'm not accusing you of anything," she quickly said, not wanting to offend him of all people. She looked down at her fidgeting hands on her lap. "It was just a stupid assumption I made after I found out that a married man, an influential and wealthy married man, had an affair with my biological mother, Tessa Bell…"

"Tessa Bell? You know about Tessa Bell? I *strongly* warned your adoptive parents against trying to expose your true identity," he responded with curt exasperation. He looked and sounded exactly like someone who was used to having his orders instantly obeyed and he didn't even try to hide his indignant disillusion with her revelation. "And I made sure that the trail ended with Alina Bruni should you or your parents be foolish enough to disregard that *simple* warning. How on earth did you get to know about Tessa Bell?"

She once again recalled her mother's final plea... *We were cautioned and now I'm cautioning you. You may not like what you uncover if you delve too deep. Please, can you try to let this go? Can you do that for me?* But she had completely turned her back on that crystal clear piece of advice, following instead that overwhelming hunger to know the truth. She started to cry and Luca's arm went tighter around her shoulders.

"My parents had nothing to do with it; I was the one who delved in things I shouldn't have. I'm so sorry," she sobbed. "I was desperate to know the truth and when I met Tom on the train...oh well...I asked him to run a DNA test and compare it to people already on your database."

"Bloody hell! My freaking fault! We had deleted Tessa Bell from the official police database and only someone from the agency could have access to the full original list; a fatal oversight on my part. But again, what were the chances of you ever meeting a secret agent like Tom and asking him to illegally run a DNA test and him being unethical enough to run it? And that is exactly what killed Tom. The test itself must have tipped off the demons from your past and set in motion this fatal course of events. Tell me, when did he run the test? Yesterday?"

"No, a very long time ago, perhaps even as long as a month ago, or perhaps two. But he never told me the result, and the other day when he was all drunk I hacked his computer and retrieved a deleted email. He caught me in the act and beat me into unconsciousness. When I came round yesterday, he told me that he had disregarded the information on the basis that Tessa had died eight years before I was born and he agreed to take me to visit Rita King in prison to confirm this, which she did at first. But then Tom left the room to answer Luca's call, and she managed to sneak in a word, telling me that Tessa was indeed my mother. After that, we went back to Tom's house. I plucked up enough courage to tell him that I wanted to end the relationship, but he had his own plans for the evening, sadistic plans, and he wasn't going to let me go."

She stopped and shuddered. She wanted nothing more than to forget what she had to go through, but she felt obliged to talk about it, to justify her decision to hit Tom on the head. "He made me do stuff to him, dirty perverse stuff. He was gagging me and strangling me...it was very painful and there were moments when I thought that I was about to break and die. I had to get away from him and at the first opportunity I got, I smashed a bottle of wine on the side of his head. But that was all I did, I did not stab him through the heart. He was still alive and profusely swearing and threatening me as I ran out of the house. *You are going to die for this, Alina*, those were his exact last words, and I was so scared. But he didn't follow me out in the street or attempt to drag me back inside, and I just ran to the underground station and went back home."

"But he must have called someone after that," Ben mused. "Tom had probably unravelled your past a long time ago but had decided to keep everything to himself, until you ran out on him yesterday. Then, in a fit of bitter revenge, he spilled all the beans. Everything backfired and he ended up dead. Whoever killed him must have transferred your fingerprints from the bottle of wine onto the knife, simple enough to do. After that your photo was released for all the world to see. Eventually someone out there would be bound to spot you and report it, and when that happens they would immediately close in and silence you."

Alina closed her eyes as a sigh of great relief escaped her pursed lips. The daunting Chief of British Intelligence had somehow believed her story too. His response gave her just enough strength to ask about her past, the past he had so thoroughly wanted to bury, the past she had a right to know about. "Why are they doing this to me and who are these demons from my past?"

"I honestly don't know. If I knew I wouldn't be standing here. Obviously, he or she or they are someone far craftier and greater than I am because they have been eluding me for years." He took in a deep breath and prepared to divulge the facts he should have told her a long time ago, but regrettably never had the inclination or the time to do so.

"Tessa Bell was indeed your mother. She was extremely bright and innovative, possessing very unique mathematical skills, just as yourself. She piqued the interest of British Intelligence after she murdered her husband and craftily swindled all his fortune at the tender age of eighteen. I believed her plea of self-defence, even though no one else did, and I offered her a second chance at life, working as an undercover agent with British Intelligence. She grabbed it with both hands and Tessa Bell died and was reborn under a brand new identity. She flourished after that. Her quarry was a wealthy lawyer dabbling in drugs, prostitution and terrorism, something our agency deals with on a daily basis. He was married but he had this great weakness for beautiful women and Tessa had no problem at all assuming the role of his mistress. She certainly knew how to keep him breathlessly tagging along and he was soon irreversibly besotted by her allure, setting her up in one of his many houses. Little did he know that she was feeding us vital information; we foiled major plots and let other minor ones pass by, just enough to keep the mission alive. This went on for some years and they eventually had a child...you...or so everybody thought."

"So, is he my father? Can I have his name, please? I will not pass this information on to anyone else; I give you my word on it. Please, I have a right to know."

"His name is not important because he is not your father either. As it happened, his wife had been trying to conceive for years. He had always assumed that the infertility problem lay with her; after all he was under the impression that he had no problem conceiving with his mistress. He eventually agreed to get himself tested just to humour his wife. He was sterile. He couldn't have been the father of his mistress' child, the child he had started to love and smother with expensive gifts. He was livid and Tessa had to bear the vicious brunt of his frustrated anger. She somehow managed to run away from him, taking you with her. I was in Paris enjoying a relaxing family holiday with my wife and kids when she called me, telling me that the mission had been compromised. I quickly forwarded her onto one of our safe houses in the countryside, just until we regroup and refurbish her with a new identity, perhaps somewhere abroad until the dust settled. I knew that it wouldn't take long for the lawyer to figure out Tessa's actual role in his life, and I gave the order to arrest him as soon as possible, having enough evidence to put him behind bars for life. I thought that I had settled the problem over the phone, but then I happened to foresee the fire and..."

"Foresee? What do you mean by that?"

The coal-black eyes shifted onto Luca. "Didn't you tell her about that blessed *Blake Curse* gene? Bloody hell, what were you doing all night?"

"We had a lot of catching up to do and that eccentric revelation was at the very bottom of my list of priorities. After all, it was too early in our acquaintance for me to reveal the fact that I am an active member of the Blake loony bunch." Luca turned his cheeky grin on her, "Don't worry about it, Becca. What my uncle actually meant to say was that he somehow got wind of a plot to burn the safe house down. That's perfectly logical, isn't it?" He was smiling widely, lifting the sombre mood and turning everything into a hilarious joke, just as she had seen him do on countless occasions in the space of the few hours she had known him. He was a whirlwind of fresh air and she would gladly walk into his spinning aura. She could believe anything he said just as long as he smiled at her, and his charismatic smile seemed to be infectious too because even the grave and serious uncle was chuckling and shaking his head in disbelief.

"Yes, OK, that is a logical way to look at it." The coal-black eyes lost their mirth as they shifted on her again and went back to the business at hand. "Anyway, as Luca kindly explained, I got to know about the plot and I secretly flew in to thwart it. Since the location of the safe house was known only by us, I had to assume that someone inside our agency wanted your mother dead, and so I avoided involving them in the rescue mission and instead I asked Luca's father to help me out. It was past midnight by the time I arrived at the house. I entered through the back door and the first thing I saw was the corpse of the lawyer lying on the kitchen floor. Someone had planted him there so as to make it look like he had set off the bomb and was caught up in its explosion. Your mother happened to come in the room and she saw me squatting on the ground beside the corpse of her former quarry. It didn't look nice from her vantage point and she immediately drew her gun on me and she wouldn't believe me when I told her that the whole place was about to blow up some time soon. I was running out of time and I had to resort to brutal tactics. I knocked her gun out of her hand and I knocked her aside too and I sprinted up the stairs to get you from your room. You and I were standing on the landing and your mother was halfway up the stairs when the first blast shook the house. At that point it was too late for your mother but I did try to help her nonetheless..."

"I know, I remember," Alina whispered as she recalled his hissed command snaking high above the crackle and the crunch...*Take my fucking hand. I can get you both out of here, I promise. Trust me for fuck's sake...* She wiped a stray tear. "But she didn't want to slow you down and compromise my safety. You did manage to save my life that day despite the injuries you sustained from the second blast. I remember your pain as we walked around a field, and then we met a man who was waiting for us in a car."

"He was Luca's father, Jake Snell."

She closed her eyes and remembered...

...*"Hello little girl. I'm Jake. What's your name?"*

"I'm Becca. Are you a good man too?" she asked as she shook his outstretched hand.

"Yes, I would like to think that I am," he smiled.

*The little girl looked at him bathed in the headlights of his car, trying to weigh up the validity of his claim. His dark blonde hair was wild and tousled, his features strong and rugged, but it was his eyes that grabbed her entire attention. They were so vividly blue and bright, so open and honest, so hypnotizing, washing her with that inexplicable sense of gentle tranquillity...*and that same warm glow touched her heart every time she looked into Luca's eyes. She dragged her mind back to what the Chief was saying.

"Jake is a surgeon, a cardiac surgeon, but nonetheless brilliant enough to fix me up in the best way he could in the security of his mansion since I wanted to avoid hospital admission, just to create the illusion that I was still in Paris. That way no one would suspect that I had plucked you away from the jaws of death. The three blasts that rocked that house annihilated everyone inside beyond recognition and the few human remains were identified through their DNA. Let's just say that I managed to slip in your DNA in the forensic report so that the little girl called Becca was certified dead. The demons who had killed your mother would never know that you still walked amongst the living. After that, I created a new identity for you, piece of cake, something we do all the time. Tessa was of Maltese descent and she spoke lovingly of the island and its people, and I happened to know the place, having gone there on a couple of holidays when I was still a boy visiting my uncle, a Sicilian writer who had emigrated to one of the Maltese islands, Kemmuna, I believe, very small, quaint and peaceful. Anyway, I knew that Tessa would want you to go back to her roots and Malta was a perfect choice. I personally handpicked the people who would raise you in the greatest love and security. I would like to think that I chose wisely for you. Did I?"

"Yes, you did. I could not have asked for better parents and for that I thank you."

"I was too ill to travel at the time and it was Jake who took you all the way to Malta and introduced you to your new life. I did visit as soon as I could, just to make sure that you were doing well..."

"I know, my mother told me, and you gave me my first dog."

"Yes, I gave you that dog. I always try to keep my promises."

"And you gave me Tessa's dodgy money too, the very funds she stole from her murdered husband."

"Tessa killed her husband in self-defence, his funds rightfully belonged to her on his demise, and after her death they became your inheritance. I just had to pass them on to you. It was the right thing to do. What you do with them is entirely up to you. Anyway, back to the story; my colleagues at the agency explained the tragedy as an undercover mission gone disastrously wrong with the quarry killing himself, his mistress and her child. I knew otherwise and I did try to discreetly find out who had masterminded that plot and why, but I never unravelled the mystery, perhaps because I could never delve too deep, needing to keep your rescue as well as my involvement with it a secret, all for the sake of protecting your new identity. I look on that case as one of my few failures in my career, which I must now detangle at all costs for Luca's sake if for nothing else. If you value his life, and I know that you do, then you must help me out and do exactly what I tell you to do. Do you understand that, Becca?"

She nodded, not really understanding his riddles which confounded her as much as his nephew's. Why should Luca's life have anything to do with all this? She didn't understand it, but she trusted him and she would blindly nod to anything he said.

"Right," the Chief continued, happy with her response. "Tom seemed to have uncovered something I never did in all these years. I have to retrace his steps from the very beginning. You said that you retrieved a deleted email. What can you tell me about it?"

"It was an email sent by the geneticist, Alan Scott, who was illicitly handling my DNA as a personal favour to Tom. It said that he had found a strong match, Tessa Bell, my mother."

"Yes, we all knew that. Was there anything else?"

"Ermmm...yes, now I remember. It said something about another match, paternal side. It was too huge to put down in writing. I had forgotten all about it because the match with Tessa Bell overshadowed its importance. And besides, Tom told me later that it was another false positive result."

"Highly unlikely, we don't get that many false positive results, contrary to what Tom might have told you. However, having said that, I did once try to run a discreet paternity test on your DNA, wanting to know if the identity of your real father was the reason behind that plot since I could not think of any other reason why anyone would want Tessa dead; she was so greatly loved and respected by all at the agency. But, at that time, the test yielded no paternal match. An arrest in later years with its consequent new addition of DNA to the database must have yielded a result for Tom. Perhaps I should give Alan Scott a ring and discreetly ask him about it; a risk worth taking." He took his phone out from his pocket and moved to the kitchen end of the room.

22. The Affair

Luca hugged her tight against his chest, knowing that she was mentally exhausted after that intense session of brainstorming. His uncle could be quite relentless and too grave, keeping the atmosphere around him on the heavy side, but he was sharp and brilliant enough to tease out a valid lead so early on in the discussion. All thanks to him, Luca could still get to see another day.

He kissed her forehead. “See, I told you. We will soon figure this out. My Uncle Ben, he is great, isn’t he?”

“Yes, he is.” She paused, “Luca, what did he mean when he said that he had to unravel the case for your sake...and that scary thing about valuing your life? Is this case putting you in any danger, like it did to Tom?”

Damn his uncle; he had such a big mouth. He really didn’t want her to know about that wacky *Blake Curse* gene he shared with his uncle which had enabled them both to dip into a future where he didn’t exist. She shouldn’t be burdened with the knowledge that he was about to die to save her life if those demons from her past managed to catch up on her. She seemed to be gullible to his twisted responses and he gave it his best shot, quickly conjuring up some soppy answer to her serious question, just to pacify her. “Of course he is doing it for my sake. I am irreversibly besotted by your charm and my life would be worthless without you.” So true, but so lame. He was spared from gagging over the nauseating sweetness of his words by his uncle’s return to his armchair. Luca looked up at him. Something was wrong, gravely wrong. He could see it all in his eyes; the shocked disbelief of a sudden catastrophic checkmate.

“What is it, Uncle?”

“That was Alan Scott’s wife. The police were at their house, breaking the terrible news. Apparently a student geneticist found Alan dead in his lab this morning. They are thinking that it is a suicide, an overdose. This is not a coincidence, this is not a suicide.”

"No, no, no, this can't be happening to me," Becca screamed as she completely lost control of all her emotions in a frantic hysterical fit. "How many people have to die because of me? I'm so sorry, I'm so sorry. I should leave, I should leave and let them take me, only then will this nightmare stop."

Luca tightened his arms around her, physically restraining her from heading for the door, cornering her to the side of the sofa. "Becca, stop this," he ordered, his voice deep and assertive, though hardly assertive enough to penetrate her manic frenzy. "Hysterics won't fix the problem. Stop this. I am NOT going to let you go out of that door, so you might as well stop struggling. STOP, NOW."

She sagged against him, crying uncontrollably against his bare chest. "I'm sorry, I'm so sorry."

"None of this is your fault, and you've got to believe that." Luca continued to hold her firmly as he turned to his uncle. "We now know the *why,"* he said above the loud wrecking sobs. "The identity of her father must be the root of the problem. We can run the test again."

"We can, but I am certain that it won't yield a match this time round. Whoever killed Tom and Alan would be clever enough to delete that specific incriminating addition to the database, and I'm sure that he must have used the murdered victims' accounts to do so, covering his tracks."

"Becca can undo what was deleted, I know she can." He clasped her face between his hands, "Becca, honey, listen to me, I need you to gather yourself together and help us out. Take a deep breath in and out, that's it baby, good. And again, breathe in and breathe out." He had finally got her to focus on him, on his eyes which always seemed to take her to some secure place somewhere inside her mind. "Honey, you said that you retrieved a deleted email from Tom's account, can you also retrieve a deleted name on a list?"

"I don't know. I can try," she sobbed.

"Thank you, honey." Luca swiftly lifted her up in his arms and carried her to the kitchen table, sitting her trembling body down on a chair. He booted up his laptop and accessed his agency account, going straight to the DNA database available only to British Intelligence personnel. "OK, Becca, here is the list. I need you to retrieve what was deleted yesterday. Come on, honey, you can do it."

Both men stood back, a pace or two behind her, watching her trembling hands perform their magic across the keyboard. The minutes ticked by and her hands eventually lost their tremble and gained their speed and confidence. This was her world, a world in which she thrived, a lonely world she was comfortable living in. In less than an hour, names started to appear across the screen, names in alphabetical order. Tom and Alan, or someone who had accessed their account in their name, had deleted more than fifty names the day before; whoever had meddled with that list didn't want to draw attention to that one single incriminating identity. But the name in question rather stood out as it finally graced the screen, it being one of the last to appear because it was way down the alphabetical list...Wills...Jessica Wills.

"What the hell!" Luca swore. It definitely made sense. Jessica was notorious for getting into trouble with the law on countless occasions and her DNA must have been added to the list in the past six or seven years, ever since she had turned on the wild side in her teenage years. That must be the reason why Ben didn't have a match in the past but Tom did in the present. Could she be Becca's half-sister? Was that the paternal link Alan Scott mentioned in his email? It was certainly too huge to put down in writing. The more he thought of it, the more plausible it seemed. The father of both girls, the Prime Minister, had access to Tom and Alan's accounts if he wanted to and he was in a fantastic position to delete whatever he deemed necessary. His decision always overrode that of the Chief of British Intelligence.

"Could Larry Wills be Becca's father? Did he know Tessa?" Luca asked as he looked at his uncle who was as deeply rattled as he was.

"He knew her in passing. Theoretically, he could be the father, though I would never have bet on it. Larry was a secret agent a long time ago before he went into politics. But that was ages ago, way before the child was born, and his contact with

Tessa was minimal to say the least. They were hardly more than mere acquaintances."

Becca stood up, leaning heavily against the table. "Yesterday Rita King told me that two men in suits visited Tessa in prison before her faked death. I assume that one of them was you. Who was the other?"

"Larry Wills, and as far as I know those few visits were the only professional contact he had with her. Shortly afterwards he resigned from the agency to pursue an active career in politics, and he rose through the ranks with incredible speed. People liked him."

"And so did Tessa Bell, that dirty home-wrecker," Becca spat in disgust. "Rita King told me that after those initial visits, one of those two men used to call her out of her cell in the middle of the night and engage in sexual activities with her and he did that on a fairly regular basis. Tessa confessed to being in love and she thought that he was too. She fiercely protected his identity because he was married and highly successful. And that was the main reason why I assumed that you could be my father. But it was the other agent who was messing about with her all along. They must have kept their affair alive when she went undercover, at least long enough to conceive me at some point. And that makes me nothing but a dirty by-product of a filthy affair."

"Damn it!" Ben hissed through clenched teeth. "How could I have missed the obvious? He has been screwing with us for years."

"Technically, he was screwing just her," Luca maintained with a grin.

His uncle frowned at him. "Do you always have to turn everything into a bloody joke?"

"Yes, why not, life is too short to dwell in anger for too long...or to live in guilt that should not be yours in the first place," and he grabbed Becca's hand and jerked her towards him, circling his arms around her waist and smiling cheerfully at her. "Honey, you are not responsible for what your parents did in bed. As for me, I can't thank them enough for what they created together because I absolutely love the beautiful by-product of their filthy affair. Come on, honey, give me a smile." He was pleased to see a slow smile spread across her face and, despite her shy reticence, she leaned against him and gave him a spontaneous brief kiss on his lips as a sign of her profound appreciation. He surprised her by retuning that kiss, a little bit deeper than was appropriate in front of an audience. He eventually pulled away, wanting to continue boosting her confidence; she most definitely needed a boost. "Honey, what you did with those deleted names was simply amazing, your skills are amazing, out of this world. I am so proud of you and you should be too."

"As I am too," his uncle stepped in. "That was a brilliant piece of work, Becca. Well done. You've got a job with British Intelligence waiting for you whenever you want it. We will pay well for skills like yours. So think about it. We will obviously have to refurbish you with a new secret identity and ship you away from here, but that shouldn't stop us from recruiting you because that type of work could be done for us wherever in the world." He turned on his nephew, "And Luca, you will also have to lose your identity if you want to stay with her. Her face is plastered all over and her *Sicilian friends* or anyone else hunting her down for her skills would know that London is the place to look for her. You wouldn't be able to live safely here, or even anywhere in the UK for quite some time. So, the choice is yours, Luca."

"That's a no-brainer; I choose to be with her wherever we have to go. So it's *goodbye* to Luca Snell and *hello* to whatever," and he turned on her, a wide smile on his face, "What would you like to call me, John, James, Jack...Whatever?"

"Are you crazy? You don't know me. How could you possibly give up your life here, your family, your career, your everything for someone you don't know, just for the sake of an impulsive whim?"

"Oh no, I know you well enough, trust me, this is not an impulsive whim. And I am not giving up anything by following you because I will certainly get to see my folk from time to time and so will you. It won't be so bad, you'll see."

"What if I don't want this for you..."

"Hey," Ben said, slicing through their dispute. "You two can discuss this later. There are a lot of things to clear up before we even get to that stage. My first priority right now has to be the downfall of the mighty Larry Wills. Now that I know who is behind all this I can easily rustle up a trustworthy team to unearth enough evidence to convict him of Tom and Alan's murder to say the least. I will eventually open the case of Tessa's murder too but that would be a bit harder to prove, if we can prove it at all. But yesterday's events should be simple enough to pin on him. In the meantime, I want you two to stay put. Becca, do you understand that? I'll repeat...you are to stay INSIDE this apartment until Larry is safely locked up where he belongs. You have to do exactly as I say if you value Luca's life. And I can't put it any clearer than that."

"Why do you keep saying that?"

"Because he's an obsessive moron," Luca frowned at his uncle. "But we can humour him and promise to stay indoors. We will find interesting stuff to do in here for a day or two or perhaps three, I'm sure."

"Day or two? But I have nothing to wear. I will need stuff and clothes and…"

Luca waved her concerns aside. "Nah, you're good the way you are. You don't need anything else."

"Yes, she does," Ben interjected. "Don't worry, Becca, I'll get my wife to call you and she can buy your new clothes and anything else you need. Right, that's settled then. I'm off." And with that he left.

"It looks as though I'm babysitting again today. So, what do you want to do?" Luca asked with a big grin on his face. "Play chess, monopoly, watch movies...whatever you want, I'm at your service, madam."

"I need a bath first, a nice long hot soapy bath to ease away the traumatic stress of this horrendous morning."

The suggestive ring in the tone of her voice was loud and clear. He swallowed hard as he pulled her towards him and started undoing the buttons on the shirt he had lent her. He slowly slipped it off her shoulders. The lacy black slip hit the ground shortly afterwards. "A nice soapy bath you say? Mmmm, that's a brilliant idea to while away all these boring hours we have to kill. I can scrub your back if you promise to scrub mine."

"Sure, that's a fair deal."

23. Let Me Go

Alina lay still on his bed, staring vacantly at the darkened ceiling of his bedroom, a niggling feeling of deep unrest keeping her wide awake. Had she been sleeping alone in her bed she would have tossed and turned and tossed and turned until she eventually slipped into that world of uneasy dreams, but she wasn't free to move wildly there in Luca's bed with him sleeping like a baby beside her. In all truth she should be sound asleep too, with nothing worrying her, because suddenly her fortunes had changed and the sun was shining brightly on her again.

It took Ben Blake three days to do the impossible and gather enough evidence to formally charge Larry Wills with Tom's murder and abetting Alan's suicide. It was the sensational breaking news of that evening, shocking the entire nation to its very core. From what she could gather from Ben's call to Luca, Tom had apparently contacted Larry and asked for an astronomical amount of privileges as well as cash to get rid of the embarrassing problem of an illegitimate child which could so easily smear the Prime Minister's good name and sway the voting public, an election being imminent in the coming few months. Larry had no choice but to agree to Tom's demands, knowing that the illegitimacy was the least of his problems. The murdered mistress was an even more serious accusation should it ever come to light, and he suspected that someone out there was already aware of bits and pieces, knowing enough to fake the child's death all those years ago, but not knowing quite enough to incriminate him as the father and murderer. When Tom's hired thugs failed to do the job, Larry quickly recruited the help of two high officials within his political party, individuals who he knew would do anything, even murder, to win that coming election and stay in power. Between the three of them they executed a quasi-perfect plot turning the blackmailer, Tom, into the victim. But every plot has its own few loose ends which were quickly picked up by Ben and his team.

Cornered and broken, Larry also confessed to orchestrating Tessa's murder. Apparently, the affair that had started in the prison rooms went on for many years and only ended four years after the birth of the child. At that time both he and Tessa were under the impression that the quarry had indeed fathered the child, Larry himself having undergone a vasectomy after the birth of his legitimate daughter, Jessica, which happened to coincide with the time of conception. He knew that Tessa was madly in love with him but he wasn't with her. It was just the naughty illegality of the secret affair that excited him and spurred him on. Eventually, Larry moved on to another mistress, one much younger and more adventurous to his increasing needs, and he cut all ties with Tessa who was livid to say the least. At first, her verbal threats to expose their past affair were nothing more than mere inconveniences since he knew that she didn't have any concrete evidence supporting her claim; he had always made sure that he covered his back well whenever he visited. Then Tessa called him, telling him about the quarry's infertility problem and the consequent certainty that the child was his. He recognised the plausibility of it all, knowing that he had indeed engaged in unprotected sex with her before he had been given the all-clear by the doctor who had performed the vasectomy. Suddenly the game play had changed and Tessa had enough evidence to back her threats. He didn't want to live under the shroud of blackmail and he set the ball rolling to get rid of her and the incriminating evidence in the form of the child. And he would have got away with it hadn't Tom run that test and chosen to exploit the result.

That evening the demons of Alina's dark past were finally laid to rest and it was indeed enough cause for celebration which the bouncing Luca seized with his characteristic flamboyant style; cracking open a bottle of Champagne of which she took mere sips, ordering lavish gourmet food which she enjoyed, and engaging in highly entertaining sex till the early hours of the morning which she greatly relished. He was a party animal at heart and she knew that he would have liked to celebrate in a much bigger style but his uncle had not yet lifted the curfew. Nonetheless, although confined in that small space with her, he seemed to be happy, extremely happy, and she was happy too. He made her happy. And that was why she should be fast asleep in that *happy* world of dreams. But she just couldn't doze off, all due to that deep unrest whose root could be traced back to his family who had all called in the past three days.

The first to visit were his parents who came all the way from Cambridge specifically to spend time with him. Both warmly welcomed her inside their family circle and were friendly enough, especially Emma Snell, whose dark beauty and bubbly personality, so much like her son's, seized the limelight and drew everyone inside her fresh spinning aura. But there was a lot of trepidation behind that sparkling facade of hers as Alina found out when she happened to overhear snippets of a whispered conversation between the mother and son...

"...Luca, darling, I'm scared for you, please be careful."

"Uncle Ben shouldn't have told you anything."

"I have a right to know; I'm your mother. It would kill me if something happened to you."

"Nothing is going to happen. I am a survivor. I always have been and I always will be. Mum, please understand, she makes me happy and I am prepared to go through hell to be with her."

And then there was that final heart-shattering hug between the two before the mother left with tears in her eyes.

"I love you, Luca, take care."

"I love you too, Mum. Everything will be fine. Don't worry. I'll be fine."

She would have brushed that aside as a perfectly rational emotional encounter between mother and son hadn't the rest of the family visited in their throngs, two brothers and three sisters with their husbands and wives and kids. It strongly looked as though they had all come to pay their sad last respects to a dying brother...chilling indeed. But through it all Luca managed to maintain his bounce and turn everything into one big hilarious joke.

Alina had to conclude that Ben had told his sister that all too soon Luca would have to permanently let go of his true identity, severing all his ties with his family and his past, all because he had chosen to live on the run with her in some obscure location or probably locations. She loved him too much to condemn him to that perilous life with her. Perhaps she should just pack her bags and leave. Luca looked like the type who wouldn't mourn any girl and he would quickly move on to other healthy relationships which would keep intact that tight-knit family feel the Snells shared amongst themselves.

She heard him murmur something in his deep slumber and she turned on her side, facing him, watching him sleep and loving him all the more. He murmured something again and this time she could just about decipher his slurred words...*I will always love you, Becca*. He was dreaming about her. She felt her heart soar with happiness and tears of joy streamed down to her pillow. What had she done to deserve his love? She moved closer and caressed the wisps of jet-black hair chaotically falling across his forehead. He responded to her light touch and he circled his arms around her, drawing her naked body close to him. He once more mumbled that he loved her before falling again in deep sleep against her flowing dark hair. Comforted by the regular beat of his heart, she too drifted off to sleep, that niggling unrest booted out by his mumbled and sincere declaration of love.

*

His phone was ringing. Alina felt him detangle himself from their intertwined warmth as he reached out for that irritating shrilling gadget on his bedside table.

"Hello," he said in a deep voice smothered with sleep. "Yes, Uncle, you have woken me up, can't you tell by the sound of my voice?" He yawned widely as he listened to what his uncle had to say. He eventually responded with that lazy carefree drone of his. "I thought that you would take the day off after your victory yesterday. Don't you ever rest, Uncle?" He yawned again. "Yes, OK, I guess," he grudgingly conceded to his uncle's demands. "See you in thirty minutes." He flung his phone aside and turned on her, kissing her good morning. "Sorry about that, but we've got to get ready. My uncle has been working all through the night, creating these new profiles for us. He will be here soon to discuss them because he wants us out of here by the end of the day."

"So soon?" she asked, her voice trembling with apprehension. "Luca, I'm not too sure about this. Can you just pause and think about it, about everything you're about to give up for me?"

"I love you, Becca. Do you love me back?"

"Yes, I do."

"If you really do, you would want to make me happy, and being with you makes me happy."

"You are so gifted with words, twisting and turning everything around to suit your needs at that specific moment in time."

"I know, I've been told plenty of times that I was lucky enough to be born with that wonderful gift of the gab. But, seriously, Becca, can you stop with this pause thing. I do not need to think about it. I know exactly what I want to do with my life. And, for the thousandth time, I am not giving up anything to be with you. I will still get to see my parents from time to time and so will you. If you do exactly what I tell you to do, we will both be safe and able to live a normal life without any fear of being picked up by the Mafia or any other organisation lusting for that brilliant brain of yours. Understood?" And he sealed his powerful and moving speech with a deep never-ending kiss.

The doorbell rang. "Damn it," Luca moaned. "He said thirty minutes, not five minutes." He dragged himself out of the bed and put on his boxers, quickly raking his jet-black tousled hair with his fingers before making his way out to the lounge.

"Bloody hell," Alina heard him swear at the door. "What the fuck are you doing here, Jessica?" His tone of voice was rough and bordering on the insolent.

Alina quickly put on her jeans and T-shirt, the clothes Ben's wife had kindly bought for her as promised. She heard

Jessica respond with a condescending haughty tone matching Luca's insolence, "Don't flatter yourself, Luca dear. I'm not here to see *you*. I am assuming that the Becca you kept calling in your sleep these past few years is none other than my baby half-sister, and, judging by your state of half-undress, I can bet a million pounds that she is in your bed right now. I want to talk to her."

"You cannot. Now, get the fuck out of here before I throw you out."

There were scuffles at the door amidst Jessica's loud strong voice, "Take your filthy hands off me, Luca. She is my sister and I have a right to get to know her, to talk to her about our father whose monstrous blood we both share."

Alina heard the slight tremor of suppressed emotions in the girl's voice despite the tough show she wanted to maintain in front of her former lover. This can't be easy on poor Jessica, transformed overnight from the daughter of a much-admired Prime Minister to the daughter of a scheming murderer and cheat. Alina self-consciously walked out of the bedroom and she came face to face with a stunning girl with gorgeous long blonde hair and the most mesmerising pair of cat-like emerald green eyes. All the photos in the trashy magazines who had preyed on her life didn't do her enough justice. Alina felt so plain standing next to her. They were sisters, half-sisters, but their appearances were miles apart, colouring and all.

"Hello, you must be Becca," Jessica said with much confidence, something her sister completely lacked, another huge difference between them. She sidestepped Luca's blocking frame and calmly approached her, stretching out her hand. "I'm Jessica, apparently your half-sister. I've always wanted to have a younger sister and I would really like it if we were to get to know each other well, be friends."

Alina looked at her outstretched hand and she could not stop herself from crying, her innate feelings of inadequacy making her shoulder all the guilt for her beautiful sister's cruel predicament. "I'm so sorry for what I made your father do. I didn't mean to mess up his life, or yours."

"Oh, honey, none of this is your fault. Surely you can see that." Jessica had abandoned the formal handshake and was hugging her close to her chest now. "Our father was the one who messed up our lives, mine and yours...mine more than yours. Believe me, Becca, when I tell you that had he tried to physically kill me like he did to you, it would have been kinder on my soul."

She broke the warm embrace and moved away from her, swaying on her high heels towards the sofa. She slowly sat down. "Yesterday night, after they arrested him, I approached Ben Blake and told him just how deep the sins of the mighty Larry Wills actually run. I was in my early teens when my own father sold my body to a friend of his, a highly influential man who could help him advance his political career, the only thing in the world that ever mattered to him. *I am doing all this for you, Jessica*, he used to tell me every time he locked me inside the room with his ravenous friend. After that I just became the sophisticated whore he always wanted me to become." She stopped to gather her composure as she looked up at Luca, holding his gaze. "Since then, all the men I've ever been with never saw any further than that single entertaining night of sex. They just used me and left, thinking that whores were not entitled to have any feelings. Not once did they try to delve within my soul and ask me why a girl like me should be acting that way. Not once did they ever tell me that they loved me."

Alina followed her powerfully green gaze towards one of the self-centred men in question. Luca was just standing there, his arms folded across his bare chest, his blazing blue eyes showing no remorse as they shifted onto Alina, trying to gauge her reaction, which seemed to be more important to him than Jessica's feelings.

Tell her that you're sorry, Alina mouthed at him across the space.

He shook his head, understanding her mime but unwilling to expose himself to any weaknesses as far as Jessica was concerned. He turned his back on them both and walked to the kitchen end of the room, busying himself with the kettle.

Alina looked back at her sister, at the green eyes now filling up with tears. It was all so obvious to her; Jessica was in love with Luca even though he had treated her so badly. *Jessica and Luca*; both were so hard-headed, so wild, so adventurous, so carefree, so confident, so similar. The more she thought about it, the more it made sense. Yes definitely, *Jessica and Luca* made more sense than *Becca and Luca.* For starters, Jessica wouldn't have to drag him away from his life, from his career, from his family. Emma Snell and the rest of the Snell family she had just met over the past few days would approve of *Jessica* more than they could ever approve of *Becca.* Her shoulders slumped down in sadness and she looked away, and as she did so her gaze fell on her teddy bear stuffed with her stolen bank accounts. She knew what she had to do. Because she loved him so much she had to leave. She grabbed her teddy and was out of the door before anyone inside the room had blinked.

She ran down the deserted street of that early morning.

"Becca, wait, stop there. Becca, please, hear me out."

She looked over her shoulder. Luca was running barefoot behind her, clad only in his boxers. She ran faster but his athletic strides easily caught up with her. He grabbed hold of her hand and jerked her round to face him.

"You slept with my sister," she hissed at him.

"At that time I didn't know that she was your sister. Not even *you* knew that she was your sister."

"It doesn't matter. You still slept with her. You two share a history that goes much further than ours. I will not stand between you two especially knowing that she is in love with you."

"But I am NOT in love with her. I love you, and only you. Becca, please, forgive me; I am begging you to forgive me. I will do anything you ask of me and if you want me to tell her that I'm sorry, then I will. Please come back inside with me and we can talk about it as much as you want."

"What's the point of discussing things with you and your *wonderful gift of the gab*," she spat in disgust, "You always manage to persuade me to do whatever you want me to do. Let me go, Luca, it is over between us."

“It will never be over between us and there will always be something binding us.” He paused to take a deep breath before plunging in, “You’ll be having my child, a handsome boy, a little devil just like his father.” He was smiling at her, a wide cheeky smile that he knew would make her heart flutter wildly.

“What are you talking about? How do you know?”

“Trust me, I just know. Besides, we’ve been having unprotected sex for the better part of three days now. Didn’t you ever stop and think about the risks involved with that?”

“You’re wrong. I’m not at that time of...”she stopped abruptly, mentally calculating the days of that past traumatic month which had flown past with incredible speed. For a brilliant mathematician she was being rather slow about it, but in the end the simple calculations tallied with his predictions and all her blood drained out to her feet. “Oh my God!”

“Will you marry me, Becca? And I’m not asking you because of the child, I’m asking you because I’m in love with you. I always have been and I always will be.”

She looked up into his bright blue eyes, lost for words. Then she saw those same eyes widen in fear as they momentarily shifted onto something behind her shoulder. He was quick to react, hugging her close to his chest as he twisted round and pushed her down to the ground so that the bullet that was meant to lodge in her spine, lodged in his flank instead. He lay heavily upon her, his body protecting her from the second bullet tearing through his chest. She felt his hand drag down to her belly.

“Tell our son...” he gasped. “Tell him...that I’ll always...” He stopped, changing the flavour of the last words he had chosen to say. “Let me go, Becca...give Mark a chance...promise me....” The light in the blue eyes was dimming, fading away, further and further away until it was extinguished into nothingness.

She shook his head, trying to ignite that spark of life inside him, “Luca, Luca, Luca, no please no, oh please dear God, no, please, noooo...” She looked up the barrel of the gun, now pointed at her face, and beyond it she glimpsed the cold grey eyes of the heartless soul who had originally started all the drama on that fateful graduation party a lifetime ago. "Steve," she whispered. "How? Why?"

"*Why*? Isn't it obvious, I fucking hate you, Alina." He squatted down beside her, circling the gun around her cheek, wanting to play with her fear. "*How*, you ask? It was simple enough; the Mafia commissioned me to bring you in, *alive not dead*, they cautioned. But I myself was aiming for dead. Some days ago I had my lucky break when I heard your boyfriend talking to Max in his office through the bug I placed there, and after that, it was relatively easy to track down a Luca Snell living in London. I camped outside his door, waiting patiently for you to emerge from his den, and you finally did so on this opportune lonely hour of the morning. And, for your information, I kept Mark in the dark because I know of the soft spot he harbours for..."

He never finished his sentence. Jessica's high and deadly heel was rammed inside his cold grey left eye making him crouch down in pain. Jessica was quick to grab his falling gun and point it as his head as she kicked him backwards.

"Move away from my sister, you bloody bastard. Are you hurt, Becca? Is that blood yours?"

"No. No. It's Luca's...oh please, Luca, open your eyes, talk to me, please..." She shifted his dead weight off her and laid him flat on the ground as she fumbled around for a pulse, any pulse, however weak it could be. But he had none. She heard a car screech to a halt and Ben was squatting down beside her, taking control of the resuscitation.

"What part of *don't leave the apartment* didn't you understand?" he growled at her as he pumped at his nephew's chest, refusing defeat.

"I'm so sorry."

"Sorry won't make him whole again," he boomed above the wailing sound of the approaching siren. "Go back inside, NOW. GO, NOW, and this time stay inside until I come for you. UNDERSTOOD?" He softened his harsh tone of voice as he addressed the other girl. "Jessica, you're doing well, just keep the gun on him for now. It won't be long, help is at hand. After that you can join your sister inside...and try to keep her out of trouble."

The pavement started filling up with paramedics and police officers and Alina moved back, clutching her teddy. "No one else will die because of me," she promised herself. She disregarded Ben's crystal-clear set of orders and she began to run down the road towards the obscure solitary life of a recluse.

24. Crossroads

Mark Deliri finished the last piece of work for the day and, with a deep sigh, he sat back on his luxurious leather office chair. It was late, past eleven o'clock in the evening, and he knew that he should be heading back home to his family. His daughter would almost certainly be asleep in her bed and his wife, Sophia...well, he wouldn't know where she would be, and he didn't care either. After the birth of their daughter they had both tried so hard to make it work but he had eventually given up, finding that arduous task too impossible to achieve, and they were now growing further and further apart. He knew that he was the sole problem behind his dying marriage, the major cause of the apathetic rift, and should he try just a little bit harder his wife would respond well to his efforts. But the phantom inside his heart kept lingering on, festering on deep wounds. He was just unable to offer closure to the first love that had rocked his life.

Eight months, a week and five days had passed from that precious last brief digital conversation with Alina. It seemed as though she had suddenly severed all contact with everyone on earth: Max, her parents, himself and the British man who he knew was sweating so hard to track her down for months on end. He had had no less than five visits from Ben Blake who claimed that the reason behind his desperate search was the fact that she was vulnerable and pregnant. She was indeed vulnerable but Mark seriously doubted the pregnancy bit, knowing that Alina was just too conservative to willingly sleep with a random person she barely knew. It was more likely that Ben's secret organisation, whatever it could be, was hunting her down for her skills, just as the Mafia were. But, in any case, Ben Blake seemed to be under the impression that Alina, exhausted and broken, would eventually seek Mark's help, and that conviction was so strong that he had him placed under constant minute by minute surveillance and he made no secret of it. Mark was made fully aware that all his conversations were listened to, all his emails read and all his steps closely followed, whether he liked it or not. It was evident that Ben Blake's organisation was a massive indestructible bullying giant so much greater than his own. However, Mark had the advantage of knowledge, knowledge of their surveillance and that would prove vital if and when Alina chose to call.

Out of sheer habit, something he found himself doing at least twenty times a day, he took out his phone and checked for any hidden folders that Alina always used to create for the purpose of a brief conversation which she would then delete when it was all over. But there was nothing on his screen. He was about to rise from his chair and drag his feet back home, when his phone sparked to life. With trembling hands, he opened the familiar folder.

Hi, Mark.

He sank back down on his chair, an incredible elation overwhelming him. He steadied himself for a moment or two, not wanting to sound too keen lest he offended her morals and scared her away. She constantly chose to call his meaningless marriage *the binding promise of the ring*, and her phobia of disrupting it was just ridiculous in his book, but apparently not in hers. He had to tread very carefully with her moral values and he chose his first words with caution.

Hi. It's really great hearing from you, we were all so worried. How are you?

Fine, I guess. And you?

Still sorely missing you. His first slip, but he quickly continued to type...*Listen, I'm under surveillance, twenty-four-seven. A bloke called Ben Blake has been looking for you and he is getting very desperate. I thought that I had better warn you just in case you let slip anything about your whereabouts and he happens to get hold of this conversation.*

He won't. I've seen some cyber-sharks around your space but I've created an invisible wall they will never be able to breach. This conversation is safe. Mark, I need your help. I am exhausted, I just can't keep on running and I have decided to come back home. Please, can you pass on a message to the Mafia for me? Tell them that I will co-operate fully and will do whatever they ask of me. If I do that the people around me will be safe. Would they?

No, they will never be safe. You will always be threatened and blackmailed with their well-being. Blackmail is brutal, believe me, it is nothing but an overhanging cloud of darkness that you can't ever escape from. In the years to come there will always be something that you can't do for the mob and inevitably the people you love most will bear the brunt. Honey, don't even go there. Co-operating with the Mafia isn't your only choice. You don't have to keep on running if you accept my offer of sanctuary in one of my places, and, before you ask, no you don't have to be my mistress, all you have to be is my friend.

Thank you, Mark. I will take up your offer, but before I do we have to meet because you might want to retract your proposal when you see me. On second thoughts, I had better tell you right away and spare you the trouble of a trip should the news change your feelings towards me. I am pregnant, heavily pregnant, the baby due any day now. I just can't keep on running, not with a child, it wouldn't be fair on him.

Mark kept staring at the words on the screen but no matter how hard he stared they did not change. Ben Blake had been right; she was indeed pregnant but she was obviously running away from the father of the child, whoever it might be, preferring a life within the arms of the Mafia to a life with him. That didn't say much for the father. He must be a ruthless monster. He must have raped her, he concluded.

Mark, are you still there? Tell me, do you still want to meet? I will understand if you don't want to.

Don't be silly. Of course I want to. He shed all attempts at moral discretion, throwing caution to the wind. *Honey, you are the light that shines in my darkest cave. You always have been and you always will be. I am nothing without you. You being pregnant will not change these strong feelings I have for you and I will love the child because it is yours.*

Thank you. This means so much to me. I'm so scared right now, scared of everything, but even more so of the birth.

There's nothing to be afraid of. The birth of a baby, any baby, is such a beautiful experience, so wonderful, so heart-lifting. It will all be worth it in the end. I should know, I've already gone through it...oh well, not the pain and pushing part but the holding hands and feeling inadequate part...

He paused, remembering the birth of his own daughter, his little princess. He had never before experienced such deep happiness in his heart. Every birth was an incredible gift of nature. He wanted more children of his own, but this time he wanted to share them with the woman he loved. *Honey,* he continued to type, *I won't let you go through this alone and I'll be there through it all, holding your hand, I promise. I'll clear my diary right away. Where are you?*

At Mara's. She's been so kind to me, offering me shelter for the past two weeks and organising everything, midwife and all. I'm having the baby here at the brothel since it would be sheer madness if I were to walk inside a hospital; it's just too risky. Mara wanted to call you straight away but I wasn't ready to meet you, and she respected my wishes but kept on badgering me until I finally took the plunge today. And I'm still having my doubts. I don't want to come between you and your wife. Have things improved between you two?

No, if anything they are even worse. Mara must have told you.

Yes she did, but...oh well, I don't know.

We'll talk about it later. I will aim to sail from here in an hour or so and I'll be there as soon as I physically can, so let the little mite know that he or she should wait for me.

It's a boy, at least that's what I've been told. Mark, I really can't thank you enough.

Please don't. It's my pleasure. See you soon xxx

With a spring in his step, he headed out of the door and went straight for his car. Through his rear-view mirror he saw the not-so-subtle black car tailing him all the way to his house. He made sure that he did nothing out of the ordinary, just a normal working man returning to his family home after a long and hard day's work. That should put them off their guard and they would hopefully loosen their surveillance for the night.

Once inside, he called for his wife and daughter, but, just as he had expected, his daughter was fast asleep in her bed and the housekeeper/nanny informed him that his wife was out again for the whole night. He went to the bathroom and shed all his clothes, suspecting that somewhere on them there had to be some tracking device. He left everything behind him; his phone, his wallet, his watch, his ring, his keys, everything on the bathroom floor. For the sake of decency, he put a towel around his waist and went out through the window, skimming down a tree in his back garden. Barefoot, he walked along the path meandering between the orange trees until he came to his neighbour's fence which he skipped over with ease. The light beaming out of the kitchen window beckoned him forward and he was soon tapping on the glass.

His neighbour, his skipper, knew the drill by now. Over the past few months Mark had so often dodged surveillance that way, needing an escape route for his secret rendezvous with the ladies he chose to take sailing with him for the night.

"So, who is the lucky lady we are picking up tonight?" the skipper asked with a grin as he handed him a pair of shorts, a shirt and shoes.

"She is waiting for me in Sicily. I need to get there fast."

"No problem, it's a good night for sailing."

*

The day had just broken by the time he was ushered inside Alina's bedroom. He expected her to be fast asleep at that ungodly hour, but instead she was alert and wide awake, pacing across the spacious room, her hands caressing her heavily pregnant belly.

She had changed dramatically, and he wasn't just referring to the obvious physical change. She had completely shed that awkward naive aura of an innocent girl and had matured into a sensual confident woman about to embark on motherhood. She no longer fidgeted with her fingers or shyly averted her eyes to some spot below his chin; instead she confidently looked him in the eye and smiled warmly at him as he walked inside the room. Her style of dress had changed too as she opted to highlight her beautiful assets with silks and lace rather than hiding them beneath casual frumpy clothes he had always known her to wear. Standing there before him in her nightclothes, even though heavily pregnant, she was the most beautiful creature he had ever laid his eyes on and his heart started to beat fast inside his chest.

"You are a very beautiful woman, Alina. You look absolutely fantastic, glowing," he said with sincere feeling.

"You are too kind to me, Mark. I'm not feeling that great."

"Why are you up at this time of morning? Are you in pain?"

"On and off, but it's very mild and bearable right now. The midwife just examined me and she said that I'm still in the very early stages of labour. It might take hours and hours and perhaps a day, and by that time the pain is bound to get worse, sending me straight to bed. Scary."

"Hey, don't worry about it. I'll be there to help you along." There was an awkward pause at his end but then he moved across the room and opened his arms for her, "Come here, Alina, give me a hug. I've missed you so much."

"You know, I've missed you too, really missed you and the conversations we used to have," she said as she slid comfortably inside his arms.

He gambled and he immediately sought her lips. She didn't push him away and she responded with enough passion. However, he knew that her heart and soul were not in that deep kiss, at least not as much as his heart and soul were. Perhaps she had been too traumatised by her experience with the father of the child to readily trust other men. He was curious to know the reason why she was desperately fleeing from him. Had he hurt her? Had he raped her? He wanted her to be able to open up to him and talk to him about everything; he wanted their relationship to be built on transparent trust rather than physical lust. Perhaps he shouldn't have kissed her so soon. He broke his kiss and gently brushed his hand across her belly.

"Tell me about the father of the child. How did it happen? Did he hurt you?" he asked in his gentlest tone of voice.

"No, no. It's not what you're thinking. He didn't force himself on me. I fell in love and I think that he was in love too."

"Then why are you running away from him? Why aren't you with him?"

"He died...he died to save my life and that of our son."

He stared at her, deeply confounded. He was positive that Ben Blake had told him that the father of the child was desperate to make contact with her but he was too poorly to travel to Malta with him and beg for Mark's help. On more than one occasion, Ben had earnestly asked him to pass on the simple message or better still call him immediately should she surface and ask for help. At that time Mark had put that down as a cunning ploy to lure the girl's gifted mind inside a trap. But was it a trap or was it the truth? "He died? Are you sure? Are you absolutely sure?" he asked her.

"Yes, I'm sure. He is dead," she answered as fresh tears started to well up in her eyes, the memory too raw for her to bear, even after all that time. "Steve was about to shoot me in the back but Luca saw him and opted to take the bullet that was aimed for me in his flank. He fell over me, protecting me from the second shot which hit his chest. He died on the spot, in my arms. That is not the version you might have heard on the media surrounding Steve's arrest, they just twisted the truth around and said that he murdered a random person on the street. They did that to protect my identity, I guess."

So the father's name was Luca, probably the same Luca Snell, the British detective, who had been desperately looking for her and had sought out Max's help a long time ago. Apparently, he had managed to find her and he had even seduced her with his charm. Things started to fit together inside his mind. "Perhaps this Luca managed to survive, after all. What makes you think that he is dead?" Mark insisted again.

"No, he didn't survive those lethal shots, I'm positive about that. He had no pulse and wasn't breathing when they bundled him onto the ambulance. After that, they kept him alive on machines. Eventually, he was pronounced brain dead and they pulled the plug on him. I hacked his hospital file and followed his progress for three whole agonising months, hoping against hope, but I guess it was inevitable. I disguised myself and went to his funeral service. They buried him in a chapel in his father's ancestral home, a huge mansion in Cambridge, his father being an Earl or something. Ben Blake, his uncle, saw through my disguise and nearly cornered me that day, but I managed to slip away just in time."

Right, so Ben Blake is the uncle, he mused. "Something doesn't quite fit. If you were so in love with each other, then why on earth are you running away from his uncle? This bloke is moving mountains to find you, I mean he actually sent out a team to track my every move and he was even honest enough to tell me that he was hacking my stuff with the sole aim of finding you."

"Ben Blake and I didn't actually part on friendly terms. In fact, Luca's entire family must hate me so much and I wouldn't want to live on their forced charity. Besides, I don't want anyone else to die because of me and that was why I went to live in solitude, hopping from one place to another every couple of days. But, with the baby due any minute now, I got so scared and well...here I am now."

Mark had to know, he had to ask, "Alina, if Luca had survived, would you be with him today?"

"I don't know. I was breaking up with him when it all happened. His uncle was about to supply us with new identities and ship us somewhere safe from the Mafia but, after meeting the rest of Luca's family, I felt that he shouldn't be sacrificing that much for me. Of course, at the time I didn't know that I was pregnant but he somehow did. It was so weird living with him, we were together for just three days but he knew so much about me, some really intimate stuff that only I should know. He even knew about this soft spot I have for you and the digital conversations we shared...and do you know what he told me before he took his last breath? He begged me to let him go and give you a chance...*give Mark a chance*...those were his exact words."

"Is that why you're here?"

"I don't know. I have to be honest with you, Mark. I like you. Really like you. Really, really like you. But I don't know if I can ever like you more than a friend because...you're married and I know that I shouldn't be doing this."

"Hey, it's OK. We can go no further than a friend if that makes you happy."

"Yeah, right. Who are you kidding?" she answered with a big smile on her face.

He had to grin back, knowing that she was absolutely right. The second awkward pause was interrupted by Mara's soft knock on the door and he seized the opportunity and took his leave because he desperately needed to think. He made his way out to the back garden and prowled the perimeter, evaluating the bits and pieces that had just surfaced.

She was under the strong impression that Luca had died, and indeed all the circumstantial evidence in the form of the hacked hospital notes pointed that way. They had even held a funeral service for him. But Ben Blake had insisted over and over again that the father of the child was desperately seeking a reconciliation, implying that he was very much alive though too poorly to travel. Mark closed his eyes and recalled the uncle's exact words...

...I am begging you, Mr Deliri, please do the right thing. Tell her that the father of her child wants to talk to her. Just pass on the message and let her decide what she wants out of her life. I can promise you that he will respect her decision whatever it might be. Please...

It now seemed obvious that Luca Snell was not just a British detective, he was something more than that, perhaps an agent working within an elite secret organisation in the UK, something the uncle seemed to be part of too as evident by the tight surveillance he had placed him under in the past few months.

Before the shooting, Ben was about to furnish the young couple with fresh identities, and from that Mark could easily deduce that the wise old owl had decided to seize the opportunity and kill off Luca's true identity when he was so poorly, making the illusion realistic. The medical notes could easily be tampered with and the funeral service could have been staged as a way to lure the mourning Alina in to pay her last respects; in fact Ben seemed to have been on the lookout for her and had nearly trapped her that day.

If all that were true, then Mark was at a crossroads. He could opt to say nothing, allowing her to continue living in darkness, under the false impression that the man she had fallen in love with had died to save her life. If he were to do that, he and Alina would almost certainly become lovers but he seriously doubted if she could ever love him as much as she had once loved this Luca. However, he could easily live with that because he would have her all for himself, raise a family with her, love her and spoil her, something he had always wanted to do from that first day he had laid his eyes on her and secretly fallen in love with her sweet innocence.

Or...he could do the right thing and opt to call Ben Blake, losing her forever to the young secret agent who had stolen her heart in the few days he had known her. He himself, on the other hand, had *known* her for most of his life, had *loved* her for most of his life, but she had still chosen to fall in love with someone she barely knew. Now, how was that fair?

*

Mark held her hand tight as a strong contraction gripped her entire being, making her moan out in sheer pain. "Oh my God, it hurts so much, it hurts so much. Argh. Argh. Mark, help me, Mark. I'm not strong enough for this."

"You're doing fine, honey. I'm so proud of you. Come on, Alina, you can do it." She had advanced in labour, the contractions increasing in intensity and giving her only five to ten minutes of respite in between. It won't be long now, thirty minutes, an hour perhaps, the midwife reckoned. The wave of pain eased and he helped her back on her pillow. "You've got to rest in between. That's it, honey, close your eyes."

She nodded and closed her eyes, trusting him, believing him, needing his reassuring presence. He glanced at the door, wondering if Luca would manage to be there on time. Yes, Mark had chosen to call Ben Blake because he loved her too much to let her live in darkness. He had played the ball in her court, giving her the choice to decide what she wanted out of her life. And he was proud of his decision, however painful it could prove to be.

As if on cue, the door opened and Mara ushered in a gaunt-looking young man whose vivacious sparkle in his deep blue eyes contrasted heavily with the sickly grey lethargic colour of his skin. He made his way slowly across the room, taking small calculated steps that seemed to rock his fragile frame with pain. Nonetheless, his smile was bright and sunny, immediately lifting the mood in that room. He clapped Mark on his back. "Thank you, my friend," he whispered.

"You're welcome," and Mark reluctantly let go of her hand and moved to the side, giving up his seat. He lingered behind the expectant father, wanting to witness Alina's reaction as she sensed a different hand holding her own, compelling her to open her eyes. Mark anticipated a bright surprise, a gasp of disbelief, incredible jubilation. He needed her happiness to get him through the difficult and selfless path he had just chosen to take. And indeed, she did not disappoint him; her euphoria touched his heart and sent goose bumps all down his spine.

"Oh my God, Luca! Oh my God, am I dreaming? But I saw the hospital notes...I saw them bury you."

"The notes were half true. I was in a coma for weeks on end but my uncle wouldn't let me go. He kept pulling me out of the grave, time and time again, until I managed to surface completely and stay afloat, and as you can see I'm still struggling with rehabilitation, but I'm slowly getting there. But no, I'm not dead; the funeral service was all an illusion, my dear."

"But I saw your mother cry, really cry..."

"My mother is an actress, she could cry whenever. My father, on the other hand, was banned from attending the mock service because he just can't act. Didn't you find his absence odd? I'm sorry for the pain you had to go through but Luca Snell had to die. My uncle thought it best and he was rather hoping to corner you that day but you managed to slip past him, and you've continued to elude him for months." He paused to kiss the back of her hand. "My uncle wasn't the only one looking for you, you know. Jessica was too. She traced you back to your childhood, thinking that she'll find you there, wanting so desperately to help you. And she met Max in the process. The last I've heard is that the two are still going very strong. Does that make you happy?"

"Oh, gosh yes. Wow, Max and my sister...speechless."

"Now that your sister is all happy and in love, can you find it in your heart to forgive me for the past I shared with her?"

"Maybe."

"OK, I'm happy with that; a maybe is so much better than a no. Ermmm…and one other thing, before I got shot I asked you a question. You never got a chance to answer it. Is it a *yes* or a *no* or a *maybe*?"

She smiled at him and raked her fingers through his jet-black hair, "A *yes,* a definite *yes.* I never stopped loving you, Luca."

Mark turned his back on the happy couple and quietly left the room. That was all he wanted to hear. She had made her choice and she was happy. Funnily enough, hearing that heartfelt *yes* offered him the closure he had so desperately been looking for all through that past year. The chains that had been weighing him down had lifted and the phantom that had gripped his heart for so long had gone to rest. The love he had for her was a strange kind of love, a selfless kind of love as she would have called it, and he would always love her that way, wanting nothing more than to see her smile. But now it was time for him to move on. By letting her go, he now felt free enough to work hard and fulfil the promise he had once made when he gave Sophia a ring. He took out his phone and called her.

“Hi, honey. Do you want to have dinner with me, tonight? Somewhere quiet, somewhere nice, just the two of us, just like old times.”

“I would love to, Mark. I thought that you’ll never ask.”

***

More From The Blake Series

THE BLAKE SOUL

Josh Blake wakes up to the sound of the chilling scream echoing inside his head. His childhood nightmares are haunting him again. But why return now after all those years of oblivion? He sets out to investigate and he changes the natural course of events, rewriting destiny and creating a whole new world for himself and for those around him. His turbulent childhood mingles with the present, unveiling the deep insecurities that lurk behind his polished exterior of fame, glory and wealth.

The Blake Soul is a gripping, emotional love story which violently collides with family feuds, guilt, betrayal and revenge.

THE BLAKE CURSE

<u>*Ben Blake*</u>, an eighteen year old British Intelligence agent brimming with gifts; intellectual genius, striking appearance, impeccable acting skills and a heightened sixth sense... gifts that all guarantee the success of his first undercover assignment. He effortlessly infiltrates university life in Cambridge and befriends Cathy, the daughter of billionaire Edward Carter, one of the most influential and politically secure titans of the time.

<u>*Samantha Black*</u>, known as the elusive and exquisitely petite Sam. She rises from the ashes and battles her dark legacy. Her cryptic past and deep secrets become firmly intertwined with Ben's investigations, shredding his carefully thought out plan to bits.

<u>*Jake Snell*</u>, the young rugged Earl of Yorkley, the enigma, the rogue full of vices....but possessing abundant resourcefulness, creativity and determination. He is Ben's only lifeline in this treacherous game.

The Blake Curse is all about heartrending choices, fast paced suspense and that faith in the thread of human goodness.

THE BLAKE MISTAKE

Three characters and a life-changing event.

Ben Blake; British intelligence agent, intellectual genius, striking appearance, impeccable acting skills and a heightened sixth sense, all concealed behind a solid impenetrable mask.

Jake Snell; the rugged eleventh Earl of Yorkley, the extremely bright cardiac surgeon, the loving husband, the devoted father, the enigma whose criminal past gives British intelligence another perspective from the other side of the fence.

Emma Snell; the talented actress who denounces her claim to fame and glory and becomes a stay-at-home mother. She finds the trapdoor in the edge of the woods surrounding her husband's stately home. She has no idea of the horror that had taken place in the hidden rooms or how this would play into her future.

The London bombing; Ben foresees it, Jake thwarts it and destiny is rewritten, spewing forth a cataclysmic course of events as all the domino pieces begin to fall. Snippets of Jake's violent and forgotten childhood start to surface his conscious mind and his perfect life begins to break apart before his very own eyes. Women he comes in contact with are found dead bearing a particular signature linked with his childhood. He starts to doubt his hidden suppressed half. He has to unlock his memories and search deep within the bowels of his vast ancestral home if he is to ever save his wife and tame the brutal destiny he himself had unleashed.

The Blake Mistake is all about insecurities, unconditional love and that desperate run against the flowing sands of time.

OTHER BOOKS BY IC CAMILLERI

WEEK OF LIES

It is New Year's Day. Beth Banks wakes up to find her father dead in their multimillion pound house in London. It appears to be a suicide, but Beth has her doubts. She looks back on her previous week, her introduction into the cryptic world of Rob Menezes, the righteous law graduate desperately seeking a living, the man she has grown to love and trust despite his many facets. She sets out in search of the truth and she uncovers a dark secret that could radically change her life.

RED TIDES

A young man flees war's bloodshed and embarks on a treacherous journey across the Mediterranean Sea. He desperately seeks solace in the decaying things around him. Preserving the life of an orphaned boy becomes his driving force to survive against all odds.

13685543R00140

Printed in Great Britain
by Amazon.co.uk, Ltd.,
Marston Gate.